P9-CAE-898

LUCKY DEVIL

A JOAN KAHN BOOK

LUCKY DEVIL

by
Arthur Maling

HARPER & ROW, PUBLISHERS
New York, Hagerstown, San Francisco, London

A HARPER NOVEL OF SUSPENSE

FIRST EDITION

Designed by Eve Callahan

Library of Congress Cataloging in Publication Data

Maling, Arthur.
  Lucky devil.
  I. Title.
PZ4.M25Lu [PS3563.A4313]   813'.5'4   77–11782
ISBN 0–06–012854–2

78 79 80 81 82 10 9 8 7 6 5 4 3 2 1

To the memory of John Berryman,
who gave hope and encouragement
to a very inexperienced young writer

LUCKY DEVIL

1

The policeman arrived shortly after three o'clock. And spoiled what had been, until then, a perfect day.

Tom, Mark and I were sitting in Mark's office. We were celebrating. Tom had brought the Hamilton National Bank into the fold. The Hamilton National Bank manages some six billion dollars' worth of trust, pension and assorted other accounts, and we were at last going to get a chunk of its brokerage business. Furthermore, we'd learned that our firm had been picked to participate in the underwriting of the Mid-North Electric bond issue. Two major successes in one morning.

So the three of us had gone out to lunch together—something we rarely did—and had had three martinis apiece before the meal. Then we'd come back to the office, where Mark had revealed the presence in his desk of a bottle of Chivas Regal, which was something else to celebrate. For while Mark is worth maybe ten million dollars, and stands to inherit another fifteen or twenty million when his father dies, he hates to part with a buck. The Scotch he serves at home and usually keeps around the office is the kind that costs like four dollars a quart and tastes as if it were made from the bark of trees. But there it was, a brand-new bottle of Chivas Regal; and he not only let us see it, he opened it.

Before he could pass it around, though, the telephone rang.

Mark frowned. He'd told his secretary not to disturb us. He put the bottle down, however, and answered. Then he handed the telephone to me. "Someone to see you."

The voice at the other end of the line was that of Helen Doyle, my secretary. And there was uneasiness in it. "A Detective Hastings is here," she said. "From the police department."

I wasn't drunk, but I had enough alcohol in my bloodstream to make me flippant. "Sell him a hundred shares of General Motors and send him home."

"Mr. Potter's in conference," I heard Helen say. "Perhaps one of our salesmen can help you."

I didn't hear the policeman's reply, but Helen reported, "Mr. Hastings would like to speak with you personally."

"Tell him—" I started to suggest something obscene but checked myself; Helen takes a dim view of obscenity. "Oh, all right. I'll be there in a minute." I hung up, and turned to my partners. "This won't take long. It's only a policeman."

Tom went pale. "You're not in trouble again, are you?"

And Mark said, "I couldn't endure that." He sounded, as he often does, like the late President Franklin D. Roosevelt. They'd had the same kind of education, a couple of generations apart.

I looked from one to the other. Tom's reaction didn't surprise me. Although he comes across most of the time as a man without a care in the world, it doesn't take much to alarm him. But Mark, who has an air of being above the scuffles of ordinary mortals, is actually very ballsy. "Don't be ridiculous," I said, and got to my feet. "Pour me some Scotch. I'll be right back."

I started down the corridor to my own office, reviewing my standard speech: Price, Potter and Petacque doesn't deal with the general public—only with banks, mutual funds and such;

and, much as I'd like to, I don't give investment advice to anyone who isn't one of our regular customers.

I paused to look in on Irving and Brian, to assure myself that everything was all right with them. They were becoming a source of real anxiety to me.

Irving had his chair tilted back and was reading a report. He didn't see me.

Brian was out.

Helen was typing. A tall man was standing beside her desk, studying the single yellow rose in the vase next to the appointment calendar. I judged him to be in his middle fifties. He had graying hair, a nose that appeared to have been broken and not properly set, and deep furrows at the corners of his mouth, which gave him the look of a confirmed pessimist. And he'd evidently lost a lot of weight recently; no one would have bought a suit which was that much too big for him.

Helen glanced up. The uneasiness that had been present in her voice was also present in her eyes. Tom and Mark weren't the only ones.

The tall man more or less came to attention. "Brockton Potter?" His voice was like gravel sliding down a chute.

I nodded.

He took a leather folder from his pocket and opened it for me. It contained his shield and identification card. His first name, I noticed, was James. And I'd been right about his having lost weight; the photograph on the identification card had been taken when he was heavier.

I nodded, and he returned the folder to his pocket. "Zone One Homicide Squad," he said.

"Pleased to meet you," I said. "What can I do for you?" Then, without waiting for a reply, I went into my speech. "As you may not know, Mr. Hastings, our company isn't equipped to deal with the general public. We confine ourselves to—"

"I'm not here to buy stock," he interrupted. "Can't afford it."

"Well, then?"

"I'd like your help in identifying a body."

Helen gasped.

I blinked a couple of times. "A body?"

"A woman who was killed this morning. If it wouldn't be too much trouble, I'd appreciate your coming to the morgue with me."

Pictures of women I knew flashed through my mind. I began to feel frightened. "What does she look like?"

"She was very old."

I relaxed. I didn't know any very old women. Not intimately, at any rate. "Why me?" I asked.

"She had your name and address in her pocket."

"I see. Well, come into my office."

Helen gave me a dirty look. I gathered that she wanted to hear more about the old lady. Nevertheless I led Hastings from Helen's office into mine and closed the door.

He looked around. "Nice," he said.

I concentrated. My mother was dead. I had two elderly aunts, but they didn't live in New York and I hadn't heard from either of them in years. No one else came to mind. "My name and address?" I asked.

He nodded gravely.

"It can't be anyone I'm close to. How was she killed?"

"She was hit by a subway train."

My stomach turned a slow somersault. "Christ! I think you'd better get someone else."

"There is no one else."

"I don't know any old ladies. And besides—"

"Someone snatched her purse before she fell. We have nothing to go on except your name and address. They were on a piece of paper she was carrying in the pocket of her coat." He gave me a smile that was probably meant to convey encouragement but that failed to do so. "It won't take long."

4

"I'm sure it'd be a waste of time. Anyway—"

"I'll drive you there and back."

My name and address, I thought. My curiosity gave a faint twitch. "You say her purse was snatched. Is that what made her fall off the platform?"

"We don't know. This is one of those cases where there are just too many eyewitnesses. The station was crowded. At least thirty people saw it happen, and everyone seems to have a different version." He sighed. "Some say her purse was snatched and she fell. Others say the purse-snatcher pushed her. And some say her purse wasn't snatched at all—she just fell. It'll take time to sort out the stories. But no matter what, she's dead, and we'd like to notify her family, and we can't until we find out who she is. We haven't been able to find her pocketbook or any means of identification except that piece of paper."

"But aren't there things like laundry marks, labels—couldn't you identify her that way?"

"Eventually. But in the meantime . . . Look, Mr. Potter, I know this sort of thing isn't pleasant, but I think, under the circumstances, you do have an obligation."

That, it seemed to me, was a debatable point. But his tone of voice was one that I myself sometimes used, when someone was giving me a hard time and I was running out of patience, and there was a stubborn thrust to his chin. However, I'm accustomed to people who run out of patience with me and I'm accustomed to stubbornness; I can cope with both. What I can't cope with, at times, is my own curiosity. And at that moment my curiosity was definitely coming alive. Who was the woman, and why had she been carrying my name and address?

"All right," I said presently, "I'll go. But let's make it fast."

Hastings nodded.

I went to the closet and got my coat. And as I was putting the coat on, the telephone rang. "Damn," I said irritably.

The call was from Carol. "I forgot to ask you," she said. "Do

5

you want onion dip or bleu cheese?"

"I don't want either one," I told her. "I want honest-to-God hors d'oeuvres. Smoked salmon and chicken livers with bacon and sturgeon and things like that. I want it to be nice."

"But, Brock, you didn't *say* you wanted hors d'oeuvres."

"Well, I do."

"It's too late to order them."

"No, it isn't." And to preclude further discussion, I hung up. "Never let your girlfriend plan your parties," I said to Hastings. "It's always a mistake."

"I don't have a girlfriend," he replied. "I have a wife." He looked around the office again. "Pretty place."

I paused at Helen's desk on the way out. "I'll be back in half an hour," I said. Then I remembered the Scotch. I told Hastings I'd meet him by the elevators and went down the corridor to Mark's office.

A shot glass had been filled for me and set aside. I drank what was in it and poured myself a refill. I felt I was liable to need it.

"Where are you going with your coat on?" Tom asked.

"To the morgue," I replied.

His face had acquired a pink glow, but suddenly the glow faded. "What for?"

"To identify a body."

"Whose, for God's sake?"

"Damned if I know." I drank my refill. "I'm simply being a good citizen." And with that I squared my shoulders, assumed a confident expression and made what was intended to be a brisk, purposeful exit.

But my shoulders sagged and the confident expression vanished when, halfway to the door, I heard Tom say, behind my back, "I hope he's not getting us into trouble again," and Mark reply, "We couldn't tolerate that."

6

2

Another man had been waiting in the car. Hastings introduced him as Detective Ryerson, who was working on the case with him. Ryerson and I shook hands through the open window; then I got into the back seat, Hastings got into the front, and Ryerson started the motor.

"Where *is* the morgue?" I asked.

"Thirtieth and First," Hastings replied.

That ended the conversation, and I gave myself up to thoughts that had nothing to do with the dead woman but were nevertheless dismal. I was remembering what Tom and Mark had said as I left. And I was feeling hurt.

Perhaps it was the two Scotches on top of the three martinis. Or the abrupt letdown from the euphoria I'd been experiencing earlier. I don't know. But it suddenly seemed to me that the two men I considered my best friends, the two men I trusted above all others, weren't my best friends, weren't trustworthy and didn't appreciate all I'd done for them.

Tom Petacque and I had known each other for twelve years. He was one of the salesmen at the brokerage house that hired me to work in its research department when I first came to New York. We hit it off from the very beginning, and he introduced me to his wife, Daisy, and she and I hit it off, too, and before long I was like a member of the family. When their son, Jerry, was born, a couple of years later, they made me his godfather.

Even in those days Tom was an exceptionally good securities

salesman. He had an intuitive understanding of stocks and bonds that many of the others lacked, in addition to which he had a great talent for making friends. And with the passing of time he went from exceptionally good to truly remarkable. He was, in my opinion, the best securities salesman in the industry. Moreover, our friendship had deepened until we were closer than most brothers. I was one of the few people who understood what went on behind the easy going front he put up. Who knew that what made him so likable wasn't the self-confidence that everyone assumed he had, but rather the lack of it. Who realized that in a tight situation he was apt to panic—and hate himself afterward. In short, who appreciated how much it cost him to do the wonderful job he did.

With Mark Price it was different. Mark was an outsider. We'd taken him in as a partner not because we liked him but because without his money we wouldn't have been able to start the company.

Mark was a bundle of contradictions. At times I thought he was one of the most admirable men I knew. But at other times he infuriated me, and infuriated everyone else too.

On the plus side, he was a hard worker. Although he was rich enough to let himself grow lazy, he'd never done so. He was the first to show up at the office in the morning and the last to leave at night. Furthermore, he had an extraordinary sense of fairness and decency. He'd put up more than one-third of our initial stake but he'd asked for no more than a one-third interest in the company, on the grounds that he'd be bearing only one-third of the responsibility. And he was no snob. Although he'd grown up in one of the most rarefied environments in the United States, I'd never heard him say one word against anyone because of the person's class, color or religion.

But there were some big minuses, too. He never seemed to understand why everyone didn't do things his way, because his way was the only right one. Moreover, he was a stickler for detail; he loved interoffice memos, lists and reports of all kinds. And he insisted that all such data be submitted in triplicate, so that he could give one copy to Tom and another to me. With the result that Tom and I were constantly deluged with trivia, including a daily inventory of the items in the supply closet, down to the last bar of soap.

Mark's most annoying eccentricity, however, had to do with the spending of money. He owned a ten-room duplex on Fifth Avenue, a five-acre estate in Greenwich and a sixty-foot yacht. But the apartment in New York, as well as the house in Connecticut, was furnished partly with cast-off antiques from his in-laws' houses and partly with bargain-basement junk that he and his wife had picked up for next to nothing. And the yacht sat idle most of the time, because Mark couldn't find a captain or crew members who were willing to work for what he was willing to pay. By the grace of God, he'd married a woman who was just as rich as he, just as decent, and just as stingy. Dinner at their house was an experience to be avoided, for the magnificent Spode china and Waterford stemware that had been given to Mark and Joyce by her mother never quite made up for the fact that you were eating cheap cuts of meat and drinking the kind of wine that's sold in gallon bottles with screw-on caps.

Yet when you got to know Mark and Joyce really well, you learned that they were very generous to certain worthy causes and were privately supporting a number of needy people whom they were in no way obligated to support. It didn't make sense, but there it was.

At any rate, Tom, Mark and I started the brokerage house known as Price, Potter and Petacque, and it's done extremely well, despite the fact that we went into business at a time when many brokers were going under. Tom and I discovered that for all his peculiarities, Mark was almost a genius when it came to corporate financing. And that while he wasn't right as often as he thought he was, he was right a surprising amount of the time.

9

And that we liked him vastly more than we'd thought we were going to. The three of us made a good team, and we knew it, and our competitors knew it too.

I had to admit that I preferred Tom to Mark. But I also had to admit that of the two, Mark was the more stable. When I had a problem, Mark was the one I turned to, not Tom. And I'd always known that both of them thought more highly of me than they did of each other.

Which, apparently, was the way I wanted it. Because, skimming northward on the East River Drive in that unmarked police car, I was disturbed as hell by the thought that maybe they didn't think so highly of me after all.

I may not be the greatest securities analyst in the world, but some very important money managers seem to consider my advice good enough to be their main reason for doing business with Price, Potter and Petacque. Tom's biggest selling point is: "If you use us, you'll be able to consult with Brock."

It wasn't only because of his personality that we now had the Hamilton National Bank; it was also because the bank's top decision-makers wanted the information that I assemble, with the aid of my staff. I knew it. So did Tom. So did Mark.

What, then, were they worried about?

Seeing the string of seldom-used piers along the East River always reminded me of the decline of New York as a port. What had caused it? Which cities were benefiting at New York's expense? How safe were any municipal bonds? And as I looked at the piers now, such questions again presented themselves. But only for a moment. I knew damn well what had caused the decline of New York as a port: the same two forces that cause the decline of whatever they touch. Greed and corruption.

And that, in a way, was what Tom and Mark were worried about. Those occasions in the past when I'd discovered fraud and exposed it. For, in doing so, I'd antagonized some powerful folks, including the folks at the Securities and Exchange Commission and a number of our largest customers.

But the backlash we'd felt had been only temporary, and in the end we'd profited from the publicity. The people who were mad at us forgave us, and people who'd previously ignored us sat up and took notice.

Could it be that Tom and Mark had never really approved of what I'd done, even though they'd backed me at the time?

I recalled something Mark had once said to me. He'd said that I was by nature a moralist and a reformer and that I enjoyed finding the worms under the stones. I'd denied that I was or that I did—and I still denied it. But his words began to bother me all over again.

I recalled the way Tom flinched whenever I said I was looking into something that didn't seem quite right to me.

And the uneasiness in Helen's voice when she'd said a policeman wanted to see me. Even my secretary seemed to fear my getting the firm into another scrape.

My thoughts grew darker, and I sighed.

"Over there," Hastings said.

Startled, I looked up. He was pointing at a turquoise brick building. "The morgue?" I asked.

He grunted an affirmation.

Ryerson guided the car into the parking lot north of the building. He remained in the car when Hastings and I got out. I followed Hastings around to the entrance, which faced First Avenue. A modest sign in metal letters said: CITY OF NEW YORK OFFICE OF CHIEF MEDICAL EXAMINER. I'd passed the place a thousand times, I realized, and never known what it was.

The lobby, with its terrazzo floor, dusty rubber plants and vinyl-upholstered benches, was like that of a hospital. Hastings escorted me past the uniformed policeman who sat yawning behind a desk, and in the direction indicated by an arrow on a sign that said: IDENTIFICATION ROOM 106. I began to wish fervently that I were somewhere else.

Room 106 was being presided over by a young woman with red hair and pink acne.

"Be right back," Hastings said, and left.

The young woman whipped out a form. "Your name?" she asked.

"Brockton Potter."

"Your address?"

I gave her the office address.

"Your relationship to the deceased?"

"I don't know."

She looked up from the form. Her acne seemed to grow pinker. "You don't *know?*"

I shook my head.

"Then what are you doing here?"

"Detective Hastings asked me to come."

She frowned. We were obviously at an impasse. The impasse didn't last long, however, for Hastings returned presently with a clipboard that had some papers fastened to it.

"He doesn't know his relationship to the deceased," the young woman complained.

"Not yet, at least," Hastings replied, consulting the papers on the clipboard. "Send up the subway case."

She lifted a telephone receiver and told someone to "send up the Jane Doe in box nineteen." Then she rose from the desk and instructed me to come with her.

My palms began to sweat, something they don't often do.

She led the way into a small adjoining room that had a plastic window in one wall. She pressed a button, and a metal screen came down to cover the window. Then she pressed another button, and a light went on. I heard the sound of machinery. I looked around rather desperately. My eyes met Hastings'. He'd come with us and was watching me intently. I swallowed. The sound of machinery stopped.

12

"Now, please," said the young woman as she pushed the button to raise the screen.

I forced myself to look.

The body on the other side of the window was covered by a black rubber sheet. Only the face and one arm were exposed. The arm was partially raised, as if the woman had died trying to fend off the oncoming train.

She had indeed been old. Her hair was pure white, and the skin of her face was deeply wrinkled. Her arm seemed pitifully thin.

I'd never seen her before in my life.

I tried to say so but I couldn't speak. All I could do was turn to Hastings and shake my head.

"No idea?" he asked, still watching me intently.

I shook my head again.

"O.K.," he said to the attendant, and she pushed another button.

I hurried back to the other room. Hastings followed. I sat down beside the desk and lit a cigarette. After a couple of drags I was able to say, "Can't imagine who."

"Think back," he said.

"I'm positive."

He read from the notes on the clipboard: "White female, age seventy plus, height approximately five feet one inch, weight approximately one hundred pounds, personal hygiene good, no indication of drugs or alcohol, teeth—"

"It won't help," I said. "I don't know who she is."

He went on reading: "Body almost completely transsected through midthoracic region. Upper and lower portions held together by skin flap."

"Stop it," I said.

He stopped. The young woman joined us. Hastings detached one of the pieces of paper from the clipboard and put it on the desk. "This is what they found."

13

It was an irregularly shaped piece of brown paper that looked as if it had been torn from a grocery bag. At its longest it was maybe four inches. It was crumpled and badly stained. The stains, I imagined, were those of the woman's blood. The writing was nevertheless easy to read. Listed, in a large, neat script, were "Hair net, Ivory soap (3¢ off), 2 Kleenex (89¢), Brockton Potter." That part of the list was written in pencil. Then, in ink, under my name, was the address of my office. Evidently the address had been added later. Perhaps she'd had to consult a telephone directory.

A mental image of the body I'd just seen made me shudder. "Must have been planning to go to the drugstore too," I said.

Hastings grunted. "Drug or grocery. Or had been." He paused. "Sure you've never seen her?"

"Positive."

He sighed and collected the piece of brown paper, replacing it under the spring of the clipboard. "Well, thank you very much, Mr. Potter." He tucked the clipboard under his arm. "I'll return this, then we'll drive you back to your office."

"We're all through?"

He nodded.

I no longer wanted to go back to my office. "Would you mind driving me home instead? I live on West Eleventh, just off Fifth."

He nodded again.

The young woman sat down at her desk, glanced at the uncompleted form, tore it in half and dropped it into the wastebasket.

3

The next day was Saturday. Because I was giving a party, Louise, my housekeeper, had agreed to come in, although she didn't usually work on weekends. So I was awakened by the sound of the vacuum cleaner.

I tried to go back to sleep, but Louise was working upstairs, and as she got closer to my bedroom the sound of the vacuum cleaner grew louder, making sleep impossible. After a while I gave up, put on a robe and left the bedroom, which was evidently what Louise wanted me to do, for she immediately rushed in and began to strip the bed.

I went downstairs to the kitchen. Louise makes delicious coffee and she always leaves a carafe of it on the kitchen table.

The carafe was there, but so was Carol, and she'd drunk most of the coffee.

"Morning," she said.

"Morning," I said.

"I need help carrying the dishes," she said.

"Hell," I said, and got a cup.

She poured what was left of the coffee into my cup, and we looked at each other the way husbands and wives do when they've been married for ten years and have run out of enthusiasm. Except that Carol and I weren't husband and wife. We were just friends who always seemed to be either breaking up because we weren't in love or getting back together because we missed each other. Sometimes I'd give her a key to my house,

15

and for a while everything would be fine. Then we'd decide that we really weren't right for each other and that our relationship had no future, and she'd give me back the key, and we wouldn't see each other for a month or two. At the moment, she had a key but wasn't using it very often. That was a state of affairs which had never existed before and it was troubling me, although we hadn't got around to discussing it.

"I talked them into the hors d'oeuvres," she said.

"Good."

"You should have *told* me you wanted hors d'oeuvres."

"I did."

"No, you didn't." She paused. "The flowers are going to be expensive."

"How much?"

"I'm not sure. I think around seventy-five dollars."

"OK."

"You don't sound very interested this morning. In anything."

"I'm sleepy. I didn't go to bed until three."

"Where were you?"

"At The Cyclops."

"Why?" The Cyclops was a bar on Christopher Street, and Carol knew I was more inclined to go there when I was distressed than when I wasn't.

"I'd seen a dead body."

Her eyes widened. Her lips parted. After a moment she said, "Whose?"

"I don't know. Some poor old lady who was hit by a subway train. And afterwards, I kept seeing her. So I went to The Cyclops."

"Oh." She seemed relieved. "For a minute I thought . . ."

"You thought what?"

"Well, you know how you are. I mean, the way you're always *getting into* things."

"Join the club. That's the way Mark and Tom feel too."

"You don't have to get angry about it."

"I'm not angry. I'd like more coffee."

"I'll make some."

She did, and we drank it. Then I got dressed, and we went over to her apartment for the dishes that she was lending me for the party. Her apartment was two blocks away, on Fifth Avenue near Ninth Street. We had to make two trips.

She helped me set the table, and when we were finished I had to admit that it looked very nice. Shortly after that the flowers came, and she helped me get them set up too. By then it was noon, and she left for the beauty shop.

The party worried me. I live more or less alone and don't do much formal entertaining at home; when I have guests I take them to a restaurant. But this time, because of the situation, I'd decided that a home environment might make a difference. And Carol, no matter what the state of our relationship, was always ready to drop everything in order to "help Brock entertain some business friends." So, for that matter, was every other woman I'd ever known. I don't know why, but nothing seems to turn a woman on as much as helping a man give a party, especially a party for people he works with.

But I was skeptical about the catering service Carol had talked me into using. It was a husband-and-wife operation, the husband and wife being a couple of Hungarian refugees. I had visions of noodles and stuffed cabbage. I was also skeptical about Carol's and my abilities to make everyone feel as comfortable as I wanted them to feel. The purpose of the party was to ease tension, and that wasn't going to be a simple task. Matters had got out of hand.

The tension had started with Irving and Brian, but it was beginning to affect the others too. I'd always been proud of the team spirit I generated in the research department, the willingness of one member of the department to help another. But the friction between Irving and Brian had grown to such proportions that everyone was now involved, and no one was cooperating with anyone else. Joe Rothland and George Cole, who'd always got along well with each other, were bickering, and Harriet Jensen, who usually held herself aloof from any sort of alliance, had begun to side with Brian and was therefore at odds with Irving.

Irving Silvers was my right-hand man. He was the first person I'd hired for the department, and I'd hired him before the company was even formally in business, because I knew him and knew how good he was. He was a small man who weighed no more than a hundred and twenty pounds, soaking wet. But he was utterly dauntless; when he was on the trail of information, no one could intimidate him or deter him from getting it. He was also scrupulously honest, a tireless worker, and the greatest authority I knew on the subject of steel and automobile manufacturers. I had implicit confidence in him, and he was in charge of the department when I was out of town, which was often, and I had no intention of ever firing him or letting him quit.

But Brian Barth was an exceptional asset to the department also. Brian was the newest member of the team. He was still in his twenties, a plump, baby-faced Virginian with blue eyes, pink cheeks and a soft-spoken manner that was totally deceptive. For he was not only enormously bright, he was quite ruthless. I called him my piranha. But he too was honest, indefatigable, impossible to frighten, and in practically no time he had become an authority himself—on chemical and oil companies. He'd supplied me with some very valuable bits of information and in many ways proved himself to be someone I could rely on to come through in any situation. I wasn't about to part with him either.

Irving felt that Brian was out to get him. Which was true.

Brian was the sort of man who would always be out to get the person who was his immediate superior and take over his job. He couldn't help it. He was like that. But that didn't make him less useful to the company. And Irving, as I kept trying to tell him, was in no way threatened.

Brian, on the other hand, felt that Irving was picking on him. Which was also true. Irving, who'd always been extremely fair, was going out of his way to make life difficult for Brian, challenging everything he said and did. Matters had come to a head a few weeks previously when, in my absence, Brian had told Irving he intended to make a trip to Louisiana, to visit a chemical plant which had recently been built there, and Irving had told him he couldn't go. The plant was turning out a new type of urethane which was more flame-resistant than any currently in use. The product had great potential and could affect a number of other industries, such as construction and home appliances. By making buildings safer, it could save lives. Brian had refused to take no for an answer and had gone anyway.

Irving was wrong to have said no. Brian was wrong to have defied him. Both of them were wrong to have invited the three other members of the department—George, Joe and Harriet—to take sides.

Now there was constant quarreling, which I couldn't seem to control. Not being able to control my own staff was a new experience for me. I didn't like it.

So I was giving a party. Because I hoped that in a social situation all the ruffled feathers would be smoothed. And because I simply didn't know what else to do.

The three married members of the department were bringing their wives. The two single ones—Brian and Harriet—were bringing dates. With Carol and me, there'd be an even dozen at the table.

And with luck, everyone would end up being friends again.

4

At three-thirty the caterers arrived in a small van loaded with boxes of food and cooking utensils of every size, shape and description.

At four Louise left in a huff, because the Hungarian woman had spoken rudely to her.

At a quarter to five two men in turtleneck sweaters and suede jackets showed up, carrying suitcases. They were the helpers, they said in thick Hungarian accents. They were going to wait table and do the dishes.

At five-thirty Carol returned, sporting a new hair style and a new dress. She looked lovely. While she checked on the progress that was being made in the kitchen, I went upstairs to shave, shower and put on my blue suit. By then the entire house was fragrant with delightful, unidentifiable aromas, and I was in an optimistic mood.

Carol and I had a drink together in the den, and at seven o'clock the first guests arrived. Joe Rothland and his wife, Florence. Then George Cole and his wife rang the doorbell, and right after them came Irving and his wife.

The last to appear were Brian and Harriet, who, with their dates, pulled up in the same taxi.

It was strange to see Harriet with a masculine escort. She was a pretty little blonde who elicited admiration from men but didn't seem to want it. It was strange, also, to see her in a dress —she always wore pants suits. But there she was, in something pale green and even rather frilly, on the arm of a man named Dennis, who was the spitting image of Henry Kissinger.

Brian's date was a stunning young woman who was two inches taller than he and looked like a showgirl. Her name was Gloria Hines. She wasn't a showgirl, however. She was a recent graduate of Columbia University. The jewelry she was wearing consisted of a pair of pearl earrings and a small gold chain, from which hung a Phi Beta Kappa key. Her occupation was teaching deaf children to speak. I found her charming.

The two helpers were more impressive in uniform than they'd been in turtleneck sweaters and suede jackets, and they passed the hors d'oeuvres trays with a distinct flair.

When I wasn't bartending I added my voice to various conversations. The person I spent the most time with was Irving's wife, Naomi. Because I was immensely fond of her, and because I knew, without even discussing the matter with her, that she was as unhappy about Irving's quarrel with Brian as I was. I recognized her as an ally and knew she'd do whatever she could to make the evening pleasant.

Naomi Silvers appeared to be nothing more than a nice little housewife and mother, and primarily that's what she was. She was utterly devoted to Irving and their three children. She loved to cook and cooked well. She did needlepoint and had a way with plants. The only outside organization she was active in was the Sisterhood at the temple she and Irving belonged to. Yet she had something in common with Gloria Hines: a Phi Beta Kappa key. She'd never earned less than an A in any subject she'd ever studied. Furthermore, while her field was child psychology rather than speech, she'd worked with handicapped children. During the first years of her marriage to Irving she'd had a job at a clinic for youngsters who were emotionally disturbed. She and Gloria would get along fine, I thought, if only I could get them together.

The problem was getting them together. Brian and Irving

had immediately positioned themselves on opposite sides of the room, and each was surrounded by his own circle. I kept trying to get people to move from one circle to the other, and failing.

Finally I took Naomi aside and said in a low voice, "Go talk to Brian and his girlfriend. He's not as bad as Irving says, and you'll love her."

She smiled. "I'll try."

At that point Carol joined us. She looked as if something was wrong. She tugged at my sleeve. "Can I see you for a minute?"

I left Naomi and went with Carol.

"The wine isn't here," she said. "Why didn't you tell me they didn't deliver the wine?"

"I didn't know they were supposed to."

"Yes, you did. You were home all afternoon. You should have realized. They promised to have it here by six o'clock. I was just out in the kitchen, and there's no wine. Oh, Brock!"

"Well, call them up."

"It's too late. And we've got all the wineglasses on the table. I don't know what to do."

"What kind of wine did you order?"

"That nice burgundy you like so much."

"Hell." I thought for a moment. "Will champagne do? I have some in the basement."

She brightened. "You do?" She dimmed. "The glasses are wrong."

"Nobody'll notice."

"Well, you'd better bring it up. We have to have *something.*"

I left her muttering about how she should have checked on the wine herself, and went down to the basement. I found the champagne and lugged the entire case upstairs. I deposited it on the kitchen floor and said to the Hungarian husband, "You'd better chill it a little."

He inspected the label on one of the bottles and nodded approvingly. "Is fine."

I returned to the living room. Naomi, I noticed, had joined Brian's group and was the center of attention. I poured myself another drink and went over to them.

Brian was giving her his innocent-little-boy smile. And was saying, "But how did you and Irving happen to meet in the first place?"

"Well, actually," Naomi replied, "we met at a Communist Party rally. I was there with another boy, and Irving was there with another girl."

I shot her a warning look, but she didn't notice it.

Brian's smile broadened. "You and Irving were *Communists?*"

I shot Naomi another warning look, but she missed that one too. "Wasn't everybody?" she replied blithely. "At the time Irving and I were going to college, no one considered you an intellectual if you weren't a Communist. Everyone was so polarized. And," she added, "Irving and I were terribly eager to be considered intellectuals."

She was exaggerating, of course. Irving had told me about his Communist phase years before. He'd never been a member of the Communist Party, and neither had Naomi. But they'd flirted briefly with it.

"What made you reject it?" I'd asked.

"Everyone in it was so damned middle-class," he'd replied.

Knowing Irving, I'd been able to accept his explanation without further question. For if there was one thing in the world he didn't want to be, it was middle-class. A part of him was suspicious of the top-level executives he was always dealing with, but a much larger part of him admired them. And I was convinced that he privately considered himself a member of their ranks.

But Brian was grinning from ear to ear, like a child with a new toy.

"Come now," I said to Naomi. "You know that both you and

Irving were never Communists." And with that, I took Brian by the arm and pulled him toward the middle of the room. I didn't know quite where I was leading him, but I felt I had to break up that particular conversation.

Fortunately, I spied Carol coming through the doorway from the hall, and I led him over to her. "You haven't talked to Brian yet," I said.

She still seemed preoccupied. But she managed to give him a big smile. And, unhappily, to say the first thing that came into her head. "You don't look like a piranha," she told him.

I wanted to strangle her.

Brian blushed, which he did rather easily. He rose to the occasion, however. "That's because I'm such a young piranha. I'm still growing."

Carol recovered her wits. "The fact is, I've been dying to have a nice long talk with you. Brock has been telling me so much about all the wonderful things you've been doing, I'm beginning to think your advice is better than his. Let's go somewhere and sit down, and you can tell me all about which stocks to buy." She guided him to the settee by the window.

I took a long swallow of my drink and went back to where Naomi was. The subject had been changed. Harriet was describing the plot of a movie she'd seen on television. It had to do with a wife who'd left her family and was seeking her identity in San Francisco. I didn't get to hear much about it, though, for presently Florence Rothland asked me for another drink, which prompted the others to request refills also, and I went off, trying not to drop any of the glasses.

Soon I noticed that Naomi was leading Gloria across the room to introduce her to Irving. Then I saw her lead Mary Cole across the room in the opposite direction, to where Harriet was. I stopped mixing the drinks and just watched. Seemingly without effort, Naomi was accomplishing what I'd worked at so deliberately and so unsuccessfully. Within minutes, everyone was chatting cheerfully with someone he hadn't been chatting with before. Except for Brian and Carol, who were still on the settee, deep in a discussion of, presumably, Carol's investments.

I made this round of drinks stronger, and from then on I just let things happen. The noise level began to rise, and the tensions I'd been aware of earlier seemed to diminish.

By the time we went into the dining room, I was certain that the party was going to be a success. The Coles and the Rothlands appeared to be the best of friends, and Harriet was carrying on an animated conversation with Irving.

The Hungarian couple had prepared a marvelous meal. The waiters demonstrated the same élan in the dining room that they'd demonstrated in the living room. The champagne was better than I'd remembered its being, and if anyone noticed that the glasses were wrong he didn't mention it.

Looking around the table, I felt a certain pride. This, in a way, was my family. The closest thing to a family that I had. And a fine one it was. Bright people. Interesting people. Winners.

My family wasn't going to come apart, I decided, because I simply wasn't going to let it do so. One way or another, I was going to patch things up between Irving and Brian. This was step number one, and it was a big step. They were seated on opposite sides of the table, and while they weren't quite speaking to each other, they were at least looking at each other without animosity. As for the rest of the group, the hard feelings had apparently vanished.

Step number two? I didn't yet know exactly what it was going to be, but I'd think of something.

Naomi was sitting at my right. She was listening to Dennis, who was explaining his theory that populations always move in a westerly direction. Suddenly she turned, and our eyes met, and both of us smiled. It was a nice moment. We were on the same wavelength.

The dessert was cherries jubilee. When we'd finished it, we sat around the table for a while. The various conversations slowed down. There was a general air of contentment. Finally I got up, and at that point everyone else did too.

The women followed Carol upstairs. George Cole and Brian went into the living room. Dennis professed an interest in my paintings, and I offered to take him on a tour of the house. Joe Rothland and Irving came with us.

I was just beginning to describe how I'd acquired the Delaunay that hung in the foyer, when the doorbell rang.

"This is a hell of a time for them to deliver the wine," I said.

"Wine?" said Irving.

"I'll tell you about it later," I said, and went to open the door.

The two men standing there weren't from the liquor store, however. They were from the police department. Detectives Hastings and Ryerson.

"Can we come in?" Hastings asked.

"Well, I guess so," I said reluctantly. "But I'm kind of in the middle of giving a party." I stepped aside to let them in.

"This won't take long," Hastings said.

I closed the door behind them. Irving, apparently sensing that the detectives weren't altogether welcome visitors, came over like an alert watchdog, in case I should need help.

Hastings looked around. "Nice place."

"Everything O.K.?" Irving asked me.

I nodded.

"We've identified the woman," Ryerson said.

My interest quickened. "You have? Who was she?"

Hastings finished his inspection. "Someone named Sarah Weinberg. Name mean anything to you?"

"Sarah Weinberg." I searched my memory. "No. I'm pretty sure I don't know anybody by that name."

"Sarah Weinberg," Irving said thoughtfully.

"The name ring a bell?" Hastings asked him.

"It might," Irving replied noncommittally.

Hastings took a notebook from his pocket and consulted it. "Sarah C. Weinberg, 658 East 26th Street, Brooklyn. That's Flatbush." He was watching Irving closely now.

Irving nodded slowly. "I know where it is," he said, and added, "Aunt Sarah."

Noting that Joe and Dennis had drawn closer, Hastings said, "Is there a place where we can talk private?"

I led the detectives into the den. Irving came with us.

"You're Mrs. Weinberg's nephew?" Hastings asked him.

Irving turned to me. "Who are these men, Brock?"

"Detectives," I said. "Police department."

Ryerson echoed Hastings. "You're Mrs. Weinberg's nephew?"

"Not really her nephew," Irving replied. "But I used to know her very well. I used to love her very much." He turned to me again. There was worry in his eyes. "What's she done, Brock? Why are these men here?"

Hastings didn't give me a chance to answer. "What she's done," he said, "is get herself murdered."

Irving turned white and took a step backward, his hand out as if reaching for a chair. I took his arm and guided him over to where a chair was. He sank into it. "I don't believe it," he groaned. "My God, I don't believe it." There were tears in his eyes.

5

I spent most of Sunday afternoon at The Cyclops. Brooding.

I've always prided myself on my ability to fit into any group, and my acceptance by the crowd that patronized The Cyclops was a case in point. For the crowd included members of every trade, political party, religion and sexual persuasion known to man. The only thing all the customers had in common was youth. The average age of a Cyclops regular was around twenty-seven. And I was forty-one. But I was treated as one of the group.

My drinking companion on that particular day was a gay activist named Milton Kaye. Milton, with his long black hair and violet eyes, looked like a cross between Prince Valiant and Elizabeth Taylor. His particular hangup was the New York Fire Department. He hated it. He couldn't forgive the firemen for the part they'd played in defeating the antidiscrimination bill which he'd worked so hard to get passed.

But Milton was only a gay activist in his spare time. Weekdays, he was a conservatively dressed, subdued, dutiful salesman at Maximilian Dover. The House of Dover, as its owner liked to refer to it, was one of the most prestigious jewelry establishments in the world, and its headquarters, on Fifth Avenue, was a sort of United Nations of the very rich. People came there from almost every country, including a surprising number of the underdeveloped countries, to trade for some small share of the earth's treasures. And Milton was well on the way to becoming a walking encyclopedia of little-known facts about millionaires. When he talked about Dover's customers he could be very amusing.

This wasn't one of his better days, however. He was depressed. The immediate cause of his depression was an appointment he had for the following morning, to have an impacted wisdom tooth removed. But in back of that was a more general depression that was prompted by the fact that Max Dover had taken the Star of Faith on tour without him. Like most of the male employees of the House of Dover, Milton was his boss's occasional lover. And his boss had chosen Milton's chief rival to accompany him on the tour.

The Star of Faith wasn't the largest diamond ever found. It weighed in at only one hundred six karats. But it was one of the most perfect. A flawless blue-white, it had been a topic of interest ever since Dover had come into possession of it and, with his usual flair, begun to use it for publicity purposes. It was not for sale. It was Dover's personal property, and he intended to use it only to raise money for various charities. But since the charity events invariably attracted the wealthiest people, Dover made more money by keeping the diamond than he would have made by selling it, for the guests at the affairs were potential customers for the other items in his bag of goodies.

Take me, for instance. I couldn't care less about diamonds or any other precious stones. They just don't interest me. But I'd seen the Star of Faith. Because Carol had threatened never to speak to me again if I didn't take her to a bash that Dover had recently given in New York. And I had to admit that I'd been awed by that single glittering rock sitting on a black velvet cushion inside a glass case that was monitored from all angles by closed-circuit television cameras.

As one of Milton's friends, I was privy to the confidential information that Dover had acquired the stone not in South Africa, as was commonly supposed, but in India, where some of the best diamonds had always been mined; and that Dover had already turned down eight offers for it. I even knew the names of those who'd made the offers—only one of which surprised me, for it was the name of the president of one of the African republics that were complaining most bitterly about their poverty.

"Where's your boss now?" I asked, hoping to rouse Milton, as well as myself, from our mutual dejection.

"Houston," he replied dully.

"And where does he go from there?"

"Los Angeles. My face'll probably be all swollen."

"Use an ice pack."

"And black and blue."

"You're making it out to be worse than it will be."

"No, I'm not. I turn black and blue very easy. Especially now. I'm in a low-resistance cycle. Everything affects me."

I gave up and let him wallow in his glum mood while I wallowed in mine.

Several things were bothering me. The first was Carol's behavior after the party. She'd gone home.

I couldn't understand it. We'd had our ups and downs. There were periods when we'd been close and periods when we hadn't. There'd been one period when we hadn't seen each other for three months. But there'd never been a period like this, when on the surface everything was all right, yet Carol just wasn't interested. Usually, it seemed to me, she was the aggressor in our ruptures as well as our reconciliations. But at the moment she wasn't being aggressive. She wasn't even being passive. She was being . . . I didn't know what. She'd knocked herself out to help me with the party, and then resisted all my efforts to persuade her to spend the night. She was tired, she'd said. That's all. Tired.

There could be only one explanation: she was getting interested in someone else.

I was also bothered by Irving's reaction to the death of Mrs. Weinberg. And by Naomi's. For Naomi had been almost as distressed by the news, when Irving broke it to her, as he was. Neither of them had given much information to the detectives or to me; they'd simply said that Sarah Weinberg had been an old and very dear friend of theirs and that although they hadn't seen much of her in recent years, her death made them terribly sad. They couldn't conceive of anyone's wanting to murder a wonderful person like Aunt Sarah. But Naomi invited the detectives to visit Irving and herself the next morning, promising that they'd tell them whatever they could. The detectives accepted the invitation and left. Shortly after that, Irving and Naomi left too.

The name Sarah Weinberg still didn't mean anything to me personally, though. I was as certain as ever that I'd never met the woman. And I couldn't understand why she'd been carrying my name around with her.

One thought led to another, and presently I was reliving my ride to the morgue. Including the state of mind I'd been in.

The conclusions I'd come to about Tom and Mark, I found, hadn't changed. To them I was someone who went out of his way to stir up trouble.

And perhaps, I admitted now, they were right. Perhaps I did have that tendency.

"From here on in, I'm going to watch myself," I said aloud.

"What?" said Milton.

I shook my head. "Nothing."

He went back to contemplating his mug of beer.

I began to feel a little better, though. I'd faced a truth and could do something about it.

"How much do you think he'll charge?" Milton asked.

"Who?" I asked.

"The dentist."

"How should I know? Let's talk about something else—OK?

I'll tell you about this party I gave last night."

Milton really wasn't interested, but I told him anyway. For the party was one thing I could still feel good about. In spite of everything, it had been a success.

6

Every Monday morning the members of the research department get together in my office. We discuss the performance of the market and pool the information we've been collecting. The opinions and facts we exchange on Monday morning form the basis of the market letter that goes out to our customers on Tuesday afternoon. Since the market letter is the main reason many of our customers do business with us, we take it very seriously, and for my staff and me the Monday meeting is the focal point of the week. Nothing is allowed to interfere with it.

But that Monday morning Irving didn't show up.

He called me at home while I was having breakfast to say that he wouldn't be in—he was going to Sarah Weinberg's funeral. He was apologetic. He said he'd try to get to the office before the meeting broke up but he doubted that he could. He read me the notes he'd prepared for the meeting and offered some suggestions as to what everyone should be doing for the next few days. I raised no objections. He was entitled. He'd never missed a meeting before, not even when he'd had something called walking pneumonia, which had driven his temperature up to a hundred and two. I merely told him not to worry, I could handle things; to take as much time as he needed.

I explained his absence to the others, and the meeting went on as usual. Everyone said something nice about the party, and then we got down to work. The market had been zigzagging up and down within a narrow range for over a month, and all of us were in agreement: it was forming a base for a substantial rise, but the rise wouldn't begin for at least another month, and perhaps longer; this was a good time to buy.

We talked for half an hour about Refrigerco, a small company that George Cole had brought to our attention some time back and was keeping us posted on. Refrigerco was the brainchild of an Omaha businessman named William Holman, who, while vacationing in Africa, had discovered that one of the big problems in some of the West African countries was keeping food fresh. Fish was an important staple in the diet of the people in those countries, and during the summer fish was plentiful. But during the winter the fishing wasn't good, and poor catches drove prices up to the point where most of the natives couldn't afford to buy. So with the cooperation of several governments he was building refrigeration plants, and the plants were turning out to be very successful. Now the company was starting to manufacture small ice chests which the native women could carry on their heads in the traditional manner when bringing perishable foods to and from market. The ice chests showed promise of being even more successful than the refrigeration plants. George thought we should recommend the stock. I agreed but felt that this wasn't the time—the company wasn't yet on firm enough footing.

"It's funny about those underdeveloped countries," Brian said. "Everyone thinks that what they need most is industrialization, and that's what their politicos keep pushing for. And in the long run they're probably right—that's what they do need. But in the meantime the people are starving. What they need first are the means of producing and distributing food."

"Look at Fairmeadow," Harriet said with satisfaction.

The rest of us nodded. Fairmeadow was one of her discoveries. It, too, had been a small company. A dairy. Its president had conceived the idea of introducing dairy products to third world countries whose land isn't suitable for raising cattle. Fairmeadow had built plants in a number of such countries to reconvert dried milk shipped in by Fairmeadow. The results had been dramatic. Tens of millions of people who hadn't previously done so were now drinking milk. And were consuming unbelievable amounts of a wonderful new product they'd never tasted before: ice cream. Some of our customers had taken our advice and had made nice profits from Fairmeadow stock.

Joe Rothland changed the subject. He'd read in one of the gossip columns that Jim Chapman was quarreling with the producers of *The Davis Family* and was threatening to leave the show. Joe had checked into the item and learned that it was true.

I glanced at the chair Irving usually sat in. So did the others. *The Davis Family* had been one of the top ten shows on television for the past three years. Its principal sponsor was an automobile company. Irving was our automotive expert. If Chapman quit the show, the ratings would undoubtedly slip. The show might even go off the air. That could affect the sponsor's sales.

"You ought to tell Irving," I said.

"I intend to," Joe said.

"Speaking of television," Brian said, "I was talking to one of my contacts over at Darby Oil Friday afternoon. They're going to change their advertising around. They're on a whole new kick. They think people are getting tired of the ecology bit. They're going to start emphasizing the employee angle. All the heroic geologists and drilling superintendents and construction foremen and helicopter pilots and people like that who are working for them in those out-of-the-way places where they have interests."

"Is that right?" I said. I thought for a moment. "By the way, how are they doing with that test well they're drilling in Indonesia?"

Evidently that was the very question Brian had intended me to ask, for a pleased look came over his face. "Very well," he replied. And he proceeded to deliver some really startling news.

Darby, we all knew, had negotiated the right to drill for oil in a large area at the eastern end of the Indonesian archipelago. So far it had drilled three wells. The drilling had been enormously expensive, for all the equipment had to be brought in by ship or plane, and the nearest major port was Singapore, some two thousand miles away. The three wells had been abandoned at fourteen thousand feet or thereabouts. No oil. The fourth well—Biawesi IV was its name—was to be the last. If it turned out to be another dry hole, the project would be abandoned. Drilling costs had been running at the rate of almost fifty thousand dollars a day. The bit was down to six thousand feet.

But on Friday afternoon, while Brian was in the Darby offices, an overseas call had come through.

Biawesi IV had struck oil.

The Darby executives themselves didn't know the extent of the find, and wouldn't for a long time. But as a result of Friday's news it was safe to predict that exploration would continue in the area. Additional wells would be drilled. And there was every reason to believe that the Indonesian concession would turn out to be extremely valuable. The gap between Darby and some of its larger competitors would narrow.

Brian was in his glory. There was no change in his voice; it remained low; he sounded almost embarrassed. But his face was flushed, and his eyes were like glowing charcoal. He was obviously proud of himself. And with Irving not there to challenge him or put him down, he could enjoy his triumph to the fullest.

He outlined in detail how the Indonesian discovery might affect Darby's crude position and earnings; what it would cost to drill additional wells, and to what extent the previous seismo-graphic surveys of the area were thought to be vindicated. Listening to him, I was awed by the extent of his knowledge. He'd managed to educate himself quite thoroughly in the work-ings of the oil industry. He'd also, apparently, established a very close relationship with someone highly placed in the Darby organization. This wasn't unusual. He had an uncanny flair for making friends with people who could be useful to him. But he was mighty close-mouthed about who they were. It was hard even for me to pry from him the names of his contacts in the various companies he studied. Partly, I knew, this was due to a desire to protect them. But partly it was due to a desire to protect himself. His contacts were great assets, and he had no intention of sharing them with anyone else.

His secrecy annoyed me. But since the information he gained was always accurate, I didn't push him. He got results, and results were what counted. In this case, however, I was annoyed not so much by his secrecy about whom he'd talked to as by the fact that he'd waited almost three days before telling anyone what he'd learned. And I said so.

"I wanted to tell you when I got back on Friday," he ex-plained, "but you weren't here."

"Then you should have told Irving."

He said nothing. The fire in his eyes went out, though.

"Or someone," I added.

"The market was already closed."

He was right, of course. Closed for the weekend.

"My feeling is this," he said carefully. "Darby isn't making any big public announcement. After all, this is just one well. It'll be a long time before the value of the field is really known. There's nothing to get excited about—yet. The potential—that's something else again. But there's no hurry. We can afford to take our time."

"I intend to say something in tomorrow's letter."

"Word it cautiously, though. I wouldn't want to get my source in trouble."

"Our first obligation is to our customers," I said sharply.

Brian's face turned a deep pink. "Naturally. But without reliable sources of information, what good are we to our customers?"

"I think you can trust me to handle the matter properly, Brian. I was doing this sort of thing when you were still in high school."

Harriet coughed politely, and directed our attention to a different subject. The Federal Reserve, she said, was planning to raise interest rates.

The rest of the meeting passed without incident. And shortly before it ended, Irving appeared.

He sat down in his usual chair but said nothing. He was paler than I'd ever seen him. He kept his eyes focused on me even when one of the others was speaking. The steadiness of his gaze disconcerted me, but I did my best to ignore it.

By a quarter to twelve we'd covered all the topics that were of moment. I told each member of the staff what he should work on during the coming week, as Irving had outlined, and they filed out of my office. Brian hesitated, as if he wanted to stay, but in the end he left with the other three.

Only Irving remained. Still in his chair. Still staring at me.

Finally he got up and closed the door. Then he came back and demanded in a quivering voice, "Why didn't you tell me that Aunt Sarah was on her way to see you when she was killed?"

"Until Saturday night I didn't even know who she was. Or that you knew her. And I still don't know that she was on her way to see me. All I know is that she had my name and address in her coat pocket."

"She was on her way to see you, all right. I'm the one who sent her to you."

37

"Oh?" I looked at him. He was standing with his legs apart. His expression was one of fury. "Well, sit down and tell me about it. And stop looking like an angel of vengeance. The poor woman is dead, Irving. Nothing is going to bring her back."

Some of the rigidity left him. "I know that. And I'm sorry if I look like an angel of vengeance. But maybe it's because in this case that's what I really want to be." He sat down and took a deep breath. "Will you help me?"

7

I didn't answer. I merely waited for him to continue. And after a moment he did.

"Everything I am," he said, "everything I have, I owe to that woman and her husband. They changed the course of my life."

I'd known Irving for eight years. He'd never even mentioned the Weinbergs. "She left a husband?" I asked.

He shook his head. He was close to tears. Then he cleared his throat and said, "He died six years ago. She lived alone."

"No children?"

He forced a smile. It was a tremulous one. "Hundreds. Including Naomi and me."

The eight years, I suddenly realized, meant less than I'd thought. We'd worked together, fought, made up again, formed a deep two-way loyalty, shared the countless ups and downs that are part of any close business relationship, hosted each other in our homes, been guests at the same affairs, become what many people would consider good friends—what we ourselves considered good friends. Yet in some respects we were like strangers. For there was a certain line that, by mutual consent, we'd never crossed. I knew next to nothing about his childhood, and he knew next to nothing about mine. I seldom discussed my childhood with anyone, because I didn't like the memories I had of it. And apparently Irving felt the same about his.

"Do you know how far it is from where I grew up to Brooklyn College?" he asked.

He'd grown up in Brooklyn. His father had been the rabbi of an Orthodox synagogue. That much I did know. So I made a guess. "Three miles?"

"Ten light-years. Maybe more." He sighed. "I grew up on a different planet. You need a telescope to see it."

I nodded. I sometimes thought that I'd grown up on a different planet too. "The Weinbergs were people you met at college?"

"He was one of my economics professors. The best I ever had. And he was one of the finest human beings I've ever known. His wife too. Even more so, in some ways. A wonderful, warm, generous woman. I loved them both."

He was opening the curtain on the area of his life that he'd kept hidden. I was pleased. But then he closed it again. He sat up straighter, cleared his throat once more and became businesslike.

"Have you ever heard of a company called Lucky Devil?" he asked.

Startled by his change of manner, I sat up straighter myself. "No."

"Neither have I. I can't find it listed anywhere. But that's what Sarah Weinberg was coming to see you about."

"Why me, Irving?"

"Because she'd read about you in the newspapers." He permitted himself a wry smile. "You have an image. A Fearless Fosdick image."

"Unfortunately."

"Anyway, she'd read about you. She hoped you'd be able to shed some light. And I assured her that if anyone could it was you."

"Why not you?"

"I would have been glad to try, if she'd asked. She didn't ask. You were the one she wanted to see. Because of your reputation, I suppose, and because—because I'm an ungrateful, self-centered son of a bitch. I let myself forget about her. We'd drifted apart. Since her husband died, Naomi and I have hardly seen her. She and Naomi exchanged cards at the holidays, but that's been about the extent of our contact the past few years. I'm ashamed now. More than you can imagine. But facts are facts. That wonderful woman who took me in when I had no one else to turn to—that—that—" He began to sputter.

"You're being too hard on yourself. We're all like that, to a degree."

"I'm not being hard enough. And if we are, we shouldn't be. But that's *my* problem—something *I*'ll have to live with. I'm not even sure she remembered that I work for you. She didn't seem to."

"I see."

"I feel like shit, Brock. But that's neither here nor there. She called me Thursday night. It was the first time I'd heard her voice in years. Naturally I was delighted. We had a nice long talk, and toward the end she asked me if I knew you. I said I not only knew you, I worked for you. She said, did I think you'd be willing to see her—she needed some advice about a stock. I said I'd arrange it. I didn't ask what stock she wanted to talk to you about, and she didn't say. I just told her to let me know when she was planning to come; I'd take her to lunch. She laughed and said she was on a low-cholesterol diet. And that was all. I intended to mention it to you, but I had no idea she was planning to come so soon. And there was so much excitement around here Friday morning."

"I know." I considered what he'd said. "Is it possible that she really did know you worked for me, and that's why she called you?"

"Perhaps, although she was anything but devious. And I can't swear that I'd ever mentioned you to her. But the important thing is that she wanted to see you and I said I'd arrange it. I thought she'd call to make an appointment, or something. She didn't *say* she was going to come the very next morning. I thought—I don't know what I thought."

"Maybe she didn't intend to come so soon. Maybe something made her change her mind."

"That's what I'm beginning to believe *did* happen. She must have had another call from that man."

"What man?"

"The one who was trying to get her to sell her Lucky Devil stock."

"Where'd you get the name of the stock?"

"After those detectives left yesterday, I went to see Nettie Hoffman. Nettie was her next-door neighbor and her best friend. According to the detectives, Nettie's the one who reported her missing and who identified her body."

"Oh."

"I've looked in *Moody's*. The stock isn't listed. It doesn't seem to be listed anywhere."

"Are you sure you have the name right?"

"Nettie seemed rather certain. Positive, in fact. Lucky Devil."

"Is it worth anything?"

"How should I know? According to Nettie, Aunt Sarah didn't think so. But she owned a hell of a lot of it. Fifty thousand shares. It was worth, she thought, about four cents a share."

"How did she ever come to buy junk like that?"

"She didn't buy it. Her husband bought it. And he'd made a small fortune on junk like that."

"She wasn't poor, then?"

"Hell, no. In addition to her husband's life insurance and her Social Security, she was worth maybe a quarter of a million dollars. That's why she could afford to sit on the stock if she wanted to." He took a deep breath and crossed his legs. "It's a long story. Morris Weinberg was really quite a guy. Brilliant mind. Great sense of humor. A sport. A liver. He liked to tell people that he'd made his money in a bar in Las Vegas, and in a way he did, but not the way you might think. He and Aunt Sarah spent a weekend there in 1957, on their way to California for a vacation, and in the bar at the hotel he met a man who was going bananas. The guy had lost a bundle at craps and was trying to raise enough money to pay his hotel bill and buy a plane ticket home. He offered to sell Morris some cheap stock he'd recently bought—for a quarter of what he'd paid for it. And Morris, on the spur of the moment, bought it." Irving paused. "Two thousand shares of Deseret Pharmaceutical, for which he paid twenty-five cents a share."

"Good God! I hope he held on to it."

"He did. For ten years. By which time his five-hundred-dollar investment was worth a hundred and forty thousand."

I shook my head in wonderment. Deseret Pharmaceutical has been one of the more remarkable success stories of the post–World War II period. Three men in Salt Lake City began packaging vitamin pills and selling them under their own brand name. From that they branched into disposable surgical and medical products. They needed money to expand. They couldn't get any brokerage house to underwrite a stock issue. So they began selling shares to their friends, at a dollar a share.

42

And in a relatively short period of time those original shares became immensely valuable. At one time Deseret's prospects were considered so bright that it was selling for one hundred twenty-nine times earnings.

"Besides," Irving went on, "as the stock got to be worth more, he was able to use it as collateral for loans. With the money he borrowed he bought more stock. As a result of Deseret, he'd become interested in the Intermountain Stock Exchange, which of course in those days was the plain old Salt Lake City Stock Exchange, where penny stocks were traded. He bought a number of those issues. Most of them went nowhere. But a few did well. He also bought some very good stuff —General Motors, things like that. And when he finally sold his Deseret—well, he left Aunt Sarah very well fixed."

"With, among other things, fifty thousand shares of this Lucky Devil."

"So it seems." Irving had begun to relax. But suddenly his expression changed. The fury returned. "Aunt Sarah was murdered. She was murdered because she wouldn't sell her Lucky Devil stock. And the murderer is a man named Barton. I'm convinced of it."

I stared at him.

"I'm going to prove it. I want your help."

I continued to stare. He wasn't making an appeal; he was issuing an ultimatum. And there was something wild in his eyes. "Why don't you just tell the police?" I said mildly.

"Because they'd *never* be able to prove it. Whereas you can. You're good at that sort of thing." He thrust himself out of the chair and began to pace the floor. "You've exposed crooks. You have an instinct, you're not afraid, you—"

"Come off it, Irving. I'm nothing of the kind. I've been in a few situations where—"

"I know the situations you've been in. I'll work with you. I'll—"

"Stop pacing like that. You're making me nervous. What makes you think the woman was killed because she wouldn't sell her stock? What makes you think she was killed by a man named Barton? You're going off the deep end. You don't know—"

"Don't tell me which end I'm going off, Brock." He continued to pace. "I'm no idiot. I can put two and two together as well as anyone else. I'm not sure the man's name is Barton. Nettie said she *thought* that's what his name was. Barton or Bartley or Barnes or something like that. It doesn't matter. I'll find him. And when I do I'm going to see that he pays for what he's done."

"For Christ's sake, Irving, sit down and stop ranting. This isn't like you."

He glanced at the chair but passed it by. "The first thing we have to do is check up on that company. It *has* to exist; otherwise why would anyone have been trying to get his hands on the stock? All right, that's the first step. One of us can do that while the other locates Barton. Nettie said she thought the man was a broker, and it makes sense that he would be."

"Damn it, sit down! Neither one of us is going to do anything of the sort."

He stopped pacing as abruptly as he'd started. He came over to my desk. He looked thunderstruck. "Are you telling me that you won't help?"

"I'm telling you you're acting like someone who's going off his rocker."

"I've never asked you for a favor before, Brock. Not once in all the years. But goddamn it to hell, I'm asking you for one now!"

"Be reasonable, Irv. What you're doing is jumping to conclusions. Because of what that woman told you, you've already tried and convicted a man whose name you're not even sure of for a crime he may very well have no connection with. The thing for you to do is tell your story to the police—or better still, get this Hoffman woman to tell her story to the police—and let them investigate. That's what we pay taxes for."

"All right, don't help me, then. I'll do it all myself."

"No, you won't, Irv. Not while you're working for this company. We've had all the sensational publicity we need. Far more than's good for us. Mark and Tom wouldn't put up with any more, and they'd be right. Price, Potter and Petacque is a brokerage firm, not a detective agency."

"I see. It's all right for you to investigate any damn thing you please, but when one of *us* wants to do it it's wrong. Well, I won't stand for that, Brock."

"Irving, I realize that you're upset. I'm trying not to lose my temper. But I'm not going to be able to hang on to it much longer. I'm simply saying that I have no intention of getting personally involved in any investigation into the death of Sarah Weinberg, and I have no intention of letting you get involved either. It has nothing to do with our company and it's not our affair."

"Brock, I'm more disappointed in you at this moment than I've ever been with anyone in my entire life. And you can go ahead and lose your temper. You can lose anything you goddamn please. But I'm telling you this: I intend to find that man and see that he gets what's coming to him. Whether you like it or not."

"And I'm telling you you're not. You're letting an unnecessarily guilty conscience run away with you. You're letting it fog up your windshield."

His face went scarlet. "Don't tell me about my conscience! Don't tell me about my windshield!" He slammed his fist on the desktop. "You can take this fucking job and shove it up your ass! I quit! I should have quit years ago! Find yourself someone else! I'm through!" And with that, he turned on his heel and stormed out of the office.

8

Five minutes later, Tom and Mark burst into my office. Together. Looking shaken.

"Irving's quit," Mark said.

"Get out!" I roared at them.

They beat a hasty retreat.

I remained at my desk. My heart was pounding. I couldn't seem to get my breathing under control. I was angrier than I'd ever been.

It was an unfocused anger. Some of it was directed at Irving. He'd behaved abominably. But some of it was directed at myself. I'd handled the situation like a clod. And some of it was directed at Tom and Mark, who, I was suddenly convinced, had no conception of the problems I had to deal with, and never had had.

I felt both righteous and stupid. Irving's outburst had been unjustified. He owed me an apology. On the other hand, I'd picked the worst possible moment to dig in my heels. What I should have done was go along with him until he was calm enough to reason with, then quietly point out the errors in his line of thinking. So perhaps I owed *him* an apology too.

Still, he was an arrogant man. Arrogant and stubborn. Always had been. Always would be. Only someone like me would have put up with him for all those years. Look at the way he'd treated Brian. There was no excuse for that.

Yet nowhere in the world was there a more loyal soul than

Irving Silvers. Or a more honest one.

I lit a cigarette. My hand was trembling. I needed a drink. I went over to the cabinet where I kept the liquor and took out the Scotch. I drank several gulps straight from the bottle.

To hell with Irving. To hell with everybody. I needed a vacation. I hadn't had a vacation in two years. Everyone managed to find time for a vacation except me. No one ever seemed to think about what *I* needed.

Except Irving. He'd always thought about what I needed, and tried to make my life easier. He'd cared.

I drank some more Scotch and put the bottle away.

I didn't go out to lunch. And Helen, who'd undoubtedly heard the shouting and guessed that I was in no mood to be disturbed, took my calls. I had forty-five minutes of solitude.

Which didn't do all that much for me. I cooled off enough, though, to realize that I couldn't leave things as they were. Irving really didn't intend to quit, and I certainly didn't intend to let him. It didn't matter who was right and who was wrong; we had to get back on a footing that was at least halfway normal. A complete reconciliation could wait, but there had to be some sort of interim settlement.

I left my office and went down the corridor to his.

He wasn't there.

I continued down the corridor to the reception desk. Clair Gould was manning the switchboard. "Where's Mr. Silvers?" I asked.

"He went home," she replied. "Almost an hour ago."

My anger rose again. "Did he say when he'd be back?"

Clair shook her head. "All he said was, 'I've had it. Goodbye.' And left."

I swore. He couldn't just walk out. He had work to do. Dozens of matters were pending. I felt myself getting hot under the collar. Literally.

The outer door opened. The rest of my staff came in. They'd

evidently decided to go to lunch together, which they didn't often do. And they'd evidently had a few drinks. They appeared to be in high spirits. They greeted me effusively.

I nodded stiffly and returned to my office. I was tempted to call Irving at home and give him a piece of my mind. I restrained myself. I'd only be making matters worse. By tomorrow he'd come to his senses.

Presently I heard a noise behind me and turned around.

"Hi," Brian said.

"What's on your mind?" I snapped.

"About Wednesday," he began. I'd followed Irving's suggestion, which was to tell Brian to spend Wednesday and Thursday putting together a preliminary report on the various companies that were involved in the manufacture of thermal-resistant urethane. Since that was the product which had caused the fight between Irving and Brian, the suggestion, coming from Irving, was an admission that he'd been wrong, almost a peace offering.

"What about Wednesday?"

"I'd like to spend some time with my contact at Darby Oil. I think by then he'll know more about Biawesi IV. I'd like to take him to lunch."

"Who the hell *is* your contact at Darby Oil, Brian?"

"I'd rather not say, Brock. You know how it is."

"I have a right to know."

Brian compressed his lips. With his round face and guileless blue eyes, he looked like a child. But a child who was about to become difficult. He said nothing.

"I think you ought to follow Irving's suggestion. Do the urethane thing. You can talk to your *contact* next week." I threw heavy sarcasm into the word "contact."

"Was that Irving's idea? I thought it was yours."

"No, it was his."

He smiled. "You know what I find hard to believe? That Irving was ever a Communist."

48

"He wasn't."

"His wife said—"

"I know what his wife said. I was there. Neither of them were ever Communists. They went through a phase. And I don't want to hear another word out of you about it. When it comes to Irving, you're always looking for something. I don't blame him for getting mad at you."

Brian's jaw dropped. Emotion usually made him blush. But this time he went pale. "That's not fair."

"It *is* fair. You've been baiting him since the day you started here. You've made it difficult for me to deal with him and you've created all kinds of dissension in the department, and I want you to quit it."

He went even paler.

I half realized that I was defending the man who'd made me angry in the first place, at the expense of one who hadn't. But I couldn't seem to stop. "Irving has been with me since the day we started this business—since *before* the day we started this business. He's my assistant. He's going to remain my assistant. If you have any ideas about getting his job, you can forget them. I'd part with you a damn sight sooner than I'd part with him, and you can remember that. Furthermore, I don't like all this secrecy of yours about where you get your information. We don't operate this department on the basis of privileged information. If you can't trust your co-workers, you shouldn't be working with them."

I paused for breath, and was about to go on. But Brian didn't give me a chance. "Apparently you've already made up your mind," he said in a very quiet voice.

"Made up my mind about what? I haven't made up my mind about anything."

"Made up your mind to part with me."

"I have not!"

"Well, you might as well have. Because I've made up my

mind to part with you. As of right now. I never thought I'd be willing to give up this job, but I suddenly find that I am. I'm sorry you feel the way you do about me, but under the circumstances it'd be pointless for me to continue. Good-bye, Brock. Thanks for everything."

He started to leave.

"Come back here!" I shouted.

But he didn't even turn around. He closed the door firmly behind him.

Twenty minutes later I arrived at The Cyclops. To get as drunk as I possibly could.

9

There were only two customers at the bar. One was a young man I'd never seen before. The other was Milton Kaye.

I sat down next to Milton. He had a mug of beer in front of him but he wasn't drinking it. He was holding his jaw.

"The Novocaine is wearing off," he said.

"Shut up," I said.

He gave me a startled look.

The bartender ambled over. I ordered a double Scotch. And when it came, I drank it quickly.

I began to feel a bit better. I turned to Milton. "I'm sorry," I said. "I've had a terrible day."

"It's only two o'clock."

"I know. But everything happened fast."

He nodded sympathetically and picked up his beer. I ordered another double Scotch.

"It hurts," he said.

"I don't know what came over me," I said.

"And it's starting to swell. I can feel the swelling."

"I lost my head."

"Can you notice the swelling?"

"I never lose my head like that. I don't know what got into me. In less than an hour I lost forty percent of my staff."

"Tomorrow I'll probably look like I have a tennis ball in my mouth."

I sighed and drank the second double Scotch. The bartender began to regard me with interest.

"Bring me another," I said.

Even Milton got interested. "You're going to fall flat on your face," he warned.

"I already have," I replied.

His prediction turned out to be wrong. I didn't fall. But I did get extremely drunk. In a very short period of time. By three o'clock I was home, in my bathroom, throwing up.

And by four o'clock I was sound asleep.

The ringing of the telephone woke me.

The room was dark. I fumbled for the lamp switch, couldn't find it, fumbled for the telephone, knocked it off the bedside table, reached down to pick it up and became aware of the fact that I had a splitting headache.

"Who is it?" I asked finally.

"Tom. What's the matter?"

"I was asleep."

"What happened to Irving? And where did you disappear to? I looked for you, and Clair said you'd left at one-thirty."

"I'll talk to you tomorrow. I'm going back to bed."

Actually, I was still in bed. That seemed unimportant, however. I found the lamp switch, put the telephone back on its cradle, the cradle back on the night table, and looked at the clock. The hands pointed to eight-twenty. I tried to figure out whether that meant eight-twenty in the morning or eight-twenty at night. I wondered why I'd got under the covers with my clothes on.

It came back to me that I'd been drunk and sick. I decided it was eight-twenty at night. My head felt like a bellows that someone was pumping too hard.

Aspirin, I thought. But the aspirin was in the bathroom, and the bathroom was halfway around the world.

I suffered for a while, then got up and set out on the enormous journey.

I took three aspirin tablets and drank a glass of water. And threw up again.

I undressed and got under the covers and fell asleep.

The next time I woke, it was one o'clock. I still had a headache, but a milder one. I longed for a glass of orange juice.

I spent the next hour and a half in the kitchen. I drank two glasses of orange juice and two cups of coffee. My headache gradually disappeared.

I came to the conclusion that the first one to deal with was Brian.

10

I'd never been to his apartment. I had to look up the address in the telephone directory.

I arrived at exactly nine o'clock, feeling reasonably competent. It was a sunny morning.

The building was located on Lexington Avenue, between Sixty-second and Sixty-third. It was a modest four-story structure with two stores on the ground floor: a pet shop and a discount drug emporium. A brass sign beside the entrance to the apartments said: VICTOR, SCIENTIFIC SCALP MASSAGE.

There were six mailboxes on the wall of the tiny lobby. Brian's was the one farthest from the front door, next to the one that said, simply, "Victor." The apartment number was 4A. I pushed the button.

A garbled voice emerged from the speaking tube.

"Brock," I said.

A buzzer sounded. I opened the door that connected the lobby with an inner vestibule. An elevator took me slowly up to the fourth floor. I found 4A and clunked the knocker. A moment later the door opened.

Brian's jaw dropped.

So did mine. For he was standing there in his pajamas, holding a baby's nursing bottle filled with milk.

He pulled himself together. "I thought you said 'Doc.'"

I pulled myself together too. "I want to talk to you."

He motioned me in and closed the door behind me.

The apartment consisted of one room with a Pullman kitchen. The accordion door to the kitchen was open and revealed a two-burner stove, a waist-high refrigerator and three cabinets. The furniture consisted of a day bed, unmade, an inflatable plastic lounge chair and a number of brightly colored wooden cubes. The cubes were tables and chests. There was a cardboard box on the floor beside the bed. I looked around for a baby. I didn't see one.

Brian seemed to realize what was bothering me. "It's for the puppy," he said. He reached into the cardboard box and lifted out the smallest dog I'd ever seen. "He's going to be a poodle. He's only a week old. His mother died when he was born. He's got nobody but me."

I took a closer look. The dog was smaller than the palm of my hand.

"He's never going to get very large," Brian explained. "He's not even a miniature; he's a toy."

"When did you get him?"

"Yesterday." He smiled ruefully. "For consolation."

"I'm sorry about yesterday," I said. "I had no business saying what I did. I apologize. I want you to come back."

He heaved a sigh of relief. "Sit down."

I eased myself into the air-filled lounge chair. I've never trusted inflatable furniture. Brian dropped onto the bed and began trying to get the puppy to take the nipple. The puppy didn't want to.

"He's not hungry," I said.

"It's not that. The nipple's really too big. I have to get a smaller one. And he seems to know he's an orphan. I think he's grieving."

"Try a saucer," I suggested.

"That might work." He got up, went over to the kitchen and took a saucer from one of the cabinets. He transferred the milk and put the saucer on the floor, the puppy beside it. The puppy attempted to drink. Brian nodded approvingly and came back to the bed. "I don't intend to keep him. I just sort of borrowed him from the pet shop downstairs. Doc Frazier was afraid he was going to die."

"Doc Frazier?"

"He owns the pet shop. He's also a vet. We're friends."

"I see."

"I'll return the pup when he gets stronger. If he survives."

"He looks all right to me."

"He's doing better since I brought him upstairs. But he cried all night. I didn't sleep a wink."

"I've been up since one o'clock myself. Thinking about yesterday. I'm really sorry, Brian. I'd just had a fight with Irving and I took it out on you."

"I didn't want to quit, Brock. You know that. It's just that —well, I am what I am. I can't help it. It's hard for me to take no for an answer, and sometimes that gets on people's nerves."

"You also don't like people to get in your way. And Irving gets in your way."

"That's true."

"You have to understand him."

"I think I do."

I nodded. "Perhaps. . . . Irving quit too."

"Oh, no!" To my surprise, he seemed genuinely regretful.

I told him about Mrs. Weinberg. Rather, I started to tell him about Mrs. Weinberg. But the puppy fell into the saucer and upset it. A large puddle of milk formed on the floor. We wiped it up with paper towels and then dried the puppy.

"Where was I?" I asked.

"This Mrs. Hoffman identified the body."

"Oh, yes." I finished the story, up to and including Irving's departure from my office.

Brian thought it over for a few moments, then said, "You're going to get *him* back too, of course."

"Of course. But in his case it's a little different. I'd like him to make the first move."

He eyed me quizzically.

"It's not just a question of getting him back. Naturally I intend to do that. But I want him to realize that he's all wrong about this thing with Mrs. Weinberg. He's simply jumped to conclusions, and I have no way of knowing, but I suspect they're the wrong conclusions. Besides, he has to realize that we can't use the resources of Price, Potter and Petacque to engage in personal vendettas. And, God knows, the company has had enough cops-and-robbers publicity. Our customers are conservative outfits. They don't like it." I told him what I'd overheard Tom and Mark say on Friday.

"But those were situations you couldn't help."

"Perhaps. I'm not really sure. I just *may* be one of those people who go looking for trouble."

"I don't think you are."

"Neither do I. But I don't want to take any more chances. And I don't want Irving to, either. So I think I'll wait a little while. He'll come around. We have too much invested in each other for him not to."

"I understand. Well, I suppose I'd better get dressed. We're already late for work."

He got dressed. But then the problem arose what to do with the puppy. Brian didn't want to return him to the pet shop, but he didn't want to leave him alone in the apartment either.

"I don't suppose I ought to bring him to the office," he said hopefully.

"I think he'd be too much of a distraction," I said.

We decided to drop him off at my house. Louise could take care of him.

So I got Brian back into the fold. And in the process I acquired a dog.

For the puppy, once installed in my house, remained there.

Louise named him Tiger, after a dog she'd once had, and the name stuck.

He's a fine little poodle, and very bright. And on account of him, Louise has become much more dependable than she used to be.

But the call I was expecting from Irving never came.

11

We didn't get to the office until almost eleven o'clock. Which made for a condensed working day. And I had a great deal to do. In addition to the usual mail and telephone calls, there was the accumulation from the day before. I'd also scheduled a luncheon with the president and one of the vice-presidents of Calloway United Insurance Company, who were in town for two days, which I couldn't change. Furthermore, unexpected distractions came my way. Principally, a lengthy telephone inquiry from one of the men at the *Wall Street Journal* about a report on the steel industry that Irving had prepared and that normally Irving would have explained, and conferences with Joe and Harriet about the projects they were working on.

Tom and Mark popped into my office separately, wanting to know about Irving, but I just didn't have time to talk to them. I said I'd tell them about it later.

Among the telephone messages from the day before was one from Carol which said, "Don't pay for wine." I didn't return that one, but at two-thirty, shortly after I came back from the luncheon, she called again. She wanted to make absolutely certain that I didn't pay for the wine, which the liquor store had delivered to her apartment late Saturday by mistake and which she'd told them they could damn well come and pick up. She didn't ask me what I'd done on Sunday or volunteer any information about what she'd done. It was a very brief conversation.

Neither Joe nor Harriet inquired about Irving. They seemed to assume that he was out on some sort of fact-gathering mission. I concluded he'd told Tom and Mark he was quitting, but no one else, and I was grateful for that.

Ordinarily, with so much to do myself, I would have given Irving an outline of what I wanted to say in the Tuesday letter and let him write it. As it was, I had to do the writing. And I didn't get started until three-thirty. Which meant that Helen had to stay overtime to finish the typing, I had to stay overtime to proofread the finished version, the girl who operated the photocopying machine had to stay overtime in order to get all the copies made, and the young fellow who handled the mailing not only had to stay overtime to get the letters in the envelopes, but had to take them in a taxi to the post office, to make sure they wouldn't be late.

It was nearly five o'clock when I got around to looking for Tom and Mark, to brief them. But by then both had gone. Tom's secretary said that he'd left at three-thirty to meet with some of the people from the Maryland Fund, and Mark's said that Mark was having a conference at the bank.

I stayed at the office until a quarter past six, when the mail boy went off to the post office. The only other person who was still around was Brian. He was at his desk, working.

"Time to go home," I said.

He yawned and stretched. "What about the pup?"

"Come on over to my place and have a drink. Then you can take him home."

Brian agreed.

There were some minutes of panic when we got to my house,

for Louise had gone and the puppy seemed to have disappeared. But presently I located him at the foot of my bed. Louise had made a sort of nest for him out of a wicker laundry basket and the pure wool blanket I'd bought at Abercrombie & Fitch for those occasions when I went to football games. I was distressed; the blanket had been absurdly expensive. But the puppy was sleeping so soundly and looked so comfortable that I simply sighed and reminded myself that there was no shortage of dry-cleaning establishments in the neighborhood.

As we drank, Brian and I discussed the puppy's future. Now that Brian was back at work, he wouldn't have time to take care of him. Yet he hated to return him to the pet shop. The puppy might die; and even if he lived, there was no telling who might buy him.

The puppy seemed healthy enough to me, but I had to admit that it would be unfortunate if whoever bought him didn't treat him well.

"What about you?" Brian suggested. "You could keep him. You have a housekeeper. She could look after him when you're away."

I protested. But I didn't protest too strenuously. And by the time we'd finished the second round the puppy's future was settled.

Brian held out his glass for a refill. I gave him one. I started to give myself one too but decided I'd better not; my stomach still felt a bit queasy.

"Heard from Irving?" he asked.

I shook my head.

"Anything I can do to help?"

I shook my head again and changed the subject. I told him how much I liked Gloria Hines. He smiled and said that he liked her too. Unfortunately, however, she was more interested in her work than she was in him.

We talked about her until he left, then I went foraging in the kitchen. I found that Louise had baked a meat loaf and made a bowl of potato salad. I sat down to dinner, but just as I was starting to eat, the telephone rang.

"Now what's all this about Irving?" Tom wanted to know. I told him the story.

"What do you intend to do?" he asked.

"Get him back, of course."

"Have you done anything about it?"

"Not yet. I've been waiting for *him* to call *me.*"

"Well, the longer you wait, the harder it's going to be."

"What do you suggest I do?"

"Don't stand on ceremonies."

I thanked him for his advice and hung up. But almost immediately the telephone rang again.

This time it was Mark. With the same question. And the same advice. Which was unusual, for they rarely agreed on any course of action, the first time around.

They were right, I knew. The longer I left the issue unresolved, the harder it was going to be to resolve it.

I debated with myself as I ate. And along with the meat loaf and potato salad, I swallowed my pride.

At nine o'clock, having decided to project mature wisdom and a sense of humor, I dialed Irving's number.

Naomi answered. There was no mistaking her relief when she recognized my voice. "I was hoping you'd call," she said. "In fact, I was just sitting here thinking about calling you."

"Irving told you what happened?"

"At great length."

"Well, I think this has gone on long enough."

"I couldn't agree more, Brock. But Irving was livid."

"Well, it's time for him to get un-livid. Better let me talk to him."

"I wish I could, but he's gone. That's what I wanted to talk to you about."

"Gone?"

"He left at noon for Salt Lake City."

12

Irving's house was a two-story red brick mock-Tudor that stood atop a steep rise near the intersection of Surrey Place and Midland Parkway, in Jamaica Estates. It had cost more than he could afford to pay at the time, but he'd bought it anyway, for he was convinced that real estate values in Jamaica Estates would hold up. And events had proved him right. The IND subway line made it easier to commute to Jamaica Estates than to the suburbs farther out on Long Island. He'd recently been offered twice what he'd paid for the house.

Climbing the steep flight of steps from the driveway to the front lawn, I smiled at the recollection of how, in the early days of our association, Irving had grumbled about the monthly mortgage payments. Well, he didn't have to grumble now; his salary had tripled since then. Good old Irving. What an asset he was.

And what a damn fool.

Salt Lake City.

For what?

A Brooklyn-born Don Quixote, no less.

The aroma of something freshly baked wrapped itself around me as I stepped into the foyer. "Something smells good," I said.

"When you said you were coming, I decided to bake some lemon cookies," Naomi said. "I know how you like them."

I kissed her on the cheek. "You're a doll. How did you ever happen to marry an idiot like Irving?"

She smiled. "Love is blind. Give me your coat. It was sweet of you to come right out. I really do want to talk to you. I feel terrible."

"Me too." I gave her my coat, and she led me into the den. "Where are the kids?" I asked.

"I made them go to bed. Sit down. I'm sure you'd like some coffee and cookies."

She went off to the kitchen and returned presently with a large tray. Not only did she bring lemon cookies with the coffee, but also a plate of pound cake, a dish of pecans and a bowl of apples. She busied herself for several minutes with hostessing, then settled down.

"I tried to get Irv to call you," she said. "He wouldn't."

I sighed. "He was wrong. So was I. But rushing off to Salt Lake City—that doesn't make any sense whatsoever. He's simply trying to appease his conscience."

Naomi's eyes brightened. She gave me a fond smile. "How smart you are."

"Irving's smart too. But he isn't acting like it."

"He's brilliant. But he lets his emotions get in his way. You don't."

"Ha!"

"No, you really don't, Brock. You're less idealistic."

"That's no compliment."

"Some people would think it was. Among them, me."

"Anyway, why's he so het up about this Mrs. Weinberg, Naomi?"

"That's a long story." She reflected. "First of all, she was murdered. That would upset anybody. I mean, a friend of yours is murdered—someone you knew well and were very fond of. Who wouldn't be upset? And she *was* murdered. There was some doubt about that at the beginning, those detectives said.

A couple of people claimed she simply fell off the platform, and one man said she jumped. But now that they've sifted through all the stories, they have a pretty good idea of what happened, and she was pushed. By a youngish man. Different people gave different descriptions of him, so the police don't know exactly what he looks like, but they do know what he was wearing. He was wearing blue jeans and some sort of leather jacket and a cap. He grabbed her purse and pushed her, just as the train was coming into the station, and then ran up the steps and disappeared. No one even made an attempt to chase him."

"It's grisly, all right. But Irving's convinced he knows who the man is. A stockbroker named Barton or something. Which in my opinion is pure guesswork on his part. The most reckless kind of guesswork."

"In my opinion too. I tried to talk him out of it, but he wouldn't listen to me either. As I said, he lets his emotions get in his way. Yet there *is* a certain logic to it, Brock. If you'd been with us, if you'd heard Nettie—"

"You went with Irving to her house?"

"Yes. Here, let me pour you some more coffee." She poured it, then returned to her chair.

"The cookies are delicious." I helped myself to another. "Had you ever met this Mrs. Hoffman before?"

"Of course. She was Aunt Sarah's next-door neighbor even then. When Irv and I were going to college, I mean. She's a dear. Her husband used to own a couple of movie theaters. He's been dead for a long time. She's a common-sense type of person. She's become a bit scattered and forgetful, but that's just old age. Underneath, she's still sound as a rock, not at all the kind of woman who would make things up, or even *mix* things up. According to her, this man had been hectoring Aunt Sarah to sell the stock for maybe six weeks. Since around Labor Day, Nettie said."

"And she isn't sure of his name?"

"Barton, she thought. But yes, she admitted she wasn't sure. It could have been Barnes or something that sounded like Barton. Aunt Sarah had only mentioned his name once or twice. Mostly she called him 'that man.' At any rate, first he offered her ten cents a share, then he kept upping the price. Well, Aunt Sarah was no fool. She hadn't understood why anyone would want to buy the stock, to begin with. But she realized that if he went to the trouble of tracking her down and getting in touch with her, there must be a reason. So she said she'd think it over, and when he called her back she said no. Then he raised the price, which made her even more suspicious, and she said no again. But he kept calling her, and finally he offered a dollar a share, at which point she decided to talk to you. She knew that something was going on but she didn't know what; she thought maybe you might."

"I've never even heard of Lucky Devil."

"Neither had Irving. That's why he went to Salt Lake City. He spent hours Sunday night trying to find out something about the company. He went through every directory we have." She pointed to the books on the shelves. "None of them mentions the company. He called a couple of friends and asked them to check. They couldn't come up with anything either. So he decided to go to Salt Lake City. He believes that's where the stock was bought. If there are records anywhere, that's where they'd be."

"Did this Mrs. Hoffman know that Aunt Sarah was coming to see me?" I frowned. Why was I starting to call her Aunt Sarah? I'd never known her.

"In a general way. They'd talked it over. But she didn't know *when*. And she didn't think anything was wrong until Friday night. She noticed that there were no lights on in Aunt Sarah's house. So she kept watching, and after a while she telephoned. She didn't get any answer. Later, she went and knocked on the door. Still no answer. She claims she sat up until after midnight, worrying and calling every half hour or so. Finally she fell asleep in a chair in the living room. She didn't wake up until the next morning. Then she called again, and when she didn't get any answer this time, she became really alarmed. She didn't know that Aunt Sarah had gone to see you, of course. She thought that she might have had a heart attack or a stroke or something. So she called the police. And they broke into the house, and Aunt Sarah wasn't there, and eventually they got around to checking the hospitals and the morgue, and—well, they took Nettie down to identify the body. You can imagine how upset she was, poor thing."

"Didn't Aunt Sarah—Mrs. Weinberg—ask the man why he wanted to buy the stock?"

Naomi smiled. "Go ahead and call her Aunt Sarah. You'd have wanted to, if you'd known her. Yes; according to Nettie, she did. He gave her some story about one of the other stockholders wanting to get control of the company. What he wouldn't tell her was why. He said he didn't know. Do you believe that? That he wouldn't know, I mean."

"It's conceivable. If he was a middleman, acting for someone else. But if that's the case—if he was a middleman—he certainly wouldn't have killed her." I glanced at the cookies but resisted the temptation to reach for another. I'd already eaten five. "What happens to the stock now? Who inherits it?"

"Barbara, I imagine. The niece. Uncle Morris's sister's daughter. There's no one else. Uncle Morris and Aunt Sarah had no children of their own. There's just the one niece. We saw her at the funeral yesterday, for the first time in years."

"I wonder if this Barton contacted her too?"

Naomi shrugged. "An apple, maybe?"

"No, thanks. Irving didn't ask her?"

"No."

"Instead he went tearing off to Salt Lake City . . . If you'd seen him yesterday, it was like—like he was some sort of vigilante."

"I know."

"He's usually so level-headed."

"This whole thing has reactivated something traumatic."

"It sure as hell must have."

"You don't really know him, Brock. Close as the two of you are, you don't really know him."

"I realized that yesterday. As far as I know, he sprang full-grown from the brow of a Brooklyn rabbi."

Naomi laughed. "Hardly." She stopped laughing. "Irving was born twice, really. Once when he came out of the womb, and once when he started college."

"College made that much difference?"

"To both of us. But especially to him. To him—I'm not kidding—it was like coming into the world all over again. It changed his entire outlook." She sighed and shook her head wistfully. "You never knew his father, did you?"

"He was already dead when I met Irving. His mother too."

"They were the dearest, sweetest people you can imagine. If there's such a thing as pure virtue in this world, they were the embodiment of it. I don't think his father ever committed a selfish act in his entire life. Everything was for other people, for 'the congregation' as he called it. But he was old-fashioned to the nth degree. Not old-fashioned the way most people think of it. I mean *really* old-fashioned. He took the Old Testament literally. He believed that God created the world in six days and rested on the seventh, and that the Red Sea actually parted, and that Moses got the Ten Commandments from the hands of God. There still are people like that, you know. Jews and Gentiles alike."

"I know. I've met some fundamentalist Christians, down South."

"You don't have to go down South. They're right here in New York. Well, Irving was brought up like that. His father sent him to a parochial school, so he shouldn't be contaminated by modern ideas. Irving was always a superb student. He was reading Hebrew when he was four years old. And he accepted the whole bit. He was as strict in his beliefs as his father was. Until he started college. Then the questions began to present themselves. It was traumatic. Have you ever heard of anyone having an emotional crisis because he doubted that God appeared to Moses in the guise of a burning bush? It happened with Irv."

"Incredible. How did he ever get to a school like Brooklyn College?"

"Deep down, I think, he'd always had a desire to know what the outside world was like. He'd already decided that he didn't want to be a rabbi, which is what his father wanted him to be. And even to his father, any college was better than none at all. Brooklyn College was a compromise between theological school and Columbia, where Irv really wanted to go. But the choice created a strain between Irv and his father, and as Irv began to change, the strain became worse. In two years he went from religious orthodoxy to"—she smiled—"to Communist rallies."

"And the Weinbergs were a link between the two."

"Their home was always a meeting place for students. They were wonderful, hospitable people. But Irv had special needs, and they recognized them. He became almost like a son to them. He even lived with them for a while, when things reached the point where he felt he simply couldn't live with his parents any longer. It was in their house that he proposed to me."

"I never knew that."

"How could you? It was part of the period that he never talks about and doesn't like me to talk about. But they encouraged him in my direction, and while neither of us had to be pushed,

67

exactly, Aunt Sarah was sort of our matchmaker."

"I'm beginning to understand."

"I hope so. They helped Irv keep his balance during a period of great conflict. They kept him from going overboard. After all, he never reverted to what he'd been before, but he didn't become a revolutionary either. He became a very good, very worthwhile, very—" Her voice began to quiver. She cleared her throat and said, "For heaven's sake, stop looking at the apples and take one."

I did.

Neither of us spoke for a while. She poured herself another cup of coffee and drank it quickly. "It's gotten cold," she observed.

I munched on the apple. Finally I said, carefully, "I sensed yesterday that what was really troubling Irving was that he'd grown away from Aunt Sarah."

"That's the tip of the iceberg, certainly. But I suspect that what I've just been telling you is what's below the surface. He *does* feel guilty, though. I do too, in a way. It's wrong to forget old friends. On the other hand, it wasn't entirely one-sided. She grew away from us too. As far as Irv and I are concerned, our lives changed considerably. There were the children, and Irv's work, and then we moved out here. I'm not excusing us; I'm merely saying that other things and other people took over. Yet, as I tried to tell Irv, Aunt Sarah could have made more of an effort to keep up with us, too. She didn't. She was getting old. She probably wanted a smaller circle. She never called. *You* understand, don't you?"

"Of course. But I don't think Irv does. He looked like he wanted to kill someone."

Naomi shuddered. "Don't talk like that."

I deposited the apple core in an ashtray.

"You will take him back, won't you, Brock?"

"You know I will. I *want* him to come back. I just wish he

hadn't left town. He was too bent on revenge. I'm worried about him."

"I'm sure he'll be all right."

"I hope so."

We let the matter rest there, and a few minutes later I left.

I was glad that Naomi and I had had the talk. I felt that I now understood Irving as I never had before. But what I'd learned didn't reassure me. For the man had certain unsafe tendencies. And he was giving in to them.

13

So the following morning I made some changes.

They weren't drastic changes, and I didn't think they'd be permanent. But I made them anyway. Because I had a hunch that Irving might not be back so soon.

I hoped that my hunch was wrong, that by the end of the week he'd once again be at his desk, carrying on as before. But the more I thought about what Naomi had told me, the more I doubted that he would. For the death of Sarah Weinberg had triggered some sort of personal crisis for him, and personal crises take time to resolve. The conflict wasn't between him and me; it was between him and himself. And even if his trip to Salt Lake City was successful, even if he uncovered the facts about the stock and the man who'd pestered Sarah to sell it, he was going to be preoccupied with the chain of events that led to her death and with his own feelings.

I called Harriet into my office and told her that Irving was going to be away for a while on some business of his own and that I wanted her to take over, for the time being, the work he was doing on the steel companies. I said that I'd handle her usual field, which was banks and financial institutions, since it was closest to my particular specialty, insurance companies.

Then I summoned Joe and put him in charge of the automotive research, as an adjunct to his other chores.

And I had George cancel a trip to Atlanta that he was planning for Friday. I also canceled a trip to New Orleans that I'd scheduled for myself.

I arranged with Clair Gould to transfer all telephone calls for Irving to Helen Doyle, and explained the new setup to Helen so that she could reroute them and at the same time keep me informed as to who was talking to whom about what.

What it amounted to was battening down the hatches in anticipation of rough weather. I'd been short-handed before. I knew how difficult it could be.

Later in the morning, I told Tom and Mark what I'd done. I didn't expect either of them to raise any objections, and neither of them did. After all, it was my department, and I was in the best position to know what moves had to be made.

I had an unusual feeling of competence. I was in charge to a degree that I hadn't been before, and my adrenal glands responded with increased activity. I was all over the place, helping everyone, making spur-of-the-moment decisions, coping with things I hadn't had to cope with in years. Nothing seemed especially hard; it was all quite stimulating.

Yet as the day wore on I found myself missing Irving. Several times I started for his office, from force of habit, and stopped short. And I realized how much I'd come to depend upon him. I trusted everyone in the department, but I trusted him absolutely, and that made a difference. I missed his physical presence, the sense of security I got simply from knowing that he was there. I could handle the extra duties, but somehow things weren't the same.

Brian was the only one whose routine I didn't alter. The decision not to alter it wasn't a conscious one. He just didn't figure in my planning. However, by midafternoon I realized that I was changing his role more than anyone else's. For I was consulting him about matters that had nothing to do with his own sphere. I was using him as a sounding board, just as I'd used Irving in the past. Brian was the newest member of the department, the youngest, the least experienced. But he was the one I seemed to want to confide in, and I wasn't sure why. Whatever the reason, though, I found myself spending more time with him than with any of the others.

My mental motor was still racing when I got home, at six o'clock.

To my amazement, Louise was still there. Except for very special occasions, she always left by four-thirty. But I burst into my bedroom, full of energy and eager for a hot shower, to find her on the floor, trying to persuade Tiger to drink some more milk. I was so surprised, I dropped my coat on the floor.

After a while I took the shower, and then Louise gave me a lecture on the care and feeding of puppies. I didn't tell her that I objected to her giving Tiger my most expensive blanket, but I did suggest that I didn't altogether approve of his sharing my bedroom, that in my opinion he belonged in the basement. She became indignant. The basement was too damp, and he was too young. He needed a warm place, and company. She made me promise that I'd leave him where he was.

We discussed what to do with him in the event that I had to go out of town. She assured me that I could always board him at her house.

She left at seven, and I poured myself a drink. The superabundance of energy I'd had throughout the day began to peter out. And presently the reaction set in. I became depressed.

I ate some of the chicken and the string beans Louise had prepared and went upstairs. Tiger was asleep. I stood there for some minutes, watching him. And somehow the pall of depression lifted.

Then I became annoyed. Was this what it had come to—a housekeeper to look after me, and a dog to keep me company? Damn it, I wasn't ninety years old. I was forty-one. What the hell was wrong with me?

I called Carol.

She sounded disinterested.

"What's the matter lately?" I asked, trying to stir something up. "Have I become boring?"

"Yes, you have," she replied.

I was too startled to say anything.

"I'm sorry," she said. "It isn't your fault. It's mine. I've about decided to go home."

Home, to her, was Minneapolis. That's where her family lived. "How can you get away? This is your busy season."

"I don't mean a vacation. I mean for good. I can't take it anymore."

"You'd better get right over here, sweetheart, and let's talk about this."

"I don't feel like it."

"I don't care whether you feel like it or not. If you're not here in half an hour, I'll come over to your place and kick down the door."

"Don't try to be masterful, Brock. But all right, I'll come. It won't do any good, though. I've made up my mind."

It was an entirely different Carol who arrived at my house that night from the one who'd hostessed my party on Saturday night. But not such a different Carol from the one who'd insisted on going home afterward because she was tired. The zest was gone.

It returned briefly when I took her upstairs to show her Tiger. "He's darling!" she exclaimed. But it didn't last. She was fed up, she said. Fed up with her job, with her analyst, with New York. She was on a treadmill—a lot of movement but no progress.

"I can assume, then, that you're also fed up with me," I said.

"I suppose I am," she said after thinking it over. "Not that I don't like you, Brock. You're by far the nicest man I've met in all the years I've been in New York. But we aren't going anywhere, you and I, and you know it. And I'm thirty-four years old. I've been in this city fourteen years. What has it got me? Nothing."

"It's got you a good job, a nice apartment, plenty of clothes, decent meals. It's got you friends. It's got you me."

"That's not what I mean. It's the future I'm thinking about. I'm getting older. What have I got to look forward to? More of the same?"

"Would that be so bad? It's more than a lot of people have to look forward to."

"It's not enough. It's simply . . . not enough." And, without warning, tears came to her eyes. One slid down her cheek.

I put my arm around her. I didn't quite know what to do. She wasn't a crier.

She put her head on my shoulder, and we sat like that for a while. Then I got her into bed.

We held on to each other. We didn't have sex. But it was nice, nevertheless. Comforting.

And eventually we fell asleep.

I awoke once, when the puppy whimpered. But I went right back to sleep.

And was still sleeping soundly at seven-fifteen, when the telephone rang.

Carol was sitting up in bed, rubbing her eyes. She took the telephone from the cradle and handed it to me.

"Who is it?" I mumbled.

All I could hear was a woman sobbing.

I propped myself up on an elbow. "Who is it? What's the matter?"

"It's Naomi." The sobbing continued.

"What's the matter? What's happened, Naomi? Tell me what's wrong."

She gasped, moaned, gasped again and said, "I just had a call from Salt Lake City. . . . Irving's been run over by a car. . . . He's dying."

14

The plane wasn't due to take off until ten, but when I arrived at La Guardia, at twenty minutes to nine, Naomi was already there. She was in the departure lounge, the only person in the room. She was sitting bolt upright on the edge of one of the chairs, knees together, hands tightly clasped around her pocketbook and ticket envelope, staring at the wall. Her face was like white marble.

I embraced her, but her body didn't yield. "Take it easy, dear," I said.

She nodded mechanically.

"Now tell me what happened."

"He was run over."

"Who called you?"

"A doctor."

"What'd he say?"

"They were going to operate."

"On what?"

"Everything. I don't know. I don't remember." She was looking at me but didn't appear to be seeing me. "He was all broken up inside. All broken up."

I tried to get her to tell me more, but she was unable to. She simply didn't know what had happened. All she knew was that the doctor had said they were doing everything possible, but he hadn't offered much hope.

I also tried to get her to come to the coffee shop with me, but she wouldn't budge.

"I'm all right," she kept saying. "You go."

Finally I did go. Not to get coffee; to use the telephone.

Tom hadn't come in yet, but I spoke to Mark. I told him about Irving and explained that I was on my way to Salt Lake City.

"But of course," he said.

I had the call transferred to Helen and asked her to cancel all my appointments for the balance of the week; and in turn I spoke to each member of my staff. I gave them the bad news and issued whatever instructions I could think of. All of them were distressed. All of them wanted to know whether there was anything they could do to help. And Brian, being Brian, inquired as to who would be in charge during my absence.

"I'm still in charge," I replied, adding, "I probably won't be gone for more than a day."

"But if you are?"

"It'll still be me," I said firmly.

The departure lounge had started to fill up while I was gone, but Naomi was exactly as I'd left her, still sitting on the edge of the chair, staring at the wall. I eased the ticket envelope from her clenched hand and checked us in for the flight.

The plane took off promptly at ten o'clock and flew for three years. Or maybe it was four years. At any rate, I'd never been on a plane that seemed to take so long in getting to its destination.

The New York–Chicago leg wasn't so bad; it was merely interminable. But the wait on the ground in Chicago, with the two of us sitting side by side in deep silence, was agonizing. And the long hours in the air between Chicago and Salt Lake City gave me the feeling that we had to be heading for a different planet; no place on this one could possibly be that far from another place.

What made the trip so God-awful was the uncertainty. I must have told myself at least six hundred times that Irving was still alive, only to decide a moment later that he wasn't. I pictured myself with Naomi on an eastbound plane, accompanying the body back to New York. Then I pictured myself with Naomi at Irving's bedside, chatting amiably with him about how the doctor had given us such a needless scare. But I couldn't stabilize either scene in my mind.

And when I wasn't thinking along those lines, I was reminding myself that whatever had happened wasn't my fault. That Irving had brought it on himself. But I couldn't altogether convince myself that this was true.

Naomi's robotlike behavior certainly didn't help. She wouldn't, or couldn't, talk; wouldn't, or couldn't, read; and, when lunch was served, wouldn't, or couldn't, eat. She just sat there, looking at nothing, as the plane flew endlessly on, above a sea of unbroken clouds.

I tried to read a magazine but found it impossible to concentrate. I made up lists of what I wanted the various members of my staff to do, but the lists came apart in my head even as I was making them up. I attempted to zero in on Carol's problem, but that didn't work either; all it did was remind me of the telephone call that had awakened me and of the fact that I'd forgotten to leave a note for Louise, and Tiger was liable to starve to death.

Everything contrived to make me feel helpless, anxious and impatient.

Until the pilot announced over the intercom that we were making our descent into Salt Lake City. Then, suddenly, Naomi came to life. She began to fidget, to check the contents of her pocketbook, to talk.

"The doctor's name was Korpf," she said. "Robert Korpf."

"What hospital?" I asked.

"Holy Cross."

"Who's staying with the children?"

"My sister-in-law. . . . I just realized, I forgot my checkbook."

"Don't worry. I have credit cards."

The airport came into view. A grinding indicated that the pilot was lowering the landing gear.

We touched ground, bounced, slowed, taxied to the gate. One of the stewardesses informed us that it was two o'clock, Mountain time, and that the temperature outside was sixty-eight degrees.

While Naomi waited for our bags to come down the chute, I hurried to a telephone and called Louise. She'd already figured out that I'd gone out of town, she said; the bedroom had been in such a mess.

I returned to the baggage claim area, to find Naomi lumbering toward me with her suitcase. I took it from her, located my own, and we went out to the taxi rank.

We reached the hospital at ten minutes to three.

Irving was in the intensive care unit. He hadn't regained consciousness. He was alive, but that was all.

15

The hospital had a chapel. I fell asleep in it.

It was after midnight by then. Naomi had refused to leave the building even for the few minutes it would have taken to check into a hotel. And I myself hadn't wanted to leave. For Irving was still hovering between life and death. That most delicate of scales, the one that weighs survival, hadn't tilted either way.

It was a long time before anyone was able to locate Dr. Korpf. And when Korpf finally did appear, he was reluctant to say much. He was just the resident who'd been detailed to contact Irving's family, he explained; Dr. William Littner was the one who could give us the most accurate information; Littner had been in charge of the neurosurgical team that had performed the operation.

Which meant another wait, at the end of which we were treated to a vast amount of medical specifics but no clear-cut answer to the big question—was Irving going to pull through? Littner was a tall, dour man with a pedantic manner and, as he put it, too much experience with the vagaries of the human body to make predictions. I realized that he was trying to be kind and that he couldn't tell us what he didn't know. But it was frustrating for Naomi and me to receive a lecture on anatomy when what we wanted was to be told whether or not Irving was going to make it through the night.

Littner did say that the team he headed had been only one of the teams participating in the operation. There'd been two others, one for the thoracic work and another for the orthopedic. Irving had been brought in with a fractured skull, a punctured lung and a broken pelvis. In addition, of course, to multiple lacerations. The skills of many people had been required.

About the accident itself Littner knew next to nothing. Merely that Irving had been brought to the hospital by the paramedical team that had responded to the police department's call. He had no idea as to where the accident had occurred or what kind of vehicle had been involved. He'd heard someone say, after the operation was over, that it was a hit-and-run case, but he wasn't sure whether that was true or not. He himself hadn't been summoned until after a brain scan showed an epidural hematoma of the dura mater. He'd rushed to the hospital, performed his portion of the surgery, then gone out to breakfast and begun his normal routine.

I made the mistake of asking him what an epidural hematoma of the dura mater is. That evoked a lengthy explanation which boiled down to the fact that it's a blood clot caused by a tear in one or more of the arteries in the outermost covering of the brain. An explanation which included such miscellaneous morsels of information as that the operation to remove the clot is like operations performed many centuries ago by the Egyptians and the Indians of Mexico, presumably to remove evil spirits.

I wasn't interested in the early Egyptians and Mexicans, but when he began to talk about the brain rather than the skull, my anxiety spread into new territory. "If he pulls through," I asked, "will he be . . . all right? I mean, his mind will be . . . ?"

"I'm only a surgeon, Mr. Potter. You must try to understand that. All I did was remove a blood clot. If there was no structural damage to the brain, then he'll have his full mental powers. I'm inclined to be hopeful, for the clot was only there a few hours, but there's no way of knowing for certain. Often, in cases such as this, the patient recovers quite dramatically. On the other hand, the extent of Mr. Silvers' injuries was such that— well, one must be prepared for the worst."

It was, to say the least, an inconclusive discussion. But before he left us, Littner went into the room where Irving lay, to check on his condition, and invited us to come along.

Irving was barely recognizable. His head was completely bandaged, his skin was a ghastly white and waxy as a candle, and he was hooked up by tubes to such a variety of devices that he resembled an inert puppet.

I groaned.

Littner seemed to realize what was bothering me. "Don't let it scare you," he said, and explained what the tubes were connected to—plasma, glucose, the electrocardiograph machine, and two bottles of water to catch the air coming from Irving's thoracic cavity.

I glanced at Naomi. She appeared to be oblivious to everything except the screen that was monitoring the rhythm of Irving's heart. The rhythm was steady but, it seemed to me, much too flat.

Littner led us back to the corridor. "You'll be notified if there's any change," he said. "Where can you be reached?"

"Right here," Naomi replied.

"But it might be days."

"Right here," she repeated firmly.

He didn't argue. Neither did I. And there we remained, our suitcases beside us, for hours. I got us some candy bars from the gift shop, and we ate them.

There was, the nurse told us every time we asked, no alteration in Mr. Silvers' condition.

Eventually I persuaded Naomi to come down to the lobby, where the seats might be more comfortable.

Soon, I noticed, she was dozing.

I began to doze too.

But presently a hysterical woman woke us. She had a gasping child in her arms. The child was choking to death—where was the emergency room—she couldn't find the emergency room—where was a doctor?

I led her to the admitting office, where an attendant took over. Then, while Naomi remained in the lobby, I wandered around. Nobody stopped me. Finally I found the chapel. It was unoccupied and quiet. I sat down for a few minutes, to think.

And fell asleep.

And dreamed about an old lady falling from a subway platform.

16

At four-thirty I went back to the lobby. Naomi was still sitting there, beside the suitcases. She was gray with fatigue but seemed more at peace than she'd been before.

"No change," she volunteered. "I checked again, a little while ago."

"We can't just camp here, Naomi. We have to get rooms somewhere. You need rest."

"I couldn't leave, Brock. But you go." She smiled. "You could use a shave."

"We'll take turns. I'll stay for a while, then you stay for a while."

"You're a lamb, but I couldn't leave. Not just yet. Why don't you get yourself a room? I don't need one. I can use the one Irv had. After you've had some sleep, come back and we'll see."

"Where was Irv staying? Do you know?"

"At the Rodeway Inn. He called me from there yesterday. Or was it the day before? I've lost all track of time."

"So've I. How can you just sit here?"

"I don't mind. I've been forcing myself to think of other things."

"You're incredible."

"Rationalization, reaction formation, regression, repression, sublimation, undoing."

"What?"

"Some of Freud's list of ego defense mechanisms. I haven't thought about them in years. I've already reviewed recipes and the Greek alphabet and the American presidents. Now I'm on Freud. 'Undoing' is what undid Irv. Go ahead and call a taxi. It's silly for both of us to sit here."

I let myself be persuaded.

The taxi came. I took the suitcases with me. I went back to the airport, rented a car and, after studying the map that the rental attendant gave me, set out on one of those confusing expressway systems without which no city in the United States is considered complete.

The main entrance to the Rodeway Inn was on Sixth Street South. The lobby was attractive. I had no difficulty in getting a room. The clerk gave me a diagram of the premises and told me to go to the swimming pool, turn right, continue to the greenery and turn left—my room was at the top of the stairs. I set out to follow her directions. The complex of buildings and driveways covered almost a square block.

Finally, shortly after six o'clock, I climbed into bed.

I didn't sleep long but I slept soundly, and when I woke I felt refreshed. I shaved, showered, changed clothes, found the coffee shop and ate a large breakfast.

After breakfast I walked across the driveway to the lobby. The room clerk who'd checked me in was off duty. I told her replacement that I was Irving Silvers and that by mistake I'd locked my key in my room. She gave me the duplicate key.

Irv's room was in the same wing as mine and, like mine, was on the second floor. Both rooms were closer to Fifth Street than to Sixth.

He'd brought an extra suit with him. It was hanging on the rod in the dressing area, along with his bathrobe. A pair of shoes stood on the rack above the rod. Various toilet articles were lined up on the countertop, beside the washbasin.

His suitcase was open. It contained nothing but the usual items of clothing a man would take on a short business trip. Except for a book.

The book was one I'd never seen before. It was bound in coarse paper and titled *Stock Annual.* An explanatory note on the cover said that it contained hard-to-find information on low-priced stocks for the aggressive investor.

I sat down on the bed and began to study the small volume.

There was a lengthy disclaimer. Neither the editor nor the publisher vouched for the accuracy of the information in the book, it said in effect; the facts were gathered from company reports, other publications, discussions with company officials and various reference manuals; the listings shouldn't be construed as recommendations; the editor and publisher assumed no responsibility for omissions or inaccuracies.

Fair enough.

I glanced at the first few entries, then turned to the *L*'s.

And there it was. LUCKY DEVIL MINERALS, INC.

The facts were few. The company's address was a post office box in Salt Lake City. The transfer agent was Gladys Jennings, 4391 South 11th Street East, Salt Lake City. No dividend had ever been declared. The capitalization was 80,000 shares, with a par value of ten cents each. The officers were: David Kisman, president; Keith Kisman, vice-president; Betsy Kisman Martin, secretary-treasurer. The annual meeting was "Decided by Directors." Total assets were $34,623.35.

A brief description stated that the company had been incorporated under the laws of Utah on June 21, 1954, as Lucky Devil Uranium Properties, Inc., that the name had subsequently been changed to Lucky Devil Minerals, Inc., that it had been engaged in the exploration of uranium and silver mining claims and the operation of a restaurant, a dairy and various retail establishments. Its mining activities had ceased in 1965.

That was all. But it was enough.

Uranium.

And silver.

I put the book in my pocket and continued my investigation of the room. On the desk was a detailed map of the city, which Irving had evidently obtained at a Conoco gas station. Tucked into the map was a sheet of hotel stationery which had been carefully folded into a small square. I unfolded it. In Irving's small, light script was written: "Gladys Jennings, 4391 S. 11 E." The stock transfer agent. I could understand that. But there were two notes written at an angle across the bottom of the page that puzzled me. One said: "Nettie–Bartten." The other said: "Brock–Albion."

I pondered. Bartten could be the name of the broker. It was probably pronounced like Barton. But Albion? The only Albion I could think of was James Justin Albion. And it was a mistake to link me with him. For he was one of the few people I knew who truly hated me.

I refolded the paper and put it in my pocket along with the book, then opened the map. The streets were confusing. There seemed to be four of everything—four Sixths, four Sevenths, four Eighths. But soon I began to understand. There was a Sixth North, a Sixth South, a Sixth East and a Sixth West. The Mormon Tabernacle was the focal point. The street numbers began there. I found Eleventh East and Forty-fifth South. Gladys Jennings lived somewhere in that vicinity. I added the map to the collection in my pocket.

I wondered where to start—at the Jennings place or at police headquarters.

It didn't occur to me not to start at all.

But meanwhile I had to go back to the hospital.

Naomi was still in the lobby. She was sound asleep. I shook her gently. She woke with a start. "No change," she mumbled. "Time to go to bed," I told her. "I'll take over now."

She nodded meekly. "No change," she said again.

The motel was only a short distance from the hospital. I drove her there, got her suitcase from my room, escorted her to Irving's room, gave her the key and saw her safely inside.

I returned to the hospital and went up to the intensive care unit. The nurse told me that Irving's condition was stable. I asked her what stable meant. She said it meant stable.

But presently Dr. Littner came along, and she gave him a different story. She said there'd been some "activity."

"Good," he replied, and turned to me. "Let's go take a look."

I accompanied him to Irving's bedside. And saw at once that indeed there was "activity." The lines on the electrocardiograph monitor were sharper, the peaks more erratic and higher. Irving's eyelids were fluttering slightly, and he was murmuring. He appeared to be dreaming.

"Excellent," Littner observed, and picked up the charts that were clipped to the foot of the bed.

I continued to look at Irving. My own pulse had quickened. His movements were undoubtedly a sign of increased strength.

Littner replaced the charts, and the two of us stood there in silence, watching the restless patient.

Then suddenly Irving groaned loudly and moved his hand. He opened his eyes, closed them, opened them again. Wide. He directed his gaze toward me.

"Am I dead?" he asked.

"No, Irv," I told him. "You're not dead."

He sighed and went back to sleep.

Littner led me back to the corridor.

I was all choked up. And although I tried to hold back the tears, I couldn't. "Damn it," I said hoarsely, "I'm crying."

But Littner merely nodded and said, "It often happens like that."

17

The Public Safety Building was less than a mile from the hospital. It was a nice-looking structure, cheerfully landscaped, next to the public library. The chief's office was on the ground floor.

I was prepared for a hassle with receptionists, secretaries and the various intermediaries who in most cities insulate public servants from the public they serve. But the hassle didn't develop. I said I wanted to see the chief of police, and the next thing I knew, I was sitting in his office.

It was a large room. The walls were covered with an assortment of maps, awards, certificates and citations. The windows offered a spectacular view of the snow-capped mountains that rose abruptly from the plains at the east end of the city.

The chief was a large, affable man who looked remarkably like the James Arness version of Matt Dillon. "Now," he said, glancing up from the business card I'd given him, "what can I do for you, Mr. Potter?"

"I want to inquire about an accident," I said. "A friend of

mine was run over by a car yesterday morning, and I'd like to know how it happened."

He asked me who my friend was, and I told him. He said he was familiar with the case but didn't know all the details. The investigation was in the hands of the hit-and-run detail.

"Then it definitely was a hit-and-run accident?" I said.

He nodded, and glanced once more at my business card. "You say the victim was a friend of yours?"

"Friend and employee. I came out from New York with his wife yesterday. It appears that he's going to recover, but he's in very bad shape. Naturally I'm concerned. I'm sure you can understand that."

He nodded again.

"He isn't a careless person."

"The hit-and-run detail is working on it. They're out at this very moment. I can't guarantee anything, but they're quite good."

"Can you tell me how it happened?"

"Not precisely."

"And when, and where?"

"In the early hours of the morning, I believe. But for anything more specific you'd have to ask the man in charge of the case, and I don't think he's in right now."

"I don't mind waiting."

He eyed me briefly with the suspicion that seems to come naturally to every law enforcement officer in the world. But the look didn't last. "Well, I can take you to his office, if you don't *mind* waiting. He should be coming in soon."

"I'd appreciate that."

He got up from his chair and escorted me down a corridor, past a conference room, to an office that was a smaller version of his own. "His name is Sessions," he said. "It shouldn't be too long." He gave me a friendly smile, and added, "If there's anything else I can do for you, just let me know."

I thanked him, and we shook hands. He left. I sat down. In every police station or sheriff's office I'd ever been to I'd felt a certain hostility in the air. This was different. It's the mountains, I thought, gazing out the window. Not only do they divide the country physically; they also divide it emotionally.

I sighed and lit a cigarette. I was very tired. The benefits from the few hours' sleep I'd had were rapidly slipping away. It was only four-thirty in the afternoon but it seemed much later. I'd stayed at the hospital until two o'clock, then returned to the motel to pick up Naomi. I'd called her earlier to give her the good news, but had insisted she continue to rest for a while. After driving her to the hospital, I went back to the motel and spent an hour on the telephone, talking in turn to Tom, Mark, Harriet and Brian; Joe and George were out. Then another trip to the hospital, to check on Irving. He'd awakened, Naomi said, but only for a few minutes; his color was better. Her color was better too, I noted. She'd totally regained her composure and was once again the quietly competent Naomi Silvers I'd always known. She'd been thinking about the children, she told me. Even if there were no relapses, Irving was going to have to be in the hospital for a long time. She didn't want to leave him, but she didn't want to leave the children either. What she thought she'd do was rent an apartment, have the children come out, and set up housekeeping temporarily in Salt Lake City.

I took the sheet of hotel stationery from my pocket and unfolded it. I studied Irving's memoranda. I tried to guess at his thought processes.

"Mr. Potter?"

I jumped.

"C. C. Sessions. The chief said you were here."

We shook hands, and I gave him one of my cards. He didn't look at it, however, so I gathered that he'd already been briefed. He sat down at his desk. "I spoke to the hospital a little while ago. Miracles do happen. How can I help you?"

"I want to know about the accident."

"There're some things I can't tell you."

"O.K., the things you *can* tell me. Like when did it happen?"

He consulted no notes; he seemed to have all the facts at the forefront of his mind. "We don't know exactly when he was hit. The call came through to us, and simultaneously to the fire department, at 3:45 A.M. A passing motorist had seen the body lying on the street."

"The fire department?"

"The paramedics are fire department personnel."

"I see. And where was the body?"

"On Fifth South, about half a block east of First West. In the middle of the block."

"Isn't that where the Rodeway Inn is?"

"Exactly. Mr. Silvers was evidently crossing from the Rodeway Inn to the Hilton. They're almost directly across the street from each other."

I nodded. I was already familiar with the area. The back entrance to the Rodeway Inn was, indeed, across the street from the front entrance to the Hilton. "Isn't Fifth South one-way westbound?"

"Yes."

"And it's a wide street."

"Yes."

"And there couldn't have been much traffic at that hour."

"Probably not. What are you getting at?"

"I don't know."

"Mr. Silvers must have been in a great hurry."

"Evidently."

"We'll interview him, of course. As soon as the doctors let us."

"You haven't located the car?"

"We will."

"Were there any eyewitnesses?"

"We're working on that."

"But have you—?"

"I'd rather not say, at this point."

"What makes you so sure you'll find the car?"

"Because of the damage-clearance sticker. It's a state law in Utah."

"I don't understand."

"Every car that's involved in an accident in this state gets a sticker which shows that the accident has been investigated. No automobile body shop will touch a car that doesn't have a sticker on it."

I thought that over. A good law to have. "Suppose somebody scrapes the door of his own garage."

"He still has to report it and get a sticker. After the car is fixed, the sticker is removed." Sessions smiled. "You'd be surprised how helpful that law is." His smile vanished. "I'm not saying that some things don't get by us. There are certain backyard body shops that ignore the law. We can't keep up with all of them." The smile returned. "But we do better than a lot of places."

"What's to keep somebody from driving the car to a different state to have it fixed?"

"As I say, we can't control everything."

I did some more thinking. "Anyone who was hit as hard as Irving was—I should think there'd be quite a bit of damage to the car."

"So should I. But in almost every case there are certain clues anyway."

"Such as?"

"I wouldn't want to talk about this case specifically, but such things as fragments of glass from a headlight which can be traced to a particular manufacturer, small pieces of grillwork, paint chips. The FBI helps. They have a spectrograph at the lab

90

in Washington. They can identify the make of a car from the tiniest flake of paint."

"In this case . . .?"

"As I said, I don't want to get specific. I don't think I should. But"—he smiled—"we *have* vacuumed the victim's clothes."

I smiled too. I found myself liking the man. "Well, I suppose you've told me as much as you can. I appreciate it. If *I* can be of any help to *you,* I hope you'll contact me. I'm at the Rodeway Inn." I got up.

He remained seated. "Do you feel that you might be helpful to us, Mr. Potter?"

"Not yet, but I'm trying."

"If you should learn anything . . ."

"Don't worry, I will."

We shook hands across the desk, and I left.

I went back to the hospital.

The only one who could explain why Irving was hurrying across the street from the Rodeway Inn to the Hilton at three-thirty in the morning was Irving.

18

Naomi had a copy of the *Salt Lake Tribune* and was reading the want ads. She'd found several listings for furnished apartments that might be suitable, she said; she planned to go out the next day and look at them.

"You'll need a car," I said.

"I've got a car," she said. "All I have to do is find it." Irving had evidently rented one, she explained; she'd come across a set of keys in the pocket of his extra suit, and the license number was attached to the key ring.

"Have you talked to him at all?" I inquired.

"Not really. He looked at me and all he said was 'Am I dead?' and I told him that he wasn't, and then he closed his eyes again."

"That's what he said to me: 'Am I dead?' "

"It's a good sign, I think. It means he remembers. The last thought he must have had was that he was going to die. So there's no amnesia. He'll remember everything."

"Let's hope so." I pondered over the car keys. "You'll probably find the car in the motel lot. He was walking across Fifth South from the Rodeway Inn to the Hilton when he was hit, so chances are he'd left the car at the motel."

"How do you know?"

I told her about my visit to police headquarters.

She frowned. "Three-thirty in the morning. A strange hour."

"A very strange hour. I'm going to have to ask him why. I'd like to talk to him."

"They won't let you. We can only see him at certain times, and only for a few minutes." She nodded in the direction of the nurse. "She's very firm."

I decided to go over the nurse's head. I found a telephone and a directory and placed a call to Dr. Littner at his home. He was having dinner, a woman said, but no sooner had she said it than he picked up an extension telephone and spoke for himself. I told him that I was at the hospital and wanted to see Mr. Silvers for a few minutes; would he please arrange it? He said he would.

Irving's eyes were closed, but he was clutching the sheet so tightly that I knew he wasn't asleep. There were beads of perspiration on his upper lip. He was obviously in great pain.

"Irv," I said softly.

He opened his eyes. He smiled. The smile became a grimace. He groaned.

I leaned over the bed. "You're going to be all right, Irv."

"Hurts like hell, Brock." But he managed to smile again. "Appreciate your coming." His voice was weak and raspy.

"I only have a few minutes, Irv. I have to ask you a few questions. Do you remember what happened?"

He clutched the sheet even tighter and grimaced again. "Oh, God!" The spasm of pain passed. "Someone tried to kill me."

"Who?"

"Don't know. Telephone call."

"Telephone call?"

Another spasm of pain gripped him. He screwed his eyes shut. The spasm passed. "Man called. Said come to the Hilton. Had information."

"Did you recognize his voice?"

"Uh uh."

"Was it Bartten?"

He opened his eyes.

"I found the *Stock Annual* in your room. I know about Lucky Devil. I also found a piece of paper you'd stuck in a map."

He didn't smile with his lips, but there was a brief flicker of affection in his eyes. "Admire you," he said. "Always did."

"Is Bartten the broker?"

"Think so. Wouldn't tell me. Almost positive, though."

"Did you talk to the Jennings woman?"

"Uh huh."

"What did she say?"

A particularly severe pain jolted him. He clenched his teeth, but a faint cry escaped nevertheless.

"It doesn't matter," I said quickly. "I plan to talk to her myself."

He took a deep breath. "Mean woman."

"You're sure you didn't recognize the voice of the man who called you?"

"Sounded strange."

"One more thing, Irv. You had my name on that piece of paper, next to an Albion."

"Saw him. Intended to tell you."

"John Justin Albion?"

"Yes. Asked about you." He screwed his eyes shut again. "Goddamn pain is awful."

"I can imagine. Albion lives here now?"

"Says so. Was going to tell you when I called. Wanted to apologize. Things I said. I'm sorry. Forgive me."

"I'm sorry too. For the things *I* said."

"Naomi's here."

"I know. We came out together."

"Look after her."

"You look after her, pal. You're going to be all right. You're going to be as good as new."

"Hope so."

"You are. You're doing fine. . . . What company is Bartten with?"

"Don't remember. Jennings woman knows. Mean lady."

The nurse appeared. "The doctor said only a few minutes," she reminded me.

"He's in great pain," I said.

"I know. I've told the doctor."

I spread two fingers in a V-for-victory sign and held them up for Irving to see, then followed the nurse out of the room.

Naomi agreed to have dinner with me, and since both of us were tired, we decided to eat in the coffee shop at the Rodeway Inn.

But first she wanted to look for Irving's car. She had the keys in her pocketbook.

The car was parked less than a hundred feet from Irving's room.

"Now how about a drink?" I suggested.

"I'd love one."

We walked over to the bar, which adjoined the coffee shop, but were told that we could only get setups—we had to bring our own liquor. There was, however, a liquor department in the gift shop, off the lobby.

I bought a bottle of Scotch. "With this, who needs a bar?" I said. "Let's go back to my room, where we can take our shoes off."

"Lovely idea," Naomi said. "And I know where there's an ice machine."

So we returned to my room. The red light on my telephone was glowing. I dialed the message clerk and was told that a Mr. Theodore North had called and wanted me to call him back.

"Do you know anyone named Theodore North?" I asked Naomi.

"No."

"Neither do I."

But when she went to get the ice I dialed the number the message clerk had given me.

A man answered.

"Theodore North?"

"Speaking."

"This is Brockton Potter. You called me?"

"I sure did," he said cheerfully. "George Gage suggested I get in touch with you."

I didn't know a George Gage either.

"He's with the Hamilton National Bank," North went on. "We do a lot of business with them, and he's a personal friend of mine. Tom Petacque told him you're out here and asked him if he knew anyone who could sort of clear a path for you, and whatever. I've heard of you, of course. I'd love to meet you."

Typical of Tom. "That's very kind of you. You're with . . . ?"

"Pioneer Trust and Savings. I'm the president, actually. It'd be a pleasure to show you the bank. How about having lunch with me on Monday?"

"I wish I could, but I have to be in New York on Monday."

"Tomorrow, then. The bank will be closed, but we can eat at my club. The grill's open on Saturday."

I hesitated. There was no reason to say no, but there was no reason to say yes, either.

"I'd like to get your opinions," he added. "Perhaps we can end up doing some business together."

The clincher. "I'd be happy to."

"Terrific. Twelve-thirtyish, at the University Club. I may be a few minutes late—my son has a track meet—but I'll leave word that you're expected. Just go up to the bar and make yourself at home."

Naomi returned with the ice.

North told me where the University Club was located. I thanked him again, and we hung up.

"North," I explained. "A friend of a friend of Tom's, and a potential customer."

Naomi smiled. "It's an ill wind . . ."

"Sometimes." I unwrapped a couple of the glasses that were on the countertop in the dressing area and poured two stiff drinks.

Naomi kicked off her shoes. "It's all beginning to catch up with me. I'm terribly tired. You must be too."

I kicked my shoes off also, and sipped the Scotch. "I am. But there's one more thing I have to do tonight. I have to see a mean lady."

She gave me a questioning glance.

I repeated what Irving had said.

"I'll go with you," she volunteered promptly.

"No, you won't. Irving asked me to look after you. You're

going to have dinner and go to bed and get a good night's sleep."

"But I'm very good with mean ladies."

"So am I."

"I doubt it."

"It's nice ladies that I have trouble with. But in any case, you're going to bed."

"If you insist." Her expression grew thoughtful. "It seems so impossible, I can't even conceive of it, and yet, based on what you said, I can't help wondering—do you think someone deliberately set out to kill Irv?"

I didn't answer right away. "It does seem inconceivable," I said finally. "But isn't it just as inconceivable that someone would have set out to kill Sarah Weinberg?"

She drank some Scotch and put her glass on a table. There was a quiver in her voice. "I've always loathed violence, Brock. Simply loathed it. But if I thought that someone deliberately hit Irv with that car—"

"Careful, Naomi. That's the state of mind Irv was in."

She blinked. "You're right. I shouldn't and I won't. I don't understand it, though. For a few shares of some silly stock . . ."

"Fifty thousand isn't a few shares, dear. And I have a feeling that the stock is a lot more valuable than Sarah Weinberg thought it was." I took the *Stock Annual* from my pocket, opened it to "Lucky Devil" and handed it to her.

She read the entry carefully. "The total assets are only $34,-000, Brock."

"That's what it says, and that may be what the books show. But think, Naomi. Uranium and silver. Do you realize how much the price of those two metals has gone up in the past fifteen years or so?"

"No. But even so." She gave the book back to me and drank some more Scotch.

"Mining isn't one of my strong points. But I do know this: the price of silver has at least tripled, and uranium, with the shortage of oil and natural gas, has increased in value even more."

"But it says that the mining activities ceased in 1965."

"I know. But they may have been started up again. In any event, I'm sure that there's more to Lucky Devil Minerals, Inc. at the moment than meets the eye."

"I have read that the utility companies are building uranium facilities," she conceded.

"The potential is enormous."

She eyed me and for a moment said nothing. Then she spoke. "Irv wouldn't like my saying this, but I don't think you ought to get involved, Brock. Any more than I thought he ought to have got involved."

"Drink up, so I can pour us seconds. I'm beginning to feel better. I don't intend to get involved, Naomi. This isn't a matter that concerns Price, Potter and Petacque. But I *am* curious, and I *do* intend to find out why someone lured Irv out of this motel at three-thirty yesterday morning and immediately after that he was hit by a car. That much, I feel, I owe him. I don't care about Sarah Weinberg. I do care about Irv."

"Which he knows, and I know, and both of us appreciate more than I can tell you. But whether it was an accident or not, why don't you just leave it to the police? You said you were favorably impressed by them."

"I was. I like the police here. They're not as uptight as they are in a lot of other places. All I intend to do is put together enough information to give them something to go on. Otherwise, even if they find the car, they may not find the driver; and even if they find the driver, they may not be able to prove a motive. And there's a hell of a difference, dear, between reckless driving and attempted murder."

She finished her drink. I refilled our glasses. We sat awhile in silence.

"Although I don't know as much as I should about mining," I said at last, "I know one thing. Since the beginning of history there's never been anything that excited human beings as much as digging something of great value out of the ground. Normally sane men go crazy at the mere prospect. Oil, diamonds, gold—it doesn't matter what. People get visions of instant wealth and become like animals. It's one of the principal causes of human progress, and human misery as well. It's responsible for the discovery of America, for God knows how many wars. The quest for minerals creates civilizations, and destroys them. And nowhere is the mining fever more intense than right here in the western part of the United States, where there's so much to mine for." I gulped some Scotch.

Naomi sighed. "Freud took a dim view of human nature. Perhaps he was right."

"Perhaps. But what you and I ought to do at the moment is put on our shoes and go get something to eat. I'm beginning to feel high."

We finished dinner shortly before nine o'clock. Naomi went to her room. I climbed into my car and drove off to find 4391 South 11th Street East.

Even with Irving's map open beside me, I got lost twice. It took me almost an hour to make a trip that should have taken no more than twenty minutes.

The neighborhood was at the far south end of the city. It appeared to be a nice one. Not magnificent, not shabby—just nice. But then, I couldn't really see that much, for the main source of illumination was the light that came from the windows of the houses.

The Jennings house was one that was dark. I got out of the car and went up to the front door. I pushed the buzzer.

There was no answer.

I waited a while, then made a circle of the building. Six or seven rooms, I decided. Not very large rooms. Attractive patio in back. Such landscaping as I could see appeared to be well cared for.

I tried to open the garage door. It was locked.

I rang the bell again. When no one came to the door, I returned to my car.

I sat there until almost eleven o'clock.

Gladys Jennings didn't return.

I got lost once more, on the way back to the motel.

It was midnight when I crawled wearily into bed. I thought about the price of uranium. I imagined a mountain of uranium. I wondered where Gladys Jennings was spending the evening. I pictured a witch. I fell asleep.

19

I'd just stepped out of the shower and started to towel myself when the telephone rang.

It was Naomi. She was on her way to breakfast. Did I want to join her?

"Meet you in the coffee shop in ten minutes," I said.

The air was clear. The sky was Wedgwood blue and without a cloud. It had evidently snowed in the mountains during the night; the peaks were whiter than they'd been before, and sparkled in the bright morning sunshine.

"How'd you make out with the mean lady?" Naomi wanted to know.

"She was out. I'm going back there this morning."

"I do wish you'd let me go along, Brock."

"No dice. But there is something you can do."

"Anything," she said eagerly.

"Call Mrs. Hoffman. See if you can get me the name, address and telephone number of Sarah Weinberg's lawyer. And of her niece."

"The niece is no problem. I know her name and where she lives. She lives in Larchmont. I can track down the exact address and telephone number. But I have no idea who the lawyer is, and Nettie may not either."

"The niece'll know. In fact, why don't you call her yourself? Don't tell her any more than you have to, but tell enough to get her cooperation. Say that I'm going to call her and that I'm a friend. I'll take it from there."

"I'll do what I can. But what do you have in mind, Brock?"

"I'm not sure. I have an idea, though. Depends on how things go. But I may need the niece's help, and the lawyer's. Will you leave the information in my mailbox?"

"Yes. I'll call as soon as we finish breakfast."

"Are you going apartment-hunting?"

"For a while. After that I'll be at the hospital."

"I'll stop by later myself. I don't know when, though. This may turn out to be a busy day."

I took a different route. I found a broad thoroughfare called Highland Drive which cut diagonally across the southeastern section of the city, and followed it. And I didn't get lost. At least not physically. But mentally I strayed quite far.

The mountains fascinated me. Perhaps ten thousand feet

high, they rose like a jagged wall along the eastern end of the city. I pictured the early Mormons struggling through the passes in their wagons. I pictured them emerging from those passes to find themselves in a vast sunbaked valley with a huge lake of intensely salty water in the middle of it. They must have felt as if they'd been guided there by providence.

Gazing at the mountains, I had the strange sensation that the East and Midwest belonged to a separate nation, a distant one.

And that those mountains represented the very essence of wealth. Gold, silver, copper, uranium, lead, beryllium, alunite and much more. No one could estimate the value of this huge area.

But someone had estimated the value of one small segment of it.

Was his name Kisman?

I parked in front of the house. The garage door was closed. I went up the walk. The impression I'd had the night before was verified. Six or seven rooms. Nice landscaping. Good maintenance. Worth perhaps sixty thousand, at today's prices. I rang the bell.

A woman opened the door. A middle-aged woman with very red hair.

"Gladys Jennings?" I said.

Her eyes narrowed, and the corners of her mouth turned down. "I am," she replied.

I smiled. The smile was genuine. For despite her look of displeasure, there was something about her that reminded me of a clown. It wasn't just the flaming red hair; it was also the face that was covered with too much white powder, the bright spot of rouge on each cheek, the scarlet lipstick that extended well beyond the lips themselves. Even her clothes seemed somehow clownish—a red-and-white-checked dress and red patent-leather platform sandals. "My name is Brockton Potter," I said. "I'm with the New York brokerage firm of Price, Potter and Petacque. I'd like to talk to you for a few minutes. May I come in?"

"No." She planted her feet and tightened her grip on the broom she was holding.

"You are the transfer agent for Lucky Devil Minerals, aren't you?"

She said nothing. Merely scowled.

"According to the information I have, you are. I think it would be in your interest to talk to me."

"I'm housecleaning."

"I'll only take a few minutes of your time. I want to discuss some shares in the company, which were owned by a Mrs. Sarah Weinberg."

"Put it in a letter and mail it to me." She renewed her grip on the broom. "And wipe that smirk off your face. I'm not funny."

"No offense, I assure you. But I have the feeling I've seen you somewhere before. Were you ever on the stage?"

It was a shot in the dark, but it struck a target. She stopped scowling. "Once." The scowl returned almost immediately, however, and became even more devastating. Yet, in spite of it, she seemed a comic figure.

"I understand that a broker by the name of Bartten was trying to purchase the stock from Mrs. Weinberg. I wonder if you can tell me where I can locate him."

"I told you: whatever you have to say, put it in a letter."

"I don't have time. I'm only here for a few days. I'd like to get in touch with Mr. Bartten, or I'd like him to get in touch with me. I'm staying at the Rodeway Inn."

She made a sudden move to close the door. I put my foot in the opening, then gave the door a hard push with my shoulder. Gladys Jennings staggered backward and almost lost her balance. I walked into the house. For a moment she was non-plused.

"What I wanted to tell you and Mr. Bartten," I said, "is that I purchased Mrs. Weinberg's stock from her ten days ago. I'm now the owner of it. If Mr. Bartten is interested in buying it, he'll have to deal with me."

She gaped. Which made her next move all the more unexpected.

She rammed the broom handle into my stomach.

I doubled up in pain.

She brought the broom handle down on my head, twice.

I cried out and covered my head with my hands.

She kicked me in both shins and whacked my hands with the broom handle.

I retreated. She kept hitting me across the head and hands until I was out of the house, then slammed the door.

I sat in the car and waited for the pain to subside.

It took a long time.

20

And even when it did subside, it didn't subside completely. I was still hurting at twelve-thirty, when I walked into the University Club.

I'd improvised an ice bag from a couple of towels and some ice cubes. That had helped a bit. But a dull ache persisted in my stomach, and I had a throbbing lump on my head and three swollen knuckles on my right hand. Along with a feeling of outrage.

The fact that I hadn't been able to reach Sarah Weinberg's niece or her lawyer didn't improve matters. Naomi had left their names and telephone numbers in my box as she'd promised. The niece's name was Deutsch; the lawyer's, Tallman. There was no answer at either number, however.

North hadn't arrived.

I ordered a double martini and wandered around the room with it, thinking of all the things I should have said to Gladys Jennings, all the things I might have done. Some of which were vicious.

But martinis are good for reducing anger, and that one was no exception. It even made me less aware of my discomfort. Gladys Jennings hadn't seen the last of me. Meanwhile . . .

"Mr. Potter?"

I turned around.

"Ted North."

Bank presidents are supposed to be middle-aged and distinguished-looking. But this one wasn't. I doubted that he was forty. And his boyish grin and air of jauntiness made him seem even younger.

We shook hands.

"Hope I haven't kept you waiting long," he said.

"Only a few minutes."

"We won."

"Won?"

"The track meet."

"Oh, yes."

"My oldest, you know. He's fifteen. Very competitive, I must say. I encourage that, in all my kids."

"How many have you?"

"Seven."

"Good Lord!"

"Keeps the wife busy. Let me get a drink." He went over to the bar and returned with an Old Fashioned. Then he escorted me from window to window, pointing out the sights.

The club occupied the top floor of one of the city's taller buildings. From any of the windows you could see for miles. The mountains, North said, belonged to the Wasatch Range. "Great skiing. Best skiing in the United States. Alta and Snowbird. We have a condominium at Snowbird. The kids love it. Let me show you the other side." We crossed the room to look westward. My host identified the shimmering expanse of the Great Salt Lake and apologized for the unattractive cloud that hung over a portion of the shoreline. "The Magna copper mine, you know. Largest open-pit copper mine in the world."

I nodded.

We concluded our tour at the south windows. My sense of outrage returned briefly as I tried to pick out the neighborhood where Gladys Jennings lived.

"Another drink?" North inquired. "Or would you rather have something to eat?"

"We'd better eat," I said. "I have stops to make this afternoon."

We went into the dining room. North ordered another drink for himself and attempted to justify the state's liquor laws. He himself didn't approve of them, he said, but he did believe that the absence of bars tended to lower the crime rate. Also the accident rate. Then he asked me why I was smiling.

I explained that the reason I was in Salt Lake City was that my right-hand man had been almost killed by a hit-and-run driver outside the Rodeway Inn.

North was shocked. "A drunken driver?"

"Who knows?" I replied.

He launched into a review of the city's medical facilities, which somehow got him onto the unrelated subjects of ballet and basketball, both of which were very big in the area, and wound up back at the beginning by offering me a list of the better clubs where I could go for drinks.

The quality of youthfulness which was the first thing I'd noticed about him seemed even more pronounced as he continued to talk. He had the eagerness to please that is characteristic of a man who isn't sure of himself. Which seemed strange, because he had plenty of cause for confidence. He was president of a bank at an age at which most bank officers are still scrambling to become first vice-presidents. Furthermore, he was extremely knowledgeable. When we got around to stocks and bonds, which he really did want to talk about, he revealed a deep understanding of the ins and outs of the market.

But his opinions were conventional, and some of the things I said shook him. Particularly what I said about real estate.

"But that's because you live in New York," he protested.

"Fortunately I do," I replied. "Living in New York is very educational." I recalled the impressions I'd had earlier in the day. "You get a different feeling out here, on this side of your Wasatch Range. You get the feeling that you're not altogether part of the rest of the United States. But actually you are. And the tendency of politicians to offer easy living in exchange for votes isn't confined only to politicians in the East. Greed destroys cities the same as it destroys everything else. Not the politicians' greed. The people's. Which the politicians cater to."

"You sound like my father."

"Your father?"

He gave me a self-deprecating smile. "He's chairman of the board of Pioneer Trust and Savings."

I suddenly understood his need to prove himself. "He must be very proud of you," I said tactfully.

And thereby moved one step closer to adding Pioneer Trust and Savings to our list of customers. "Thanks," North said.

I let that matter rest temporarily. "There's one thing I wonder if you can help me with," I said.

"Name it," he said.

"There's a stockbroker in town by the name of Bartten. I'd like to get some information about him."

He frowned. "The name doesn't register. Who's he with?"

"That's one of the things I'd like to find out. I've looked up the name in the telephone directory. There are several Barttens."

"What else?"

"What he specializes in, if anything. Where he comes from. Just general information. I'm trying to get a profile of him before I meet him. But in confidence, of course."

"I'm sure someone at the bank must have heard of him. Where can I get in touch with you?"

"I was hoping you might be able to tell me something now."

He jumped up. "Wait here. I'll make a couple of phone calls. I don't know what luck I'll have. The hunting season starts this weekend. Nine-tenths of my people have taken off for the mountains. And the remaining tenth is probably playing golf. But I'll see what I can do." He tossed his napkin onto the table and hurried off.

Leaning back in my chair, I gazed out the window. The city seemed to be growing in all directions. Perhaps I'd been too pessimistic in my statements about real estate. After all, Salt Lake City was still on the way up. It would be decades before—

"I thought I recognized you," a voice said.

I turned. And was thoroughly startled to find James Justin Albion standing beside my chair. "For God's sake!" I exclaimed, and started to get up.

He put his hand on my shoulder. "Don't bother." He dropped into the chair North had vacated. "You haven't changed a bit. Not a bit."

I studied him with interest. And with genuine awe. For he

108

was a phenomenon. A man who had started from scratch and in ten years built himself an empire worth one hundred million dollars and then, in the eleventh year, gone broke.

21

In no way was I responsible for Albion's downfall. It was as much his own doing as his success had been.

But you couldn't convince him of that. He believed that if it weren't for me he'd still be on top. He'd told me so, at length and with passion. To him I was the world's worst son of a bitch.

He'd come to me when he was desperate. He'd pleaded with me to recommend Cougar Consolidated. He'd gone beyond mere pleading; he'd threatened me and, when that failed, he'd tried to bribe me with stock in the company and with cash.

I'd refused. Joe Rothland had told me, at one of our staff meetings, that he'd heard a rumor to the effect that Cougar was in trouble. I'd assigned Irving to investigate the rumor. Irving had done so and reported that the rumor was well founded.

Chances are, I wouldn't have recommended the stock even if Joe hadn't heard the rumor. I'd avoided doing so throughout the years. I didn't trust Albion and I didn't trust the company he'd created. Not that I thought him dishonest. I simply thought that he'd risen too fast and was flying too high. I'm skeptical of men who own ten million dollars' worth of houses, private jets and elongated limousines, whose wives appear regularly in sables and diamonds, who acquire strings of race horses, charter yachts to cruise the Greek islands and never appear at conferences with less than ten frightened assistants to attend to their wants. And I'm especially skeptical when I know that the lifestyle of such men is supported by legions of trusting stockholders.

Yet Albion had made a lot of money for his stockholders. His basic idea had been sound. The syndication of oil wells, mines and concessions of every sort from marble quarries to teakwood forests. It gave small investors an opportunity to participate in the sort of ventures that previously had been open only to large ones. And Albion had produced for them. He'd developed oil fields. He'd negotiated with third world governments and gained the right for Cougar Consolidated to explore for minerals, and Cougar Consolidated had found them. He was an incomparable salesman, as effective with the president of an African country that was in the process of emerging from the Stone Age as he was with bankers, brokers and security analysts from one end of the United States to the other. He'd tried like hell, he'd succeeded magnificently—but ultimately he'd failed.

He'd failed because he'd gone too far. Because he'd got to believing that failure was impossible, that his magic touch was actually magic. He'd begun to overpay for everything and to conceal the fact that he was overpaying by overstating the value of the properties in the company reports. He hit a string of expensive losers. Costs had escalated. Some of his concessions were nationalized. A group of disgruntled stockholders sued him. His empire started to topple.

At which point he came to me. To get me to shore up the price of Cougar Consolidated stock by touting it to the large purchasers who were Price, Potter and Petacque's customers.

I doubt that I was the only securities analyst he approached. But I was a relatively hot item at that moment because of recent successes, so he may have tried harder with me. In any event, the treatment didn't work. I stuck to my guns.

Cougar Consolidated was now in the hands of a court-appointed administrator. Albion himself was the defendant in lawsuits amounting to over eight million dollars. He owed everyone from the Internal Revenue Service to his liquor dealer. He'd had a heart attack. Folks who had once considered him a likely candidate for sainthood now called him a crook and a phony.

But he looked fine. And I told him so.

"Doctor's orders," he said. " 'Take off thirty pounds and keep them off.' "

"What brings you to this neck of the woods, Justin?" He liked to be called by his middle name.

"This is where I had my heart attack. Collapsed on the sidewalk at Temple and State. The good doctors here saved my life. I feel I owe the city something." He smiled. His smile had always been great. "So I'm giving it my presence."

I wanted to ask him how he was supporting himself, but decided that the question would be in poor taste. So I asked him one that was in even poorer taste. "Are you still mad at me?"

He continued to smile. "Yes."

I sighed. There are some things a guy just has to learn to live with. "I was sorry to hear about your heart attack."

The smile vanished. "Don't be patronizing." There was real venom in his voice.

I shrugged. "All right. If you prefer, I was glad to hear about your heart attack."

"That's better. You don't like me any more than I like you, and you know it."

In addition to everything else, he'd become paranoid. "To be perfectly frank, Justin, I neither like you nor dislike you. I simply don't give a damn about you."

The smile returned. "That's more like it. Now you're being honest."

"I've always been honest."

He let that one go by. "I saw your man Silvers the other day."

"Really?"

He waited for me to say more, and when I didn't he inquired what I was doing so far off the beaten track.

"There is no beaten track these days," I replied. "But you—this is a long way from home for you."

"I never really had a home. Or perhaps I should say I had too many homes."

That was true. He'd started his operations in Tulsa, where he'd been born and raised, but he'd eventually moved the company headquarters to New York. He'd bought an apartment on Fifth Avenue, three blocks from where Mark lived. But that was just one of his roosts. He had others in Bel Air, Palm Springs, Antibes, Lausanne and County Cork, Ireland. The one in Ireland, I'd heard, was a three-hundred-year-old castle. "You're right, I guess. Where you really lived was in your plane."

"I miss the plane more than anything else," he admitted. "Once you get used to having one . . . But tell me—does Silvers need a back-up man these days?"

I noticed that the lower lid of his left eye had begun to twitch. "I can't get over how much better you look without the extra weight," I said.

The twitch got worse. "You're the same secretive bastard you always were."

"Not at all. I publish my innermost thoughts once a week. They go out to all our customers. . . . Look, Justin, this is silly. There's no reason for us to be enemies. I did what I thought was right, and you got hurt. But you would have got hurt anyway. Nothing in the world could have saved you at that point. So why can't we be friends? I'm staying at the Rodeway Inn. Come around in the morning, and I'll buy you breakfast. At least—"

"I'm not a charity case yet, and even if I were I wouldn't eat with you. Do I make myself clear?"

112

"Perfectly. So why don't you just get up from that chair and walk away? I don't need your animosity, and I don't need you, and you're keeping me from enjoying my coffee."

He did as I suggested.

You can win 'em all, I told myself. Yet in his case it seemed a shame. He probably had the same brilliant mind and kinetic personality he'd always had, but now they were being wasted. He couldn't accept the fact that he himself was responsible for his fall.

I tried to recall the last item I'd read about him, and partially succeeded. It had to do with one of the lawsuits. It had mentioned the fact that he was living out West and that he'd had a heart attack. It was natural, I supposed, that he would have gravitated to the West. He'd started in Oklahoma; geology was his specialty; the West was the land of spectacular comebacks.

The twitching of his lower eyelid . . . Eyestrain or emotional tension? Most likely emotional tension. He certainly had enough to be tense about. Nevertheless . . .

And perhaps I was exaggerating the extent of his fall. Perhaps he'd managed to stash away a comfortable nest egg. Secret bank accounts in Switzerland, the Bahamas, Mexico. Anything was possible.

I couldn't help feeling sorry for him, though. And for his wife. Limousines, maids, diamonds . . .

His private plane was gone. He missed it, too. . . .

What did a man like that consider a comfortable nest egg to be? A man like that didn't think in ordinary terms.

I sighed. And looked up to see Ted North approaching the table. He was obviously disappointed.

"I tried half a dozen people," he said before he even sat down. "No one was home." He slid into his chair and gulped some cold coffee. "You have no idea what the opening of the hunting season does to us around here. People come from as far away as California. *Everybody* hunts."

113

"What do they hunt for?"

"Deer. But then, I suppose that, being from the East, you don't approve."

I shrugged. "Easterners hunt too. Mostly they end up shooting each other. But that's their business. I have no strong opinions on the subject." I was beginning to feel depressed.

"I'll have the information for you on Monday, though. Bright and early."

"I'll be back in New York on Monday."

"I'll call you at your office."

"O.K."

I didn't want dessert, and neither did he. We finished the conversation with the same topic on which we'd begun it: the track meet.

But as we were riding down to the ground floor in the elevator, North said that he'd like to give us some business.

I said that that would be wonderful and that I'd have Tom get in touch with him on Monday morning.

I drove back to the motel and went up to my room. I opened the telephone directory and turned to the B's. There were five Barttens. I wondered whether any of them was my man, and if so which one.

I put the directory aside. Irving would be disappointed, I thought, if I didn't try to find out as much as I could. On the other hand, perhaps Irving had learned his lesson.

There was nothing for me to do in New York over the weekend. I might as well stay here.

I decided to go to the hospital and discuss the matter with Irving. Or, if I couldn't get in to see him, with Naomi.

I put on my coat. I gingerly touched the lump on my head. A woman like Gladys Jennings was capable of anything. I started for the door.

The telephone rang.

I went back and answered it.

"Brockton Potter?" a man said.

"Yes."

"My name is Gary Bartten. I understand you've been trying to locate me. When would you like to get together?"

22

It was a storefront brokerage office in an old three-story building on First South, near the Salt Palace, next to a men's haberdashery store. The sign painted on the window said, in large gilt-and-black Gothic letters, JONES & MC CABE, STOCKS. The front door was unlocked.

The room was the size of a twelve-chair barbershop, which, for all I knew, it may once have been. There was a rack of investment literature near the entrance and a quotation board on one wall, with the quotations posted in chalk. Two rows of desks faced the quotation board. An ancient glass-enclosed ticker-tape machine stood silent against the window, basking in the Saturday-afternoon sun.

Except for the man who sat at the desk behind a waist-high partition in the back of the room, the place was empty.

"I'm over here," he called.

I approached, and went through the little swinging door that was set into the partition.

Ted North had been younger than I'd expected, and Gary Bartten was older. He was, I judged, about seventy, a broad-shouldered, jowly man with a ruddy complexion, a fringe of white hair around the dome of his bald head, and shaggy white eyebrows. He was wearing a Hawaiian-type sport shirt boldly printed with blue and white flowers and was nibbling on something. He extended his hand without getting up from the swivel chair.

His grip was like a vise.

"Sit down, sir," he said, indicating the only chair other than his own in the area, a straight-backed wooden one of the sort that I always associate with history teachers.

I sat down.

By way of hospitality, he offered me a peppermint Life Saver from the almost empty package beside the telephone. I declined.

"So you're Brockton Potter," he said, making it sound as if Brockton Potter were one of nature's wonders, on a par with the Grand Canyon.

I nodded.

"Well, I'm pleased to meet you. I'm sure pleased to meet you. A man of your stature doesn't often walk through our humble door."

I tried to compare him to someone—anyone—I'd met in the past, but I couldn't find a suitable person. He was a rare breed. "Come off it," I said.

He chuckled. "And modest too," he said.

I took a deep breath and crossed my legs. The Barttens of this world require patience.

He stopped chuckling. His expression became grave. "Permit me to apologize," he said. "I understand you had an encounter with poor Mrs. Jennings this morning. I can't tell you how I regret her behavior. A man of your stature—"

"That woman ought to be locked up."

"She's a bit mad, of course." He tapped his head with a cucumberlike finger. "A bit mad. Poor soul. She's had a difficult life. But she's harmless."

"The hell she is."

"Please accept my heartfelt apologies. And hers too."

I said nothing.

He took one of the Life Savers, put it in his mouth and began to nibble again. He regarded me with what would have passed for benevolence if his eyes hadn't been so cold. "Gladys mentioned that you own some stock in Lucky Devil Minerals," he said presently.

"That's right. You want to buy it?"

"May I ask when you acquired it, sir?"

"A week ago last Wednesday. All fifty thousand shares."

"And may I ask why?"

"Because Sarah Weinberg told me that you were pressuring her to sell it, and I figured that if it was valuable to you it was also valuable to me."

He tried to chuckle but he just couldn't do it. So he swallowed the Life Saver instead. "And may I ask what you paid Mrs. Weinberg for her shares?"

"You can ask anything you want to ask."

He waited. When I didn't go on, he said, "May I say that I don't believe you?"

"You can say anything you want to say."

"Or at least that I'm skeptical."

"It was a perfectly legal transaction. She wanted to sell, I wanted to buy. The stock isn't governed by SEC regulations. She endorsed the shares, I paid her for them, and now I own them. You want to be skeptical, it's all right with me."

"But a man of your stature . . . a company like Lucky Devil . . ."

"You find it incongruous?"

"Ah, thank you. The perfect word. Incongruous. May I compliment you on your vocabulary?"

"Sure." I smiled. "It seems to me that the question isn't so much why I bought the stock but why *you* were trying to buy it."

"That's very simple, sir. I have a client who wishes to acquire the company."

"And Mrs. Weinberg owned the controlling shares."

His ruddy complexion got ruddier.

"And now I own them."

He turned almost purple. Especially his nose.

"Who's your customer?" I asked.

"Surely, sir, you don't expect me to reveal that to you."

"Why not? Is there something secret about it?"

"Aren't such matters always secret?"

"No."

He seemed shocked. He reached for another Life Saver, discovered that it was the last in the package and decided to save it for a rainy day. "Well, I'm afraid with me they are."

"Different strokes for different folks," I remarked.

He said nothing.

"You needn't worry," I said. "I won't do you out of your commission."

He drew himself up. To the extent that a man of his bulk could. "You New Yorkers are very blunt, sir."

"I'm afraid I got my bluntness in the Midwest, where I was born and brought up. I took it to New York with me when I moved there."

"Well, it's not the commission I'm concerned about. It's a matter of business ethics."

"It was hardly ethical to push Mrs. Weinberg off a subway platform."

He sagged. "I didn't know about that. I just found out about it. . . . I was stunned. The poor soul."

"I bought her stock just in the nick of time." I changed course. "Tell me, how did you happen to become involved in Lucky Devil, Bartten?"

He drew himself up again. "I'm the one who put the stock

on the market. I'm the one who made the market in it. When there was a market in it."

"You mean Jones and McCabe?"

"No. I wasn't with this company then. I had a modest company of my own—Bartten and Company. I was a member of all the major exchanges but I specialized in the stocks of this region."

"Did you have dealings with Morris Weinberg?"

"Not personally. He dealt with one of my salesmen. But I met him once. He was a fine gentleman, sir. A fine gentleman."

"Bartten and Company is no longer in existence?"

"Unfortunately, no. The recession. Many things. No, the company is no longer in existence." He sighed heavily.

"What's your connection with Jones and McCabe?"

Once more he drew himself up. "I manage it."

"On whose behalf?"

"Mr. McCabe's. Mr. Jones is dead. And Mr. McCabe is quite elderly. He's in a nursing home." He gazed longingly at the remaining Life Saver. After a moment he decided that the rainy day had come. He popped the candy into his mouth and gave the empty wrapper a vicious twist. "A fine gentleman, sir—Mr. McCabe. But sadly"—he tapped his head again—"failing."

Could he be acting for McCabe's family? Possibly. He could even be acting for himself. Trying, desperately, to stage a comeback. "Does David Kisman still run Lucky Devil?" I asked, changing course again.

His eyes widened. But went back to their normal size almost immediately, when he chuckled. "I do admire you New Yorkers, sir. You're all so"—he groped for the word—"aggressive."

"Does he?"

"No. He never did. Not while the company was active."

"I don't understand."

"Lucky Devil Minerals, sir, was the creation of David Kisman's father—Ethridge Kisman. It was Ethridge Kisman who developed the properties. And a fine gentleman he was. One of my nearest and dearest friends. David Kisman was just a lad at the time. He contributed, you might say, nothing to the family fortune. None of the Kisman children did. When their father passed on, they inherited his stock. But by then the company had suffered reverses. It was scarcely more than a shell."

"What do the children do?"

"The daughter lives in California. She's married to, if my memory serves, an oceanographer. Keith is with the federal bureaucracy—the name of the agency escapes me; I believe it's either HEW or HUD; I've lost track—in Washington. Only David remains in Salt Lake City. But you surprise me, sir. Being a New Yorker, and being, if you'll permit me to pay you a compliment, fast on your feet, I should have thought you'd have checked on all that before you bought Mrs. Weinberg's stock."

"Why should I? You were badgering the poor woman, so obviously you wanted it, so obviously it was worth something. That's all I needed to know. And being a New Yorker, I'm also impulsive. What does David Kisman do?"

He turned purple again, but only briefly. He delayed answering. He plainly didn't want to be the one to supply the information. But, just as plainly, he knew that if he didn't, someone else would. "He owns Happy Hours," he said at last, "in Cottonwood Mall."

"Happy Hours?"

"An establishment devoted to hobbies and creative arts."

"I see. But is he still president of Lucky Devil?"

Bartten delayed answering that question too.

"I'm the company's largest stockholder," I said amiably. "As such—"

"Yes," the old man said quickly. "He is."

"Then," I said, "that about wraps it up. All that remains is for you and me to make a deal for the stock."

He tried to conceal his eagerness but failed utterly. His eyes lit up like a couple of Bunsen burners. He laced his fingers together. He moistened his lips with his tongue. I was reminded of the wolf in Little Red Riding Hood. "And how much are you asking?" he said.

"A hundred dollars a share."

He gasped. Loudly. "But that's—that's five million dollars!"

I nodded. "On the button."

"You're insane!" He forgot to tap his head.

"On second thought, you'd better make it a hundred and one dollars a share. Five million for the stock, and fifty thousand for the assault on me by Mrs. Jennings. I'd rather collect this way than take her to court."

"You—you—you're—"

"One hundred and one dollars a share. That's my price. Take it or leave it." I got up. "You know where to reach me when you make up your mind."

I pushed through the swinging door and left him.

23

A suburban shopping center on Saturday afternoon.

A regiment of women in slacks. A battalion of men in Eisenhower jackets. Three companies of babies in strollers. Twelve platoons of teen-agers in jeans. And three thousand paper bags filled with the spoils of victory.

Upper-, middle- and lower-class Americans joined democratically in the pursuit of their favorite weekend pastime: invading stores.

The excitement was greater than it might have been, for this was one of the Lucky Value Days. There was to be a drawing at four o'clock for a Hammond organ. And twenty fortunate people would win tropical fish. The fish were on display in well-equipped tanks. Presumably the twenty fortunate winners would have tanks of their own.

I bought a taffy apple and proceeded down the immense covered mall, wondering whether it was pure coincidence that Gladys Jennings' house and Cottonwood Mall were only a mile apart.

Happy Hours was at the far end of the mall. Its sign was hobbylike: the letters appeared to be burned into a large piece of wood with equipment from a kit like one I'd bought Tom's son for his last birthday. And indeed there were such kits in the window. Along with kits for leather tooling, string art, decoupage, oil painting, sandcrafting, bead stringing, candle decorating and basket weaving. A sign in the corner of the window said: MACRAME LESSONS.

I threw the taffy apple stick away and went inside.

I admired the toy racing cars, and moved on to the stamp-collecting kits. A serious-looking young man of ten or twelve was considering one of them. The store was fairly crowded. Most of the customers appeared to be under fifteen or over sixty. There were two salespeople, a man and a woman. The woman was explaining to a prospective purchaser the many possible combinations of colored stones that one might use in making a bracelet. The man was lining up tubes of paint for an elderly lady who seemed indecisive about what she wanted. He was a tall, rangy man of about thirty-five with a long face and sad eyes and a cowlick that stood up like the ear of an alert terrier.

122

I paused at a large display of model airplane kits, and got a lump in my throat. There had been a period during my childhood when I desperately wanted one. My father said he couldn't afford to buy it for me. I became angry. Everybody can afford things except us, I said. The incident wouldn't have been important, except for the fact that shortly afterward my father committed suicide.

I swallowed, and wondered whether Tom's son would like a model airplane kit. It would make a nice Christmas gift.

Moving along the aisle, I stopped at a counter that had a banner over it. The banner said: SPY AND PRIVATE EYE EQUIP-MENT CENTER. Under it was a variety of compasses, false mustaches, toy guns, handcuffs, gyroscopes, walkie-talkies and pedometers. The only private eye I knew was a Chicagoan named Philip Quick, a man who wore loud sport jackets and talked incessantly. I couldn't imagine him decked out in a false mustache or using a gyroscope. In fact, I couldn't imagine any private investigator using a gyroscope. I was tempted to buy one for myself, though, as a reminder that nothing is stable for very long.

I overheard the salesman say, "But carmine and scarlet are practically the same," and the elderly lady say, "Well, all right, then."

They concluded their transaction.

I went back to the model airplane kits, picked one out and took it over to him.

"Will there be anything else?" he asked.

I shook my head, and as I reached for my wallet I said, "Is your name David Kisman?"

"Yep," he replied.

"I'm pleased to meet you," I said. "My name is Brockton Potter. I'm your new boss."

Furrows appeared between his eyebrows.

"I own Lucky Devil Minerals."

123

He put the model airplane kit down on the counter. His lips formed an O.

I placed a twenty-dollar bill and one of my business cards on the model airplane kit. He seemed not to notice them; he kept looking at my face. "As of last week," I said. "And I'd like a few words with you."

He continued to stare at me as though hypnotized. But then he snapped out of it. "About what?"

"My plans for the company. Is there someplace where we can talk privately?"

He blinked and looked around, as if he really had been in a trance. He saw all the customers but apparently decided that I was more important. "Watch the register, Del," he called to the woman. "I'm going out." He started to come around the counter.

"The model airplane," I reminded him.

He went back, put my card in his pocket, made change and wrapped the package.

"Coffee?" I suggested.

"O.K."

We went down the mall to a restaurant. Neither of us spoke until we actually had the coffee in front of us. He just kept looking at me.

Finally I said, "The controlling shares in Lucky Devil, as you're undoubtedly aware, Mr. Kisman, were owned by a New York widow named Sarah Weinberg. She died last week. But shortly before she died, I bought her stock, on a hunch—the hunch being that the stock is more valuable than she thought it was."

He glanced at his steaming coffee, then began to study my face again. "What do you want with me?"

"You're president of the company."

"But I was never active. There was never anything to be active *in.*"

"You own stock in it."

"My father's, along with Keith and Betsy."

"You must have annual meetings, or semiannual meetings, or biannual meetings. Meetings of some sort."

"We never discuss it. Never."

"I find that hard to believe, Mr. Kisman."

"Dave. Everybody calls me Dave."

"I find that hard to believe, Dave."

He decided that his coffee was cool enough to drink and sipped some. Slowly. Then he put the cup down and shook his head. His sad eyes become positively melancholy. "Camelot," he said.

I did a double take. "What?"

"Camelot. It existed. It exists for everyone. One brief happy period that comes and goes and never returns. That's why we don't discuss Lucky Devil. For a few short years we were rich. Then we were poor, and we never became rich again. Do you understand?"

I nodded.

"Lucky Devil—do you know how the company got its name?"

"No."

"My father named it after himself. After how he thought of himself. He thought he was a lucky devil. He called himself a lucky devil. He really believed in his luck. That's what ruined him."

"He's not the only one. I met a man when I was having lunch this afternoon who ruined himself in the same way. Your father was a prospector?"

"My father was a pharmacist. He owned a drugstore."

"But—"

"A pharmacist with a dream of becoming rich. He used to take off from work whenever he could and go prospecting. He had a Geiger counter. He used to take it with him. People were finding uranium. People like Charlie Steen. My father believed that if people like Charlie Steen could do it, he could too. You didn't need any money. Just a Geiger counter and a pair of boots and a dream. Well, my father's dream came true."

"The mine—"

"He called it Lucky Devil. And it was a pretty good mine. We moved into a house with a swimming pool. I had my own horse. It was . . . Camelot."

"What went wrong?"

"Just what you'd expect. My father wasn't a businessman; he was a pharmacist. That's all he really knew. But he suddenly began to think he was a businessman. Someone talked him into selling shares in the mine—going public. Someone talked him into diversifying. He had too many eggs in one basket was the way it was put, I guess. So he sold stock, and with the proceeds he went on a spending spree. Some people buy cars and clothes and wrist watches. My father bought businesses. Lousy businesses." He drank some more coffee. "A restaurant, a dairy, a toy shop—and a silver mine. The silver mine was the straw that broke the camel's back."

"But the uranium—"

"Ran out, Mr. Potter. You never know, when you begin digging, how much is actually there. The same thing happened to a lot of other people. They thought they'd found an inexhaustible supply, and then woke up to the fact that they hadn't. Furthermore, the price of uranium went to hell. The main customer in those days was the government, and the government suddenly decided that it had enough."

"But now—"

"We're not talking about now; we're talking about then. But the same thing holds true now. That's why mining today is in the hands of big operators instead of little ones like my father. The big operators can afford to take the losses and go on digging."

126

"It's possible, though, that there's more uranium in the mine than your father thought there was, that with new techniques the mine could again become valuable. The price of uranium has quadrupled since your father's time."

He laughed. The sound was a bitter one. "Anything is possible, isn't it, to a dreamer? But I can tell you this, Mr. Potter: if you bought that lady's stock with the expectation of finding more uranium in Lucky Devil than my father found, you threw your money away."

"And the silver mine?"

"Don't even mention the silver mine. It was played out long before my father bought it. Everybody seemed to know that except him. He thought like you do—that it could be revived. And maybe it could, but the cost of getting the silver out is five times what silver is worth. My father learned that, the hard way. Now, I guess, it's your turn."

"Where are the mines located?"

"Lucky Devil is down around Moab. Bertha K—that's the silver mine—isn't far from here, up above Park City." He smiled. It was the first time he'd done so. And it was a strange smile. It conveyed no amusement. Only pity. "I guess Barnum was right: there's a sucker born every minute."

"Too much pessimism is as bad as too much optimism," I said.

"Don't talk to me about pessimism and optimism, Mr. Potter. I know more about both than you do."

"And the other businesses?"

"The other businesses? What other businesses? The restaurant folded six months after Dad bought it. The dairy—who the hell knows? It's probably still there. A dozen cows and some old equipment. I haven't seen it in years. The toy store—well, you were just in it, or what it's become. But Lucky Devil Minerals doesn't own that. I took five thousand dollars' worth of inventory and beat-up fixtures which I bought from the

127

company and, with my father-in-law's help, turned it into a pretty good thing. Not because I'm an optimist or a pessimist, but because I worked like hell. I have a family to support, and it was a case of work or starve."

"You still own your Lucky Devil stock?"

"A hundred shares. A hundred-share certificate. I have it framed. It hangs in the bathroom. I look at it every morning when I brush my teeth, as a reminder to stick to what I know. My father would have been a lot better off if he'd just stuck to his drugstore."

I tried to picture him in a leather jacket and a cap, on a New York subway platform. "When did you sell the rest?"

"A few months ago, the same time Keith and Betsy did." He frowned. He seemed suddenly to be having doubts. "Why?"

"Just curious. Who bought it?"

"How should I know? A sucker like yourself, I guess." But he continued to frown.

"You may have made a mistake."

He said nothing.

"Gary Bartten was the broker?"

He nodded.

Neither of us spoke for a while. Finally I asked, "Who's this Gladys Jennings, Dave?"

He stopped frowning. He got red in the face. His cowlick appeared to stand up straighter. "That's none of your damn business," he said angrily. "That's a family matter."

I was startled.

"Furthermore, Mr. Potter, you can take your Lucky Devil stock and shove it. And you can get yourself a new president. I quit. I've been wanting to quit for years, but there was nobody to quit *to.*" He got up. "I'm sick of schemes and dreams and rainbows and pots of gold and people who think they can dig holes in the ground and wake up the next day as millionaires. Enjoy your coffee."

128

I noticed, as he strode away, that he had long legs.

I finished my coffee. Then I went to find a telephone.

I called Philip Quick, the Chicago detective. I gave him Gladys Jennings' name and address, and asked him to find out whatever he could about her.

He said that he couldn't get away but that he'd contact someone in Salt Lake City who'd look into the matter.

I asked him whether he'd ever worn a false mustache.

He said he never went to costume parties.

24

The nurse was willing to let me see Irving, but Naomi wasn't. He was still in great pain, she said, and it was a strain on him to talk.

So we stood in the corridor for a few minutes and compared notes on the day. She told me she'd found an apartment and rented it. It wasn't exactly what she wanted—it had only one bedroom—but she thought she could manage. It was near a school. She'd already talked to her sister-in-law, and the children would leave on Monday.

"You work fast," I said.

"I don't like the family to be separated. . . . What happened with you and the mean lady?"

"Don't ask." But I proceeded to tell her.

She was appalled. "I knew I should have gone with you."

"It wouldn't have made any difference. Not with a woman like that." I rubbed my head. It was still sore. "How about coming back to my room with me for a drink? Then I'll buy you dinner."

"I don't know. I thought I'd stay here a while longer."

"I need your advice."

"Well, in that case . . ."

We drove back to the motel in our separate cars. I got there before Naomi. She didn't arrive for almost twenty minutes, and I began to worry. But presently she showed up, with a grocery bag in her arms. "I stopped," she explained, and unpacked the bag. Two kinds of crackers, three kinds of cheese and a package of cashew nuts. "So we shouldn't feel so far from home," she said.

I took off my shoes. She examined the lump on my head and clucked over it. She also examined my knuckles and pronounced them swollen.

"I know."

She took off her shoes and sat down with the drink I'd poured. She looked at me expectantly.

"The problem is this," I said. "I'm going back to New York tomorrow. I have to be there for the meeting on Monday and to get the letter out on Tuesday."

"And you should stay there," she said emphatically.

"How did you know what I was going to ask?"

"Because I've been thinking about it and hoping that you *would* ask. You think Irving will be disappointed if you don't try to find out all you can about that ridiculous stock."

"It isn't just that, Naomi."

"Yes, it is just that. You feel obligated to him and, in a way, responsible. But you shouldn't. He had no business coming out here in the first place, and you have no business spending your time on something that really doesn't concern any of us."

"That stock is valuable. I don't know why, but it is."

"So it's valuable. So what?"

I didn't answer.

"Brock, if you come back here, it won't be because of Irving; it'll be because of you. I trust you realize that."

"I'm a moralist and a reformer and I enjoy finding the worms under the stones. Mark told me that once. I've never forgotten it."

"Do you? Enjoy finding the worms under the stones, I mean."

"I swear to God I don't, Naomi."

"Well, then."

"I'm afraid I've got myself in a bit deep. I went to see the broker Irving was looking for. I told him I bought your Aunt Sarah's stock. I also went to see the son of the man who built Lucky Devil and told him the same thing."

She didn't ask me why. She simply said, "That was very unwise, Brock."

"Perhaps. But it seemed like a good idea at the time."

She said nothing. I didn't pursue the matter. There was really nothing further to discuss. She'd given me her opinion. The rest was up to me. Both of us knew it. So we just drank, and ate cheese and crackers and nuts, and after a while I turned on the television set. I watched the screen and listened to the voices without any notion of what the program was all about. Mentally I was in New York, in my own house, having a drink with Carol.

I thought of the puppy. Me with a dog—a dog that, even when full-grown, would never be any bigger than one of my shoes. It was absurd.

Damn it, I was homesick.

I looked at Naomi. "Have you any idea what's happening on that screen?"

"Well," she said, "at the moment two Alka-Seltzer tablets are dissolving in a glass of water. But I haven't been paying much attention either."

I got up to turn off the set, and at that moment the telephone rang. I picked it up and answered it.

"I'm paranoid," a man said.

For a moment I didn't recognize his voice. "Who is this?"

"I have a persecution complex. I imagine enemies. I'd like to apologize. This is Justin."

I laughed, and motioned for Naomi to turn off the television set. "You certainly do," I said.

"Well, I'm sorry. I behaved like an idiot this afternoon. You're not the only one—I understand I'm the same way with others. I hope you'll forgive me."

"Sure. I understand."

"And that you're still free for breakfast tomorrow."

"I guess so. Sure."

"Good. But instead of me coming there, why don't you come here? I'm living at the Hotel Utah. I'm not so broke that I can't afford a couple of plates of bacon and eggs."

"O.K."

"Shall we say around ten?"

"Fine."

We hung up. Then I called the airline to make a reservation for a Sunday-afternoon flight to New York.

25

Marble pillars, a stained-glass skylight, glittering chandeliers—the Hotel Utah is turn-of-the-century splendor. Like the Brown Palace Hotel in Denver, it evokes images of touring opera sopranos in big bonnets and long skirts, of lusty millionaires with muttonchop whiskers and gold watch chains, of horse-drawn cabs and private railroad cars.

I was half an hour early. I decided to go up anyway.

Albion opened the door himself. He was momentarily flustered, and a flash of anger appeared in his eyes.

"I know I'm early," I said apologetically, "but the only reservation I could get was on the twelve-fifteen plane, and I wanted to allow myself enough time."

The anger disappeared as quickly as it had come, and he gave me a warm smile. "I'm glad. The more time, the better. It'll take me at least an hour to tell you how sorry I am I behaved like such a fool yesterday."

Again I was impressed by the way his face changed when he smiled. He became instantly younger and totally your friend. "Forget it," I said.

He put his arm on my shoulder and led me into the living room of the suite. He wasn't alone. A woman was seated on the sofa. At first I took her to be his wife, whom I'd never met, but then I noticed, through the partially open door, that there was another woman in the bedroom. She was sitting up in bed, wearing a pink bed jacket trimmed with marabou, reading the newspaper.

"Allow me to introduce Miss Paulette Evans," Albion said. "Paulette, this is Brockton Potter, whom I'm sure you've never heard of but who probably knows more about stocks and bonds than anyone in the business."

The young woman gave him a startled glance, then turned to me and said, "I'm pleased to meet you." She had titian hair and brown eyes and was pretty.

"How do you do," I said.

"Paulette is one of those beautiful people who saved my life," Albion said.

133

I looked from one to the other.

"She was one of my nurses when I was in the hospital," he explained.

"There you go again," she told him. "Exaggerating."

"And there are a lot of people who know more about stocks and bonds than I do," I added.

"Why does everyone insist on putting himself down?" Albion said. "You're both experts at what you do, and you know it."

The bedroom door closed softly.

The young woman got up. "Well," she said, "I'm sure you two want to be alone, so I'll be running."

Albion didn't try to detain her. He walked her to the door, kissed her lightly on the cheek, and when she left came back to me. "You can't imagine," he said, "how attached you can become to people who see you through something like a coronary."

"I'm sure."

"Your perspective about everything changes." He seated himself at the end of the sofa, where the Evans girl had been sitting, and motioned for me to sit beside him.

I took in the details of the room. It was more generously proportioned than the rooms of most newer hotels. There was nothing special about the furniture, but I noticed certain choice items that were obviously not hotel property. Pictures, bric-a-brac, plants. One of the pictures I recognized as a Mondrian, another as a Utrillo. On the coffee table in front of us was a beautiful Meissen bowl, and beside it were a pair of etched Steuben sculptures that were worth at least two thousand dollars apiece. Odds and ends hastily snatched from the various Albion residences before the creditors closed in.

"All of the things that seemed so terribly important," he went on, "suddenly don't seem so important anymore, when your life is hanging in the balance. And you begin to appreciate things that you took for granted. Friends, family. Tell me,

Brock, have you ever married?"

"No."

He stretched his arm across the back of the sofa, as if to bridge the gap between us. "That's a shame. You're very much alone, aren't you?"

"I suppose. I don't have much time to think about it. I'm always too busy running to catch planes." Which, of course, wasn't true. I did have time to think about it. Often.

"That's the way I used to live. Always on the move. But at least I had a family to come back to. You—correct me if I'm wrong—have nobody. No wife, no children, no brothers or sisters. You're completely a lone wolf."

I was beginning to grow uncomfortable. He had, in no time at all, reached the central irritant of my existence. Not many people could do that. "Tell me," I said, "how are your children?" I couldn't remember how many he had, or anything about them.

"Not children. Child. She's fine. She's living in San Francisco. Has a little place of her own. She's made the adjustment better than I have, I believe. All the problems—they haven't touched her."

"How old is she?"

"Twenty."

"Really, Justin, you don't look old enough to have a daughter of twenty." He looked like a man in his early thirties.

"I'm forty-eight."

I started to say that bankruptcy agreed with him, but bit my tongue. Besides, it wasn't the bankruptcy; it was the loss of weight. His stomach was now flat, and he had virtually no hips.

"It's the exercises," he said. "The doctor has me doing all kinds of calisthenics. Calisthenics are my religion."

The bedroom door opened, and the woman I'd seen in bed joined us.

"I don't believe you've ever met my wife," Albion said, beaming. "Vivian, this is Brockton Potter."

She smiled and extended her hand. She'd replaced the bed jacket with a hostess gown of pale-blue velvet. "A pleasure," she said.

A buzzer sounded. Albion went to the door. Two waiters wheeled in a large table and began taking the covers off various plates. Albion signed the check. The waiters finished their work and left.

We sat down to eat.

"I've been trying to tell Brock that he ought to get married," Albion said to his wife.

"You're not?" she asked me.

I shook my head.

"How awful," she said. "I'm one of those women who hates to see a man single. I'm an incurable matchmaker." She poured coffee for all of us. She was wearing one simple gold bracelet; no other jewelry. She too, it seemed to me, had considerable charm.

I felt a need to justify myself. "It's not that I'm immune," I said. "I just never seem to have had the time."

"He's like I used to be," Albion told her. "Always running. He's one of those big success stories that make such nice reading—as long as they leave out all the private stuff. He's making a great name for himself, and all kinds of money." He turned to me. "What good is all the money, Brock, if you have no one to share it with? If you were to have a heart attack like I did, if you were to drop dead tomorrow, God forbid, who'd inherit —some charity?"

I sighed. "My university."

"I hit the nail on the head, didn't I? Not that I have anything against universities or against charities—God knows, I gave to enough of them when I had it—but it points to the emptiness of a person's life when—well, you know what I mean. Or am I embarrassing you?"

136

"You're not embarrassing me, but you're making me think about things I'd rather not think about."

"Justin has a way of doing that," his wife said quickly. "Fortunately he has me around to change the subject when he goes too far. Tell me, how long have you been in Salt Lake City and what have you been doing?"

"I only got here on Thursday and I haven't been doing very much. One of the members of my staff was run over by a car here and very seriously hurt. I've been spending most of my time at the hospital."

"How unfortunate! Is he better?"

"A little, but he's still in intensive care."

"How sad. It's a shame you couldn't get around and see the sights. This is really lovely country." She went on to list some of the attractions of Salt Lake City and the nearby mountain resorts.

The conversation then veered to various parts of the world where the Albions had traveled—and there were very few parts of the world where they hadn't traveled. Albion was a marvelous talker, and I enjoyed listening to him. But I couldn't altogether shake the feeling that I was getting some sort of treatment, that he hadn't invited me for the sheer joy of my company, that he wanted something. Money, most likely. Or a big favor of some sort.

But the request didn't come. When we finished the meal, Mrs. Albion excused herself and returned to the bedroom. It was eleven o'clock by then, and I began to think about catching my plane.

"You've been very discreet," Albion said suddenly, a propos of nothing.

"Discreet?"

"You haven't asked me what it's like to be broke."

"I wanted to," I confessed with a smile.

"Well, it's not the greatest. But it's not so bad, either. It gives you something to hope and plan for."

"What are you doing with your time?"

"Aside from ducking summonses, you mean? Well, I'm dabbling in stocks. This is a great place for that, you know. That's why I came. It doesn't take much capital to get into the market out here, and some of the stocks jump around like crazy."

Here it comes, I thought. The bite. I glanced quickly at my watch. "I really have to be going," I said.

"Must you?"

"I'm afraid so."

He made no effort to detain me. "I'm glad you came. I hated myself after I left you yesterday."

"Forget it," I said, and got out as quickly as I could.

I felt as if I'd had a narrow escape. A man of his sort would think nothing of asking for a couple of hundred thousand dollars, with no collateral.

But as I sped along the expressway toward the airport I began to wonder whether he really had intended to ask me for money. He'd had ample opportunity to do so, if that was what he'd wanted. So I began to wonder, instead, whether he was as broke as he was reputed to be.

I went over the conversation, looking for something I might have missed.

My thoughts shifted to the other people I'd met in Salt Lake City. Bartten, the police officer Sessions, the Jennings woman, Kisman.

I pictured Irving in his hospital bed. I recalled what he'd told me.

The pieces didn't fit. Yet they had to fit.

Then, suddenly, I felt a chill. Because the pieces did fit.

26

I had an hour between planes in Chicago. I telephoned Philip Quick. As usual, his answering service took the call and said he'd call me back. Normally it was only a matter of a few minutes before he did. But this time it took three-quarters of an hour. I stood beside the telephone in the concourse at O'Hare Airport, smoking cigarettes, shifting my weight from one foot to the other, and trying, with no success whatsoever, to control my impatience.

Twelve minutes before my flight to New York was due to take off, the telephone rang.

Quick had taken the afternoon off to go to the football game. The Chicago Bears had played the Green Bay Packers, and lost.

"Damn it," I said, "I'm only here between planes and I've got to run. Any word on the Jennings woman?"

"She must be nuts. The guy I located in Salt Lake City went out to her house to talk to her. She hit him with an ashtray and gave him a black eye."

"It figures."

"What?"

"It figures. She's a wild one."

"You should of told me. I'd of told him, and he'd of handled it different. He went out there as a pollster, figuring he'd get acquainted. How should he know? Now he's mad. Honestly, Potter, when you know a thing like that you're supposed to tell me, otherwise how'm I gonna know? Next time—"

"Look, Quick, I haven't got time to argue or explain. I want everything you can find out about that woman, and I want it fast. This is important. Time is running out. Go to Salt Lake City yourself if you have to."

"I can't go to Salt Lake City myself if I have to. I've got six cases going here. This is the first afternoon I've had off in three weeks. There's a woman whose husband—"

"Then get more than one man working on it out there. Get as many men as you need. I want information by tomorrow. Call me at my office in New York—I'll be there all day. I want to know whether she's been married and whether she's ever had children and when she bought her house and where she gets her money, and I want her followed."

"It takes time to get all that. You want her followed?"

"Yes. I don't care how many people it takes. I don't care what it costs. I think I'm in danger."

"Danger?"

"Danger. So long, Quick, and get moving."

I hung up and ran to the gate. I was the last one to board the plane.

Everything in the house was as it should have been, except that Tiger and his basket were gone. There was a faint odor of puppy in the bedroom to remind me of him, but that was all.

I dug from my wallet the slip of paper with Barbara Deutsch's telephone number, sat down on the bed and dialed.

She answered, and when I told her who I was she said that Naomi had spoken to her about me twice in the past two days. She didn't quite understand what it was all about, she said, but evidently there was some stock. . . .

"Exactly," I said. "It's called Lucky Devil. I'd welcome the opportunity to explain about it to you and your aunt's lawyer.

Could the two of you come to my office tomorrow around noon?"

"I have a Hadassah luncheon tomorrow." She paused. "Of course, if this is important, I suppose I could forgo that. I don't know about Mr. Tallman, though. He may be busy."

"I think it's quite important, and it would help if I could see both of you at the same time. Will you ask him?"

"Yes. Twelve o'clock, you say?"

"At my office." I gave her the address. "Meanwhile, if anyone should ask you, or if anyone should ask him, tell them that I bought the stock, or that you don't know anything about it, or something to that effect. In other words, I don't want either of you admitting that you own it. Do you understand?"

"Not at all. But Naomi said I should trust you."

"Good. Then trust me. I'll explain tomorrow." I hung up.

I unpacked my bag, took a shower and poured myself a drink. As I sipped it I asked myself whether I'd covered all corners.

I decided that I hadn't. So I got out the telephone directory. But there was no listing for Milton Kaye.

27

It was not one of our better staff meetings. For one thing, Irving's unoccupied chair reminded us that we were an incomplete group. And for another, there was hostility in the air.

The hostility was aimed at Brian. At first I couldn't understand it. As the meeting progressed, however, I began to sense what the trouble was. In the absence of both Irving and myself, Brian had tried to direct the activities of the department, and the other three were annoyed.

In a way, it was amusing. For I was sure that Brian wasn't aware he'd done anything wrong. I'd told him that I was still in charge, and he'd accepted my dictum. But there'd been a vacuum of leadership, and he'd stepped in to fill it, because to do so was as natural to him as breathing. Furthermore, his suggestions had probably been right, which must have made them all the more irritating.

Yet it was a situation that I couldn't allow to continue. The department had just got over one round of dissension; it didn't need another.

Again George Cole brought up the matter of Refrigerco. Again I tabled it.

Joe Rothland told us that Jim Chapman had ended his feud with the producers of *The Davis Family;* a new dressing room was being built for him at a cost of fifty thousand dollars, and he himself could direct some of the shows.

Harriet reported that more than half of a ninety-million-dollar issue of Indiana Fuel bonds remained unsold and the underwriters were worried.

Brian, of course, was full of information about everything. He'd evidently been working twenty hours a day, covering all the companies he was supposed to cover, and a number of others besides.

But Brian couldn't keep the meeting going single-handedly. He needed help from me, and since I'd been out of touch with my usual sources for the better part of a week I wasn't able to offer much. I didn't even know that Friday's issue of the *Wall Street Journal* had carried an article on Darby's Indonesia discovery and the stock had jumped five points in one day. In addition, I was finding it difficult to concentrate. Normally I can shut out other thoughts during a meeting and devote myself wholly to the topics at hand, but at that particular meeting I couldn't. My mind kept straying backward to Salt Lake City and forward to the interview with Barbara Deutsch.

We limped along. Enough facts emerged to build the Tuesday letter around, but I wasn't happy. Not with my staff, not with myself.

I almost forgot to give them instructions for the week—Harriet had to remind me. And when the others left, she didn't leave with them. She planted herself in front of my desk, feet apart, hands shoved into the pockets of her jacket, and said, with her usual directness, "I like Brian very much, Brock, but I'll be damned if I'm going to take orders from him."

"There's only one source of orders around here while Irving's out, and that's me."

"Then please tell that to Brian." She turned briskly and strode to the door.

I sighed. I was going to have to straighten Brian out again, and I really didn't want to.

I tried to estimate how long Irving would be away from work. At least two months, I decided.

Suppose something happened to me during that period. Civil war would erupt in the department. Mark didn't have the personality to handle my people, and Tom had his hands full with his own department.

What could I do to protect myself?

I couldn't think of a single thing.

Helen brought in the telephone messages that had accumulated during my absence. The stack was thick. I groaned and began to sort the calls in the order of their importance. But before I could finish, Helen announced that Barbara Deutsch and Sidney Tallman had arrived.

I told Helen to say that I'd be with them shortly. I glanced once more at the stack of messages. Well, they could wait.

I picked up the telephone, called the House of Dover and asked to speak with Milton Kaye.

Barbara Deutsch didn't look anything like Naomi Silvers, yet she reminded me of her. She had the same unassuming manner and common-sense way of assessing things.

The lawyer impressed me less favorably. His name described him physically: he was a tall man. But he had an annoying habit of raising and lowering his eyebrows, so that his expression was continually fluctuating between surprise and displeasure. And he made a big point of telling me how busy he was and how it was an imposition for him to be asked to come on such short notice.

I apologized to both of them for the short notice. "However," I said, "I believe that a lot of money might be at stake."

Tallman's eyebrows descended until they almost met at the bridge of his nose.

"Before her death," I explained to Barbara, "a stockbroker from Salt Lake City by the name of Gary Bartten was pressuring your aunt to sell some stock that she owned and that she considered to be almost worthless. She was on her way to see me, to ask me about it, when she was killed."

"I know," she said. "That she was on her way to see you, I mean. The detectives told me. There were two of them—Hastings and someone else. They'd talked to Irving Silvers and Nettie Hoffman and got the story from them."

"So actually you're covering ground that's already been covered," Tallman put in, and his eyebrows shot up.

I ignored him. "The stock in question is called Lucky Devil Minerals. It's a defunct mining company and is ostensibly worthless. Yet somebody is trying to get control of it, so it must have some unrecognized value. Irving went out to Salt Lake

144

City to investigate and was almost killed by a hit-and-run driver."

Barbara nodded. "Naomi told me. I'm terribly sorry."

"It was no accident. I'm convinced of that. Someone tried to kill him, to keep him from finding out the truth. Irving has quite a reputation, you know."

The eyebrows came down. "It appears to me that you're trying to make Mrs. Deutsch feel guilty."

"Nonsense," said Mrs. Deutsch, and smiled at me. "Go on."

"I've spoken with Mr. Bartten and with the president of Lucky Devil, whose name is David Kisman. I lied to both of them. I told them that I bought the stock from your aunt two days before her death. I told Bartten that I was willing to sell it for a bit more than five million dollars."

When Tallman's eyebrows should have risen, they didn't. He simply stared at me.

"Good heavens!" Barbara exclaimed.

"From my standpoint, it was a foolish thing to do, and I'm sorry I did it. But from yours, it may be a boon."

"Do you mean—?" Tallman began.

"No," I said, certain of what he'd intended to ask. "I have no idea what the stock is actually worth. I was simply telling whoever is trying to buy it that I believe it's worth more than he was offering Sarah Weinberg, and I was trying to force an issue."

"But wasn't that dangerous?" Barbara asked.

"I didn't think so at the time," I replied. "I do now. In any case, I need your cooperation. If anything is to be accomplished, either for you or for me, the lie has to be maintained. I'm almost certain that an offer will be made to you, directly or through Mr. Tallman, for the stock, if for no other reason than to find out whether or not I actually bought it. I'd prefer for you to say that I did; but if you can't bring yourself to say that, then say that you don't know anything about it—that your aunt's safe-deposit box hasn't been opened yet, or something to that effect."

"It really hasn't been opened," she admitted.

"It wouldn't be ethical to say that," Tallman asserted.

"Ethical? It would be the truth." I gave him a long look. "You've already been approached, haven't you?"

His eyebrows went up and down like a pair of yo-yos. He said nothing.

"Mrs. Weinberg gave Bartten your name. She said you were her lawyer and she was going to discuss the matter with you. Bartten called you. He probably offered to make a deal with you."

Barbara turned to him. Questioningly.

"You urged her to sell the stock," I went on. "But she still wasn't sure. So she was coming to see me."

"Don't make any accusations you can't prove," the lawyer warned.

"I'm not making any accusations. I'm merely offering my theory of what happened. But I will add that if my theory is correct, you might have a difficult time convincing the law that you weren't an accessory to murder."

"That's preposterous!"

"Or the American Bar Association that you weren't, at the very least, guilty of the sort of behavior that gives lawyers a bad name. What you should have done is investigate the stock yourself. You didn't." I smiled. "Of course, the law doesn't have to know, and the Bar Association doesn't have to know. But in order for them not to, I need your cooperation. Do I make myself clear? If you don't cooperate, I'll see that you find yourself in a mighty awkward position." I turned to Barbara. "I don't think I have to point out to you, Mrs. Deutsch, the advantages of following my suggestion."

She nodded. "I'm very grateful to you, Mr. Potter. But I still think you've done a dangerous thing."

"I acted impulsively. But let's hope that you benefit." I stood up. As far as I was concerned, the interview was over.

I closed the door behind them and placed a call to Philip Quick.

His answering service said he'd call me back.

Then I went down the corridor to Mark's office.

Tom was in there with him. "Welcome, stranger!" he greeted me. "We were just talking about you."

"Favorably?" I asked, pulling up a chair.

He grinned. "Hell, no."

But the grin was misleading. He was serious.

28

The two of them had got wind of the bickering that was going on in the research department and they didn't like it.

"I know that you have a high opinion of Barth," Mark said, "but I don't think you realize how much he antagonizes the others by his pushiness."

"Pushiness is one of the requirements of the job," I replied.

"Well, the others do resent him," Tom said.

"Not nearly as much as you think," I said. "They'd defend him against either of you, for instance."

"We don't want to tread on your toes," Mark said. "It's your department. You have to run it as you see fit. And frankly I rather like Barth myself. But hard feelings can get out of control. Now tell us about Irving."

I started to, but before I could get going, the telephone rang. Mark answered, then handed the instrument to me.

"It's Mr. Quick," Helen informed me, "from Chicago."

"Put him on."

"What's up, Potter?" Quick demanded. He sounded irritable.

"You know what's up. I want a progress report."

"Goddamn it, Potter, it's not even noon yet in Salt Lake City. What the hell kind of miracles do you expect? These things take time. When I have something to tell you, I'll be in touch. Quit bugging me." He hung up.

"Who was that?" Tom asked as I banged the telephone down. "You're red in the face."

"Philip Quick."

"The Chicago detective? What did he want?"

"It's not what he wants; it's what I want. I want information. I've hired him to get it for me."

"But his prices!" Mark protested.

"I don't care about his prices," I snapped. Then I pulled myself together and gave them a report of my trip.

They began to look as if their worst suspicions about me were being confirmed. Seeing the expressions on their faces, I was tempted to edit my account. I didn't, though. I told them everything, up to and including my interview with Barbara Deutsch and the lawyer. Then I braced myself for the howls of disapproval.

Which came.

Mark even called me a ninny. No one except my grandmother had ever called me that.

I didn't try to justify what I'd done. I just sat there. And presently they began to offer the justifications themselves. I felt very close to Irving; it was natural for me to want to help him.

Mrs. Weinberg's murder was a crime that shouldn't go unpunished. Barbara Deutsch deserved to get the best possible price for her stock.

I said nothing. I was used to the way they jumped from one side of the fence to the other—I often did the same thing myself. By the time they were finished, they'd presented a better case for me than I could have presented for myself.

The longer I listened to them, the more objective I became. Both of them were missing the key point, which was that while none of us had started this chain of events, all of us were caught up in it, and all of us were behaving in ways we couldn't entirely control. Irving was Irving—no one else would have reacted to Sarah Weinberg's death exactly as he had. And by reacting in that fashion he'd provoked a second crisis, which had drawn me to the scene, whereupon my own personality had asserted itself. For better or worse, all of us were victims of our particular range of responses.

"I may have been right or wrong," I said at last, "but I did what seemed best at the time. Now I have to see it through."

"Is there anything I can do to help?" Tom asked.

"Or I?" asked Mark.

I smiled. I suddenly liked both of them very much. "Not really. Just mind the store while I'm gone."

"Back to Salt Lake City?" Mark asked.

"For a few days," I replied. "I have a hunch it won't take very long." A new idea hit me. "Especially if I have Brian along." It would get him out of the office, and I could use his help.

"What about the department?" Tom asked. "With only three people—"

"They'll manage," I said. "It'll be tough, but they'll manage."

Tom and Mark sighed in unison, and Tom said, "If you must, you must."

I told him about Ted North, then returned to my own office and sent for Brian.

I spent twenty minutes briefing him.

His knowledge of mining was sketchy, he said.

I told him to spend the next twenty-four hours learning as much about it as he could; we'd leave the following evening.

He said he would, and took off from my office at a fast gallop.

I felt sorry for whomever he intended to pump.

Helen brought me a sandwich and some coffee, and I settled down to the accumulated mail and telephone messages. My powers of concentration returned. I became absorbed, and lost track of time. I worked for what seemed like no more than an hour and was amazed, when I finally looked at my watch, to discover that it was almost five o'clock. My wastebasket was filled with torn envelopes, discarded message slips and memos that I'd written myself and acted upon.

Helen was exhausted but happy. She enjoyed it when I kept her busy. "Would you like me to stay for a while?" she volunteered.

I stretched. "I don't think it'll be necessary. It looks like we have everything under control." The events of the past week had been crowded from my mind, but now they came back. "There are a couple more chores you can do, though, before you leave, if you don't mind. Call Holy Cross Hospital in Salt Lake City and see if you can locate Mrs. Silvers for me, and make a couple of plane reservations. Mr. Barth and I are going to Salt Lake City tomorrow evening."

Helen nodded and went to her desk. Presently she reported that Mrs. Silvers was on line 1.

Irving was better. Dr. Littner was planning to have him moved from the intensive care unit to a private room. Naomi had already taken possession of the new apartment and was about to leave for the airport, to meet the children.

"I'll be there myself tomorrow night," I said. "I'm bringing Brian with me. Can you get us a couple of rooms at the Rodeway?"

There was a silence.

"I have no choice, Naomi."

"Very well," she said finally. "I'll get the rooms. Call me when you arrive." She gave me her new address and telephone number. I jotted them down. We hung up.

Helen reported that she'd made the plane reservations. If there was nothing else, she'd be going home.

I considered the evening ahead. And called Carol.

Carol was angry at me. The least I could have done was call her from Salt Lake City to let her know how Irving was. Did I think she wasn't interested? Why was she always the last one to know what was going on in my life?

I apologized on all counts and invited her to have dinner with me.

She couldn't have dinner with me. Perry, her boss, was entertaining a customer and had asked her to join them.

"How about later?" I suggested. "After dinner."

"I really don't think I want to, Brock."

"Aw, come on now, Carol. I'm not as bad as all that."

"Yes, you are." And she proceeded to tell me just how bad I was. Then, having enumerated my faults, she relented. About ten o'clock, maybe. Just for a few minutes.

"Good," I said. "You'll restore my sense of balance. Because my cocktail date is a gay activist."

29

The building was located on Christopher Street, a block from The Cyclops. It looked as if it had been built in the days when New York was still called New Amsterdam. The entrance to the apartments was next to a leather shop. The garments in the window of the leather shop consisted of fringed deerskin jackets and black calfskin vests. The vests had slacks to match.

It was so dark in the vestibule that I had a hard time reading the names on the mailboxes. Milton's apartment number was 2. I pushed the buzzer, and since the door to the stairway was unlocked, I went on up. There was a strong scent of incense in the stairwell. I knocked on the door at the second landing.

"Who is it?" Milton called.

"Brock," I replied.

There were sounds of bolts and chains being manipulated, one after another. Finally the door opened. Milton greeted me with a cigarette holder in one hand and a cat on his shoulder. "Come in," he said. "I hope you like cats. I have three."

"I have nothing against them," I said, and stepped into the apartment.

He began to refasten the bolts and chains.

The living room astonished me. It was gorgeous. Dove-gray walls with white molding, charcoal-gray velvet upholstery, crystal sconces and a dozen pieces of Lalique glass scattered here and there on tables and chests.

Milton completed the security measures and joined me, the cat still on his shoulder.

"You have a beautiful place," I said.

"Bentley did it."

I looked at him. "Meredith Bentley?" Meredith Bentley specialized in jobs like hotel lobbies and houses that cost a million dollars.

"When we were lovers. I hope you like sherry. I've been in a sherry mood for three days. Besides, I'm out of everything else."

"Sherry'll be fine."

He removed the cat from his shoulder. The cat came over, eyed me critically, decided I wasn't up to snuff and stalked out of the room. Milton busied himself with a decanter and glasses. Then, handing me one of the glasses, he invited me to make myself at home.

I gazed around the room again. I couldn't get over the contrast between the exterior of the building and the furnishings of the apartment.

Milton seated himself in a chair on the other side of the glass-and-chrome cocktail table, fitted a cigarette into the holder and lit it. "I always wanted to live in a dream world," he said with a sigh. "Reality bores me." He picked up his drink. "Cheers."

The sherry was excellent. I regarded Milton over the rim of the glass. He caught me doing so and smiled. "Is it the outfit?"

It was, partly. Black velvet slacks that fitted him like a second skin, a white satin shirt unbuttoned almost to the navel, black patent-leather loafers, two gold necklaces, a gold bracelet . . . I couldn't think of any man I'd ever known who could get himself up in a rig like that without appearing ridiculous. Yet Milton didn't. What intrigued me even more, however, was the way he really did seem to have banished reality. He was his own dream figure come to life. "Those are nice necklaces," I said, not knowing what else to say.

He fingered the shorter of the two and told me who had given it to him. I was startled. The man had been one of the top ten box office attractions for years.

"You *know* him?" I asked.

"We've tricked," he replied, and fingered the longer necklace. "And this one is from Max. The cunt."

"You're still mad at him?"

"He hasn't even called me, the whole time he's been gone."

"You're not easy to call," I said. "I tried to reach you last night. Your number isn't listed."

"Of course not. What do you think I am?"

I quickly drank some sherry.

All three cats marched into the room, single file, and deposited themselves on the sofa.

"What were you able to find out?" I asked.

"He bought a few things from us," Milton said. "The best was a diamond and ruby set. Necklace and earrings to match. For his wife's birthday, I believe. She picked it out."

"How much did it cost?"

"Ninety-six thousand. But generally they shopped at Cartier's. Charles over there used to take care of them."

"How much would you say they owned altogether?"

Milton put his drink down, sat up straighter and folded his arms across his chest. We were now approaching the subject on which he was an expert: the habits of the rich. "There's no way of knowing. Some people with that kind of money like jewelry, others don't. And those who do, like it for different reasons. Some think it's a good investment—the nervous ones, who think the world is going to pot. Others use it to impress other people or to prove to themselves that they're successful. And some buy it just because they like the way it looks. There are connoisseurs, who really appreciate beautiful stones, and clods, who'll buy anything as long as it's expensive and flashy. Albion, I'd say, didn't know a ruby from an emerald—but his wife did. She was the one with the taste. He just came along to write the check. And he was kind of show-offy about it."

"Show-offy?"

"You know. 'How much is it?' 'A hundred thousand.' 'O.K., wrap it up, we'll take it with us.' Then he'd turn to his wife. 'See anything else you like? We might as well make the day worthwhile.' " Milton made a face. "Nouveau riche."

"But all in all—could you make a guess?"

"I really couldn't."

"As much as a million dollars' worth?"

"Probably." He exhaled a cloud of smoke and frowned thoughtfully. "Judging by the way they shopped, I'd say, over the years, between three-quarters of a million and a million and a half."

"And the other thing?"

Milton nodded. "He and Max couldn't get together on the price."

"How long ago?"

"About six months." He put his cigarette out, an elaborate process that involved removing it from the holder, stubbing it in the Lalique ashtray, blowing the accumulated smoke from the holder and placing the holder carefully on the cocktail table. "Max doesn't make a practice of buying back pieces that he's sold. He's no fool, though, and sometimes, if he can buy something cheap enough . . . You know what I mean. At any rate, he and Albion couldn't get together."

"Somebody else, though . . . I mean, how much would a million dollars' worth of jewelry be worth if you wanted to sell it?"

"Come on now, Brock. How can I answer a question like that? You're always talking about your paintings. A piece of jewelry is like a painting. The value is theoretical. It depends on how badly the seller wants to sell and how anxious the buyer is to buy. A really good piece of jewelry, if the seller is in no hurry, can bring him a lot more than he paid for it. But some things aren't worth what the person paid in the first place, or they're out of fashion—or you name it."

He was right, I knew. A piece of jewelry was like a painting —or for that matter, a share of stock. The price was whatever you could get. Except that for stock there was an established marketplace where masses of buyers and sellers could meet, which made things easier for both sides. A million dollars' worth of jewelry could, at resale, bring half a million or it could bring two million. I sipped my sherry and did some mental arithmetic. But there wasn't enough to go on, so I finally had to come up with an arbitrary figure: three-quarters of a million. Then there were the paintings. I'd seen only what was left; I didn't know how much more there had once been. For the jewelry and paintings together—somewhere between a million and a million and a half, probably. "Well, thanks," I said. "About six months ago?"

"April or May, I believe."

One of the cats suddenly sprang from the sofa, walked haughtily across the room and began to rub itself against Milton's leg. He picked it up. The other cats followed. Presently he had a lapful of cats. Which reminded me of my dog. I hoped that Louise had brought him back.

"My family," Milton said, stroking the cats in turn.

"I just got a poodle," I said proudly.

He gave me an enigmatic smile. "Do you think it's true what they say about animal-lovers?" he asked.

"What do they say?"

"That they're not people-lovers."

"Certainly not!"

"That they don't trust other people."

"That's absurd!"

"That they don't relate well to other people."

"Nonsense. You relate well to other people, don't you?"

"Not when there's a full moon."

I tried to figure that one out, but failed. I finished my sherry and got up. "I appreciate what you've told me, Milton. I hope I'll be able to return the favor sometime."

"Don't go. There's no full moon tonight."

"I'm afraid I must." I started for the door.

He emptied his lap of cats and caught up with me. He put his hand on my arm, gently. I made a negative gesture with my head. He sighed and began to open the various locks. We shook hands, and I left.

But I kept wondering, as I walked slowly up Christopher Street toward Avenue of the Americas, whether what they said about people who love animals had some truth in it.

30

Louise, who knows that Monday is the one night of the week I'm always in town, had made some lamb stew. It was in the slow cooker on the kitchen table, and beside it was a note which read: "Dog is ate."

I hurried upstairs and was relieved to find Tiger dozing in his basket. He seemed pleased to see me, and I immediately forgot what they said about people who like animals. I took him down to the kitchen with me and discussed my problems with him while I had dinner. He nibbled on my shoelace as he listened. We decided that there was no alternative: Brian and I had to check out the two mines.

After dinner we went into the den, and Tiger continued to nibble on my shoelace while I made some notes for the Tuesday letter.

The ringing of the telephone startled both of us.

The call was from Quick. The information he was about to give me, he said, was very expensive; it had been necessary to employ four men in order to get it.

"O.K., O.K.," I said impatiently. "Let's hear it."

Her full name, he told me, was Gladys Cornelia Jennings, and she was fifty-five years old. She'd been born in Denver but had been brought to Salt Lake City by her parents when she was four years old. Her father had been employed by the Denver, Rio Grande & Western Railroad. Both her parents were dead. She'd studied to be an opera singer but had developed polyps on her vocal cords, or something of the sort. At any rate, a badly done operation had put an end to her operatic career, and she'd returned to Salt Lake City, where for a while she supported herself by giving piano lessons.

"She's evidently a nut," Quick said, "but I feel kind of sorry for her."

I was astonished. I hadn't thought that Philip Quick was the kind who ever felt sorry for anyone. And as far as I was concerned, Gladys Cornelia Jennings elicited about as much sympathy as a rattlesnake. "Why?"

"She's had to work hard, and nothing has ever gone right for her. First there was the operation, then there was a time of sweating to make ends meet, then she fell in love with some joker who was already married and whose kids she taught, and he wouldn't divorce his wife, and she had a child by him, and she raised the child and put him through school, and—"

"Who was the man?"

"A fellow who made a lot of money, then lost it, name of Kisman."

"Ethridge Kisman?"

"Kisman's all I know. Got rich in uranium, gave her kid some stock in the company to pay for his education, but then the company went down the drain, and she had to pay for the kid's education herself. She hasn't had it easy. And she hasn't got anything now either. But except for the mortgage on her house, she doesn't owe a dime."

"Where's the kid now?"

"Somewhere around Salt Lake City. Couldn't find out exactly where. But he's a real brain. Biochemist. Ph.D., awards . . . he's all she has, and she's very proud of him."

"What's his name?"

"Andrew Jennings."

"Married?"

"How should I know? You said check up on her, not him."

"Well, now I want to know about him too."

"That'll cost more. Anyhow, she doesn't teach piano anymore. Taught herself stenotyping, and now she's a legal stenographer. Very good at it too, I understand. That's where she was today, all day: at work. Left home at eight o'clock this morning, just got home a little while ago."

"Did she drive to work?"

"Yes."

"What kind of car does she have?"

"Toyota Corolla, two years old."

"Any dents in it, or damage?"

"What the hell, Potter?"

"I want to know. It's important."

"Well, I'll have to find out."

"Did she leave the office at any time today? Did she meet anyone?"

"Just for lunch. Ate at some little soup place in the basement

159

of the Hotel Utah. The Bowl' n' Basket, it's called. My man says it's very popular. She met a friend there. My man doesn't know whether it was by accident or on purpose. Could of been either."

"Got a description of him?"

"Old fellow, kind of big. Mostly bald, a little white hair around the edges."

"Gary Bartten," I said.

"Didn't get the name," Quick said. "But my man got the feeling that they both eat there a lot. They talked."

"What'd they say?"

"My man couldn't hear. What the hell do you expect, Potter? Some things are possible, some aren't. You want the man followed too?"

I considered. "No, I don't think so. I already know enough about him. But I'd like to know about the son. And I want her followed on a twenty-four-hour-a-day basis."

"That's what I figured, and those are the orders I gave."

"O.K., keep me posted. I'll be in my office most of the day tomorrow, then I'm going back to Salt Lake City. I'll be at the Rodeway Inn there."

"Will do. You like opals? Bought myself a pair of opal cufflinks today."

"Wear them in good health," I said, and the conversation ended.

I picked Tiger up. "Opal cufflinks," I told him. "The guy's always bragging about his clothes and his money."

Tiger put his wet nose against my finger.

I went back to work, and twenty minutes later Carol arrived. She was in a state that was unusual for her: drunk. Or at any rate, almost drunk. She couldn't remember the name of the restaurant she'd been to, she said, but she'd had three martinis and two glasses of wine, and the lamb chops had been served in a paper bag, which she thought was very funny. She called the chops "shops" and claimed that that was the only restaurant she'd ever been to where they give you the doggy bag right with the meal. She seemed to have forgotten that she was angry at me, and she desperately wanted a Coca-Cola. I gave her the Coke and tried to talk seriously with her, because I was in a mood to talk seriously, but she kept giggling and telling me that one of my eyes was browner than the other, and when I asked her whether she was still thinking of moving back to Minneapolis she replied that I needed a haircut. Since our moods conflicted more often than they coincided, I wasn't perturbed; and since she gave every indication of wanting to go to bed with me, I let her mood prevail. In practically no time, we were between the sheets and in the same mood.

I've never won any awards for love-making. I've been told, at times, that I'm very satisfactory, and at other times that I'm a disappointment, and I haven't disputed either opinion. But on that particular evening—either because of Carol's lack of inhibition or because of accumulated tensions within myself—I reached a peak that I seldom achieve, and I knew it. And when it was all over I felt wonderfully exhausted. Apparently Carol did too, for she fell into a deep sleep. I remained awake for a few minutes, enjoying the way her hair felt on my shoulder, then I fell asleep also.

I was sleeping so soundly that when the telephone first rang, the noise seemed to be occurring within my dream. But presently I began to sense that it was external and woke.

Carol stirred. "Answer," she muttered against my arm.

I reached for the telephone, missed on the first try but connected on the second. "Who is it?" I asked thickly.

The voice at the other end was so muffled that I could barely make out the words. "Brockton Potter?"

"Who is it?" I asked again.

161

"Someone intends to kill you," the voice said.

The web of sleep disintegrated. I sat bolt upright. "Who is this? What did you say?"

"Be very careful. Someone intends to kill you."

I jumped out of bed. "Who the hell is this? What the hell are you talking about?" I was suddenly as alert as I'd ever been in my life.

"I can't tell you. Your line is being tapped. Everything we say is being recorded."

I could feel my heart slamming against my rib cage. This is it, I thought. It's happened. Don't panic. Be calm. But my heart continued its slamming. "I see. Very well. Thank you for telling me. What can I do?"

"Meet me. I'll explain. But come very quickly. There isn't much time."

"Where are you?"

"At the corner. At Blimpie's."

I knew Blimpie's. It was half a block from my house, on the other side of the street—at the southeast corner of Eleventh Street and Avenue of the Americas. A deli, with delivery service. I often used it on weekends and other occasions when Louise wasn't around. "I'll be there in ten minutes."

"No longer than that," the voice said. "There isn't much time. And be careful." There was a click.

I put the telephone down.

"Who is it?" Carol murmured.

"No one. Go back to sleep."

She turned over. A moment later I heard her breathing evenly.

I found my clothes and put them on in the dark. My hands were shaking. I tried to recall the voice, to identify it. I couldn't. It had sounded as if the mouthpiece of the telephone had been covered with a fabric of some sort. I couldn't even be positive whether the speaker had been a man or a woman. A man, I guessed. But I didn't really know.

I felt my way down the steps, guiding myself by the banister. On the ground floor, I turned on the lights and went into the den. Call the police, something cried urgently. Don't, something else cried, just as urgently; if you do, it won't work.

I took my address book from the desk and looked up Blimpie's number, then dialed.

A familiar voice answered.

"Gus?" I said. He was the night counterboy.

"Yep."

"Listen carefully, Gus. This is Brock Potter. Don't look around—just tell me. Did anyone use the telephone there a few minutes ago?"

"I don't know, Mr. Potter. I been trying to fix the slicer. It's broke. You want something?"

"This is important, Gus. Who's in there with you right now?"

"Who do you think is here with me right now, Mr. Potter? It's 2:30 A.M. There's nobody here with me right now. Pete didn't show up tonight, which pisses me off, so I'm here alone. There's not even anybody here to make a delivery, and the slicer's broke."

"I don't mean that. I mean customers."

"There's no customers. Only Danny, if you can call him a customer. You know Danny. All he ever does is drink coffee."

I knew Danny. He was one of the interns at St. Vincent's Hospital, in the next block. "No one else?"

"No one else. What's the matter with you, Mr. Potter? You sound funny."

"Do me a favor, Gus. Check the washroom. See if anybody's in there, and let me know. I wouldn't ask, except it's really important, Gus."

I heard him put the telephone down. There was a long silence. Then Gus returned. "Honest, Mr. Potter, there's nobody here in this whole damn place except Danny and me. Pete didn't show up tonight, and Danny's reading the paper, and I don't know what's wrong with the slicer. . . . are you drunk or something?"

"No, I'm all right. Thank you, Gus. I'll be over there in a few minutes." I hung up, and went to the window.

Eleventh Street, I estimated, was twenty-five feet wide. But cars were parked almost bumper to bumper along both curbs, so that the clear space in the middle was considerably less— perhaps fifteen feet. Since it was a one-way street, westbound, the car would have to come from the direction of Fifth Avenue. The headlights would probably be off.

I'd have to move fast.

I looked around for something small but heavy enough to break the windshield. I noticed the candy dish on the table beside the lounge chair. It was made of marble. I picked it up. It weighed at least three pounds. It would do.

Opening the front door, I paused for a moment on the stoop. The sidewalk was deserted and silent. There was no car double-parked between Fifth Avenue and my house.

I closed the door and started down the steps, pausing again when I reached the sidewalk. I listened for the sound of the engine.

Nothing.

I worked my way carefully between two parked cars and started across the street.

Nothing.

I forced myself to stop for a few seconds in the middle of the street. I looked in both directions.

Still nothing.

Puzzled, I continued to the opposite sidewalk and turned toward Avenue of the Americas.

And presently I was at Blimpie's.

Gus glanced up and offered me an uncertain smile. I gave the

164

room a quick inspection. Except for the intern, who had a paper cup in his hand and a newspaper spread out on the table in front of him, there were no customers. I gazed briefly at the telephones that were mounted on the wall at the end of the counter, then walked over to where Gus was standing.

His smile vanished. He frowned. "What you got there in your hand?"

"A candy dish. You're sure no one called me from here a little while ago?"

"I'm not sure of nothing. What's with the candy dish?"

"Give me a cup of coffee, Gus. Regular. The candy dish? I thought someone was going to try to run me over with a car a few minutes ago."

His frown deepened. He poured the coffee and handed me the paper cup. I paid him and took the coffee to a table. A moment later he emerged from behind the counter and went over to the intern. They conferred in low voices. The intern got up and came over to me.

"Hi," he said. "Are you O.K.?"

"Sure I'm O.K., Danny."

He pointed to the candy dish. "Gus said—"

"It's a long story, Danny." I picked up my cup. "I don't want to go into it."

"Your hand is shaking."

I sighed. I wasn't anxious to get hauled down to St. Vincent's as a mental case. "One of the men who works for me was almost killed by a hit-and-run driver a few days ago. It appeared that someone might try to do the same thing to me just now."

"But the candy dish."

"I thought I could break the windshield or one of the windows. If I could force the car to crash—or even if I couldn't—I mean, it'd probably be a rented car, and the police could trace it." I looked at him. He was scratching his head. "I know it doesn't make much sense, Danny, but it would've worked. But nothing happened. I guess somebody's playing games with me."

"How could you know?" He continued to scratch his head. "I mean, wouldn't it be better to call the police, or something like that?"

"Not in this case. If I'd called the police, nothing would've happened. But nothing happened anyway. . . . Forget it, Danny. I'm not nuts. I'm just uptight. How are things at the hospital these days?"

He stopped scratching his head, regarded me narrowly, decided that I wasn't a menace to society and relaxed. "Not bad. It's been quiet for the past week or so. It's the time of year, I think."

"I appreciate your interest, Danny, but everything's all right. Go back and read your newspaper."

He nodded and returned to his table. I tried to figure out who might have placed the call, and why. To get me out of the house for a few minutes? What would be the point?

I thought of Carol.

She was alone.

I shoved my chair back, grabbed the candy dish and hurried out of the restaurant.

I stopped for a moment on the sidewalk and looked toward my house, but in the darkness I couldn't pick it out. Then I headed into the street.

I heard the engine and the squeal of tires as the car started around the corner. For a fraction of a second I was too paralyzed to move. Then in one convulsive movement I hurled myself into the air and backward. The candy dish flew out of my hand. I landed with my shoulder against the curb, my head on the sidewalk.

The engine roared as the car swept the wrong way down Eleventh Street.

I blacked out.

Then I was conscious, and Danny was helping me into the restaurant.

Gus brought me coffee, but I couldn't get it down.

Danny insisted on taking me to the emergency room at St. Vincent's.

They examined me and took x-rays. No bones were broken. I didn't even have a concussion. All I had was an aching head and a feeling of immense stupidity.

No one had noticed the license number of the car. No one could explain exactly what had happened. Not even me.

It was five-thirty when I finally got home.

Carol was still asleep.

I crawled into bed beside her.

31

It was much clearer in retrospect than it had been at the time.

The car had been parked on Avenue of the Americas, its motor running. The driver had been watching me through the plate-glass window of the restaurant. If I'd been alert, I might have been able to see him sitting in the car, although I wasn't altogether sure of that; it had been bright inside the restaurant and dark inside the car. He'd checked the neighborhood. He'd discovered that there was practically no traffic on Eleventh Street at that hour of the morning and little danger in his going the wrong way down the one-way street. Also that there were few police cars patrolling the area.

He'd counted on the fact that I'd be suspicious when I left the house but not when I returned; that I'd expect the car to be coming from the direction of Fifth Avenue. He'd been smart.

What had saved me was my crossing the street at the corner rather than in the middle of the block, as I might have done. He hadn't been able to get up enough speed.

I explained all this to Brian on the plane between New York and Denver. Brian listened soberly. His normally cheerful expression was grave. His blue eyes seemed darker than usual, and his lips were a thin line. He had only one comment to make, and that was, "The cocksucker!"

After a while I changed the subject. I began to question him about the results of his research. I'd expected that he'd have picked up a great deal of information in a short period of time, and he had. But there was an absence of enthusiasm in his manner that I couldn't account for. In the past, whenever I'd involved him in a project that I myself was working on he'd been so eager that I practically had to tie him down to keep him from racing ahead faster than I wanted him to go. Not this time, however. He was totally restrained. Almost disapproving.

Finally, as we waited for our connecting flight in Denver, I asked him what was bothering him. At first he was reluctant to tell me, but then he came out with it.

He said, "I think we're on a wild goose chase."

Nothing could have surprised me more. My jaw dropped.

"I'd like to feel that you're right," he went on unhappily. "That someone's found a new vein of uranium or silver in those mines. I just can't, though."

"But why? That's the only explanation that makes sense."

"I don't know. Maybe it's just a gut reaction on my part. But it's hard to keep a discovery of that sort secret. Look at Darby

168

Oil. In less than a week the news of their find got all the way from the Java Sea to New York, and the market's begun to react to it."

"That's oil, Brian, and people are more conscious of oil these days than they are of anything else. Besides, Darby's a well-known company. And everybody knew they were drilling in the Java Sea and that other companies had found oil in that area. This is different. Lucky Devil is an unknown company, and there aren't many people involved."

"I know. I've thought about that. And I'd like to feel that you're right—it would make everything so easy to understand. But somehow or other I keep having doubts."

"Well, we're going to check out the mines ourselves," I said firmly. "It shouldn't be hard to tell whether there's any activity going on now, or whether there's been any recently."

"That's true," Brian agreed. "We have to see for ourselves."

"All we have to do is find the goddamn places," I added.

Brian nodded. "That we'll do," he said with conviction. He was once again the old Brian. "I promise you."

They announced our flight, and we boarded the plane.

It was almost ten o'clock, Mountain time, when we reached the Rodeway Inn. Since I'd had less than three hours sleep the night before, and it was now midnight, Eastern time, I was exhausted. Nevertheless I dug out Naomi's new telephone number and called her.

Irving had been moved to a private room that morning, and the doctor had permitted the police to interview him briefly during the afternoon. He was still in considerable pain, but stronger.

"Were you there when he talked to the police?" I asked.

"No," she replied. "I'd gone to the school with the children, to talk to the principal. How about you and Brian coming over for dinner tomorrow night? I've shopped and I have everything organized."

I laughed. "I'm sure of that. But I'll have to let you know. We're going prospecting tomorrow, and I don't know what time we'll be back."

"Prospecting? Oh, Brock!" She sounded dismayed.

"Not to worry, dear. Just a little jaunt into the mountains."

Her sigh came through loud and clear.

"You have your job, I have mine. Chin up. I'll talk to you tomorrow. Thanks for getting us the rooms." I put the telephone back on its cradle.

It rang almost immediately.

"Tried to get you in New York," Quick said, "but they told me you'd already left. The Jennings woman spent today just like she spent yesterday—at least as far as I know. It was three o'clock in Salt Lake City when my man called me. She'd gone to work at the usual time and was still there. He's going to call me in the morning and let me know what she's doing tonight. He checked on the car. It's a black one. No damage that he could see."

That proved nothing, I decided. She'd had almost six days to have the damage repaired. "Did she meet the same man for lunch?"

"She went to the same place but she ate alone. He wasn't there."

I considered. It might mean something or it might not. "What about the son?"

"It's been tough to find out about him. He works for some kind of company that has to do with food. Not sure what he does. My man is still working on it. Lives in a place called Logan but comes in to see his mother and his girlfriend."

"Girlfriend?"

"He's engaged to a girl who works in Salt Lake City."

"I want him followed too. Twenty-four hours a day."

"Do you know what you're spending, Potter?"

"I have a general idea, but don't tell me. It'll keep me awake."

"The son is important?"

"Could be. Especially the girlfriend."

"O.K." Quick hung up.

I started to get undressed, then changed my mind, put my clothes back on and went next door to Brian's room.

"You've got a roommate," I said. "Just in case."

"Good idea," he said. "Never can tell. But from New York to Salt Lake City—"

"There's more than one person involved in this thing. There has to be."

Brian pulled the spread off the other bed and invited me to make myself at home. Then he took a flask of Scotch from his suitcase and suggested we have a nightcap. "Since this is one of those states," he added.

"How did you know this is one of those states?" I asked.

"I checked."

I realized I'd asked a dumb question. Of course he'd checked. Brian always checked on everything.

32

And the next morning I had a chance to see him in action. Usually we worked independently, getting together only to compare notes. But when it came to tracing mining claims, neither of us had had any experience, and I felt that two heads would be better than one. So we went down to the Federal Building as a team, and after a few minutes I came to the conclusion that two heads were barely enough.

Brian's initial research had turned up the information that such matters are under the jurisdiction of the Bureau of Land Management, which is a division of the Department of the Interior, so we went to the right office. Once there, however, we immediately got lost in the maze of cross-referencing that every government agency delights in constructing for itself. And the pert little old lady named Angela Deacon who was in charge of the office and was used to dealing with people who knew exactly how to find what they were after soon became exasperated with us. If it hadn't been for Brian's little-boy smile and deferential manner, I think she would have thrown us out.

What we needed, but didn't have, was the serial number of each of the two claims. Fortunately there was another file, which contained company names, and Lucky Devil Minerals was listed in it. From that file we got the mineral entry numbers, which enabled Miss Deacon to use the mineral survey file and produce the Master Title Plats, which showed the townships in which the claims were located. Then, by consulting the historical index for those townships, she was able to come up with the plats showing the exact locations of the claims, descriptions of them and the dates on which the claims had been filed.

What caused us the most trouble was translating the locations as shown on the various Bureau of Land Management documents into locations Brian and I could relate to a road map. As far as Miss Deacon was concerned, the state of Utah was divided into townships and ranges, and that's all there was to it. There are, she insisted, two meridians—the Uintah meridian and the Salt Lake meridian. Townships are measured north and south from the meridian lines, whereas ranges are measured east and west. The Lucky Devil uranium mine, for instance, was in Township 26 South, Range 22 East—which meant everything to Miss Deacon but nothing to Brian and me. To complicate matters further, she informed us that each township consists of thirty-six sections of six hundred and forty acres each, or six square miles. We not only had to find the correct township and range, but also the correct sections within them.

While Brian continued his discourse with our irritated mentor, I went out and bought road maps. But when I got them back to the Bureau of Land Management office, it turned out that they were as incomprehensible to Miss Deacon as her township and range maps were to us. She knew Salt Lake City like the back of her hand, she said, but the only place she ever went on her vacations was Dallas, where her sister lived, and she took a plane.

It was past lunchtime before Brian and I, poring over the various maps and plats, figured out that the original Lucky Devil mine was situated at least three hundred miles southeast of Salt Lake City, in the general vicinity of Moab, whereas the Bertha K, as David Kisman had said, was somewhere around Park City, which was less than fifty miles from where we were sitting. Also that there was no foolproof way of finding them. The only thing we could do was drive as close as possible to where we thought they were and then start questioning the locals. Both the Lucky Devil and the Bertha K had been, in their day, operating mines—it wouldn't be like looking for a couple of gopher holes. There'd be signs, fences, equipment—*some*thing.

It would take at least eighteen hours to make the roundtrip to Moab and locate the Lucky Devil and another four or five hours to check on the Bertha K. Therefore, we agreed, it would be better if we split up. Brian volunteered to make the trip to the Lucky Devil, and since I didn't feel any more competent to do the job than he, I said O.K. He telephoned a car rental

173

agency and by two o'clock, fortified with his share of maps, a photocopy of the Master Title Plat of the Lucky Devil and my good wishes, he set out. And a few minutes later I was skimming eastward along Interstate 80 toward the Wasatch Mountains and Park City.

The drive was easier than I'd expected. Interstate 80 is a well-marked multilane highway that follows a narrow valley with mountains on each side. It's the main road between Salt Lake City and Denver, some five hundred miles to the east, and traffic is heavy. The scrubby vegetation on the lower slopes of the mountains was like a color chart of autumn shades ranging from gold to pale purple, and the snow-capped peaks in the distance glittered in the afternoon sun.

In what seemed no time at all I came to a large overhead sign indicating the Park City exit. I turned off Interstate 80 onto Route 224, a two-lane hard-surface road that winds southward past complexes of new condominiums and advertisements for a nearby ski lift. I began to wonder which would be more important to the future growth of the region—minerals or skiing. The revenue from skiing was enormous. It was even possible, I thought briefly, that the value of the Lucky Devil properties consisted not of what was buried beneath the surface of the ground but in their proximity to ski resorts. However, as I drove into the outskirts of the old mining town and saw the dilapidated remnants of a couple of mines, that notion faded. Skiing was profitable now, but precious metals had been profitable for thousands of years and always would be.

From the weathered gray frame Union Pacific railroad station with its shingled roof to the battered old stores and cafés, Park City was an authentic nineteenth-century Rocky Mountain mining town. It was still alive but it was an anachronism. Its best days had come and gone. The overall impression was one of dirt, grime, poverty and memories of a turbulent, get-rich-quick past. Its only hope for the future seemed to be the ski lift.

I parked on the main street and looked around for a place to get into a conversation with some of the town residents. There wasn't much to choose from—Rosie's restaurant or the hotel, which was called the Treasure Mountain Inn. I picked the hotel.

There were two people in the coffee shop: a waitress, who was about twenty-two and, with pale hair, skin and eyes, was almost an albino, and her customer, a young man of more or less the same age, who reminded me of some of my acquaintances at The Cyclops. His hair was pulled back in a ponytail, and he was wearing jeans, a blue denim jacket and several pounds of silver-and-turquoise jewelry. Unlike any of my acquaintances at The Cyclops, however, he spoke with a classic cockney accent.

The two of them were discussing a movie they'd seen. It dealt with a train robbery. Their discussion involved not only the movie but the things they'd do with the stolen money if they had it. Each of them would buy a large house or maybe even several large houses.

After a while the waitress noticed me and sauntered over. I ordered a bacon-and-egg sandwich and coffee. She disappeared into the kitchen for a moment and then came back to resume her conversation with the young man. Presently I joined in. I described a thirty-room house I'd once seen at Sands Point, Long Island, and both of them seemed to feel that that was exactly the sort of place they'd like to own. One word led to another, and before long I was part of the group. When the waitress went into the kitchen to get my sandwich, I asked the young man whether he lived in Park City. He replied that he didn't really live anywhere, but that he'd been in Park City since April. I asked him what he did. He said that he skied. I asked him whether he did anything besides ski. He said that he made jewelry. That opened up a whole new avenue for us, because if there's anything that The Cyclops regulars do more than anything else, it's make jewelry. He said that he came from London and was working his way around the world. I gathered that he was seeking, primarily, the perfect ski slope. He hoped to save up enough money by spring to go to the Andes.

He was a bright guy, though, and he seemed to have picked up a certain amount of local lore in the various places he'd visited on his odyssey. I asked him what he knew about Park City and was surprised by the amount he could tell me. In 1868 soldiers, checking a ridge above Parley's Peak, had found some yellow quartz. When assayed, it was found to contain ninety-six ounces of silver per ton, with substantial portions of gold and lead mixed in. During the 1880s the town had flourished. The Hearst fortune originated there. Fires were frequent in the mining camps, and in 1898 the entire town burned to the ground. But it was rebuilt, and the mining continued for another thirty years or so, until it became unprofitable. Over the years, more than four hundred million dollars' worth of silver had been dug out of the ground thereabouts, in addition to many more millions of dollars' worth of lead and zinc.

"Mining's one of my interests," I said finally. "I'm looking for an old silver mine called the Bertha K. Would you happen to know where it is?"

He shook his head.

There were a couple of mines still in operation, the waitress put in. I asked her where they were. She pointed in the direction of the hotel lobby and said, "Up that way, the other side of town." She couldn't be any more specific than that.

I finished my sandwich and coffee and left to look for a real estate office.

The real estate broker wanted to sell me a condominium. When he realized that I wasn't about to buy one, he lost interest in me. He didn't know anything about old mines, he said. But he did say, pointing in the same direction the waitress had, that most of the mines were up that way.

I tried Rosie's restaurant and the grocery store. It was the same story in both places. No one knew or cared about old mines. Although the town had come into being because of the mines, its citizenry had little interest in them now. Condominiums and skiing were its current preoccupations. But everyone seemed to agree that my best chance of finding the Bertha K lay toward the south, along the road that led to Brighton. One of the women I spoke with in the grocery store warned me to be careful—the road was open only when the weather was good, and there'd been snow recently at the higher elevations.

I climbed into my car and continued through Park City. I soon came to one of the mines the waitress had mentioned. It was a silver mine and appeared to be flourishing. The chain-link fence that separated it from the road was obviously new, and all the equipment had been recently painted. Encouraged, I continued around a hairpin curve and up the steep grade of the pavement that hugged the side of the mountain. But presently the feeling of encouragement died. A sign said: ROAD CLOSED. I pulled over to the side and looked around. I could see the silver mine below and, farther down, the town. I was surprised by the height to which I'd climbed in a short span of time.

I consulted the Master Title Plat of the Bertha K and attempted to figure out how close I was to the acreage it described. The intersecting lines and numbers meant nothing to me. South seventy-three degrees twenty-six minutes east, fifteen hundred feet—it showed how the property had been divided for survey purposes and where the shafts were located, but to my untrained eyes it said nothing about where the property actually was. I knew that I was in the right general area, but that was all.

Unfolding the road map, I found my present position. I was still on Route 224, just beyond Park City. Brighton was some twenty-five miles to the south and west. The elevations of the mountains shown on the map varied from nine thousand to eleven thousand feet. The road leading to Brighton was, from this point on, unpaved.

My common sense reminded me that I was a city driver. Unpaved mountain roads weren't my bag. But another voice, less rational, insisted that this was neither the time nor the place to quit. Kisman had found the mine, and he'd probably traveled by car; I could too.

A Pontiac came around the bend beyond the ROAD CLOSED sign, bumping along in the direction of Park City, and passed me. The two men in the front seat were wearing bright orange vests, and a dead deer was lashed to the roof. I decided that if the road was good enough for them it was good enough for me. I shifted into second gear and put my foot down gently on the gas pedal.

The road was steep and twisting, but as far as I could determine it was safe enough. In summer the car would have kicked up clouds of dust, but now the main hazards were potholes, which were filled with water from melted snow. The water seemed shallow until the car hit it and sank several inches before sloughing out on the other side. After two or three hard jolts I made a point of edging around anything that even looked like a puddle. There were patches of snow on the ground between the tall trees, and some of the branches were dusted with it, but the late-afternoon sun was strong, and the air was warm. Looking toward the west, I tried to estimate how much daylight remained. An hour to an hour and a half, I concluded. And by then I either would have found the mine or I'd be in Brighton, from which, the map showed, a hard-surfaced, all-weather road led through Cottonwood Canyon back to Salt Lake City.

But I was going to find the mine. I was certain of it. Not by any process of deduction. And not because of any knowledge I had. I was going to find it simply through dumb luck. I was getting closer by the minute—I could feel it in my bones.

Another car passed me, going in the opposite direction. This car also had two orange-vested men in the front seat. And a few hundred feet farther along the road I came upon a parked station wagon. A man in a plaid shirt was sitting on the tailgate, slicing a salami. His rifle was propped against the side of the wagon, and his orange vest was spread out on the hood. He waved to me. I waved back. For a road that was supposed to be closed, I thought, this one had an awful lot of traffic. But then, hunters were intrepid souls. Which made me intrepid too, because I was as much of a hunter as any of them. And what I was hunting was a hell of a lot more valuable than a deer. Furthermore, I was new to the territory.

Valiant, brave, noble Brockton Potter, bumping along an unfamiliar mountain road that he had no right to be on, facing the dangers of the forest. Dangers like hidden potholes and men who slice salami with hunting knives.

Inexperienced, city-bred, office-oriented Brockton Potter, armed only with a plat that he couldn't understand and a road map that said nothing about minerals, was going to find the Bertha K silver mine. Because a voice kept whispering in his ear that he was on the right road.

And I'll be damned if the silly son of a bitch didn't do exactly that.

At five minutes past five he saw a pair of ruts that led off the road and had a rusty wire strung across them between two trees. A weather-beaten sign hanging from the wire said: LUCKY DEVIL MINERALS, PRIVATE PROPERTY, NO TRESPASSING.

Brockton Potter, of course, trespassed. He got out of his car, climbed under the wire and followed the two ruts to their terminus, some fifty feet up the slope.

What he found there was an utterly dead and deserted mine.

He didn't know much about mining, but he did recognize failure when he encountered it. And the Bertha K, at this point

179

in its history, reeked of failure. There'd once been activity at the site—that was obvious. But the activity had taken place long ago. There was no indication that anyone had been around, or had had any reason to come around, in many years. Whatever equipment remained had been corroded by the elements, and some of it had actually fallen to pieces. Nature was in the process of reclaiming this tract of land which really had been hers all along.

I poked about for a few minutes, hoping to find some clue that would tell me that what I was seeing and feeling was false, that there had been, after all, some recent discovery on the property.

No such clue appeared.

The Bertha K was as worthless as Kisman had said it was.

So the answer to Lucky Devil's value had to be uranium.

I thought of Brian speeding toward Moab.

I refused to admit that he, too, might draw a blank.

33

The message light was on. I dialed the message clerk. Detective Sessions had called and wanted me to call him back.

I did, but he was out. I left my name. Then I called Naomi.

She'd made a pot roast, she said. She and the children were just sitting down to eat. They'd wait, though, if I'd come right over.

I said I would.

And when I got there I was glad I'd accepted the invitation. Not only because Naomi had prepared a delicious meal, and not only because it was a pleasure to see the children again, but because sitting around the table with them gave me a sense of normal family life that I seldom had even in New York.

The dining area was too small for all of us; we were jammed together like anchovies in a jar. The furniture was shabby. We could hear a man and woman quarreling in the next apartment. Nothing was quite what any of us was used to. Yet we were a man, a woman and three children having dinner together in the traditional way, and for a couple of hours I felt like the head of a household.

Memories of Park City and the Bertha K vanished completely as I tried to keep up with the rapid flow of conversation among the children and to answer the questions they kept putting to me. All three of them had been precocious ever since I could remember; I didn't know what their IQs were, and if Naomi knew, she'd always kept the information to herself; but intellectually, with them, I was very much on the defensive.

Elaine, the oldest, was the most difficult for me to cope with. She was going on fourteen and was, as she put it, in a period of transition: until now she'd always been a Freudian, like her mother, but she was beginning to find that she was really more in tune with Carl Rogers. She wanted to know which of the two schools of thought I favored.

"Do I have to make a choice?" I countered. I'd never heard of Carl Rogers.

"Well, you can't really believe in both," she said.

"You can too!" Frances said hotly. Frances was twelve. "They're both personality theorists!"

"You can not!" Elaine told her emphatically. "Rogers is completely nondirective." She turned to her mother. "Isn't that right, Mom?"

181

Naomi nodded.

"I mean," Elaine asked me, "don't you feel terribly self-actualized, and don't you think being self-actualized is really the most important thing in a person's whole existence?"

"I hate to have to ask," I said, "but what's 'self-actualized'?"

She'd been about to spear a piece of potato but she put her fork down. "To be everything a human being is capable of becoming," she explained.

"Is anybody, ever?"

She nodded vigorously. "One percent of the population. That's what Maslow says. One percent of the population is completely fulfilled."

"Well, I'm afraid I fall into the other ninety-nine percent," I said.

She seemed disappointed but she went ahead with the potato.

"It's a nice goal, though," Naomi said tactfully.

"If I had a million dollars," Joel said, "I'd be fulfilled." Joel was nine.

"You wouldn't be fulfilled if you had a hundred million dollars," Elaine told him. "Money has nothing to do with it. Isn't that right, Mom?"

Naomi nodded and smiled.

Joel ignored them. "Do you think General Motors is going to declare an extra dividend this year?" he asked me.

I gaped at him.

"Dad thinks so," he explained, "but I don't."

"Your dad's a General Motors expert," I said when I found my voice.

"The Buick Division is the problem, in my opinion," he said.

"Eat your string beans," his mother told him.

He took a forkful of them and began to chew.

"Dad says you're not a Keynesian either," Frances informed me.

"He's right," I said. "I think that John Maynard Keynes is

one of the most destructive thinkers the Western world has ever produced."

"My goodness!" Naomi exclaimed. "Such conviction!"

"You're damn tootin'," I said.

"We have sponge cake for dessert," she said, and while she and the girls cleared the table, Joel told me what he felt was wrong with the Buick Division.

The children went off to bed at nine.

"They're too much," I said.

Naomi smiled. "It'll do them good to get away from New York for a change. Just looking at those mountains . . . How did the prospecting go today?"

"My end of it was disappointing." I described my trip to the Bertha K and told her that Brian was on his way to the Lucky Devil. "The answer has to be uranium," I concluded.

She reached for a piece of needlepoint she was just getting started with. She remained silent for a while. Then, when she did speak, what she said caught me totally by surprise. "I heard this afternoon that you almost became a hit-and-run victim yourself, night before last."

"How in God's name did you find out about that, Naomi?"

"The hit-and-run detective, Mr. Sessions, came to the hospital this afternoon to see Irv again. I talked to him. He told me."

"But how did *he* find out?"

"From those detectives in New York who questioned us about Aunt Sarah. Detectives Hastings and Ryerson."

"But—"

"Some intern took you to the hospital, they said, and he insisted on filing a report. Apparently the detectives saw it and recognized your name. They must have traced you through your office and found out you were in Salt Lake City. They sent a message to the police department here, and Detective Sessions got hold of it. He called them. They told him about you, and he told them about Irv—they didn't know about Irv's accident.

Now everybody's wondering about everything."

"There was a message from Sessions when I got back to the motel."

"He wants to ask you some questions."

I sighed heavily. "Good old Danny."

"Who?"

"The intern. How much did Irv tell Sessions?"

"I don't know. I wasn't in the room with them. I hope he told them everything."

Knowing Irv, I was skeptical. I decided that it would be a good idea to talk to him before talking to Sessions.

Naomi seemed absorbed in the design she was working on, but evidently she wasn't. "The man who tried to kill you and who tried to kill Irv is the same man who killed Aunt Sarah," she said. "I've been thinking about it, and I'm almost certain."

"So am I."

"He's a strange personality."

"All murderers are strange personalities."

"Not necessarily. But even so, this one is especially strange." She paused. "He has a peculiar sort of conscience."

I looked at her. "Conscience? That's what he's lacking."

"I don't think so. Everyone has a conscience, even murderers. But this one doesn't want to feel that he personally did the killing. I mean, most murders today are committed with guns or knives or weapons of some sort. Mostly guns, I think—at least in this country, where guns are so available. In other countries it's different. At any rate, the killing is a direct act. In this case, the killer doesn't want to feel that he was directly responsible for a death. He can tell himself that he didn't kill Aunt Sarah—the train did; he didn't mangle Irv—the car did."

"A car is as much of a weapon as a gun. So, when you shove someone in front of one, is a train."

"Perhaps. But not for a certain mentality. That mentality

says that he gave the victim a chance, that the victim could have saved himself."

"What chance did Sarah Weinberg have?"

"None. And the killer certainly wanted her to die. But I think that in a strange way he managed to kill her and appease his conscience at the same time."

"I wish I could agree with you, Naomi, but as far as I'm concerned, this is a cold-blooded man who planned to kill, killed, planned to kill again, almost succeeded, and then tried a third time and missed. What you can say about a car you can say about a gun: 'I didn't kill him; the gun did.' The only difference between this killer and any other is that he's smarter. He managed to hide his identity—the first time, because there were too many witnesses; and the second and third times, because there weren't any, or it was too dark. And even that may have been luck. The important thing for him, as for anyone who deliberately kills, was to get someone out of the way."

"I feel sorry for him." She frowned at the needlepoint. "I certainly don't like this shade of green I bought. I don't know what made me buy it."

"Would you rather that he got away with killing your Aunt Sarah and almost killing Irv, if you feel so sorry for him?"

Naomi thought it over. "No," she said at last. "No, I don't think anyone should be allowed to kill another human being on purpose and get away with it."

"Especially when he does it for money, as this man did."

She put the needlepoint aside and studied me. "You know who he is, don't you?" she said quietly.

I was about to say yes, when I remembered the abandoned, worthless silver mine. I had a moment of self-doubt. Was it possible that Brian would find at the Lucky Devil what I'd found at the Bertha K, and that I was wrong about everything? I didn't see how it could be, but I was suddenly less certain than

I'd been before. "I like to have all the facts before I make up my mind," I said. "And I don't yet have them."

"I'm glad you feel that way," she said, and returned to her needlepoint.

Shortly after that, I left.

And when I got back to the motel, the message light was on again.

34

I hoped that the message was from Brian but feared that it was from Sessions.

It was from neither. Philip Quick had called.

The red light went off, and I dialed Quick's number. The woman at his answering service said that he was out for the evening and wouldn't be available until morning. I gave her Brian's name and room number and told her that I could be reached there. Then I went into Brian's room and settled down for the night.

I didn't expect to be able to fall asleep immediately, but I didn't think it would take me as long as it did. At one o'clock I was still awake, stewing over the day's events. Doubt and conviction played tag at that level of consciousness where they usually operate. Brian would find that someone had recently been digging at the Lucky Devil. Brian would find nothing. I was right. I was wrong. I had the answer. I didn't have the answer.

Damn Philip Quick. The least he could have done was give

me the names of his Salt Lake City detective friends, so that I could talk to them myself. But to be fair about it, I hadn't asked. He was the one I'd always dealt with; whatever information he'd got he'd given me himself. In that way, he probably figured, he could charge me more. I had to be fair about that too, though: he'd never really let me down; his information had always been worth whatever he'd charged for it.

I tried to imagine where he was and when I'd hear from him. It didn't require much effort. Most of his clients were sent to him by divorce lawyers. He usually had several cases going simultaneously. He refused to hire an assistant. So he was out tearing around from one motel or apartment to another, checking on who was spending the night with whom. Depressing work, but he had it down to a science—and his income was enormous. The trouble was, he had nothing to spend it on except clothes and jewelry; he was too much on the move to enjoy the normal pleasures of life. He wouldn't get home until six or seven in the morning, probably. Then he'd go to sleep for a few hours, probably. I wouldn't hear from him until maybe ten o'clock, Salt Lake City time—probably.

Sessions hadn't located the car, otherwise he wouldn't still be questioning Irving. The FBI crime lab undoubtedly had marvelous equipment, but the equipment was of value only if there was something to analyze, and I guessed the hit-and-run detail had found nothing to send it.

Opal cufflinks . . . jewelry . . . Milton Kaye . . .

I had to be right.

But was I?

Come through for me, Brian. Come through for me, kid.

I fell asleep. I didn't sleep soundly, however. And I was already awake when the telephone rang at seven o'clock.

I grabbed it on the first ring and said, "Brian?"

"No—Quick," said the voice at the other end. "I've got some information for you. Hurry up and take it down before I go to sleep sitting here. I've been out all night and I'm beat."

I got a pencil and paper. "Go ahead."

"There's absolutely nothing on the Jennings woman. My Salt Lake City contact has been having her watched day and night. She doesn't do anything. Nothing. Zilch. She goes to work in the morning and comes home at night. It's no wonder she's a screwball. Either she knows she's being followed, or else she's one of those women who just don't do anything except work and take care of the house. And I don't think she knows she's being followed, because there's been a lot of different men working in shifts, and they're all pretty good. Last night she cut the grass and trimmed a hedge, and that's absolutely all she's done all week—except eat lunch, of course. She goes to that same place in the hotel every day, but every day she goes at a different time. It depends on her jobs, I think. Most of her work she does right in the building where she has her office, but sometimes she goes to other buildings."

"What about the man she met having lunch the other day? Has she met him again?"

"The old guy? She met him yesterday, but not on purpose, I don't think. They certainly know each other, and when they meet they talk, but that's about it. Today she's having company. Her son. That's about all who ever comes over, I guess."

"Her son is coming over today? How do you know?"

"One of my man's men got to talk to him. Something about making a survey for an insurance company. They got chummy. Andrew Jennings is kind of interested in insurance these days, because like I told you, he's getting married. That's what he's going into Salt Lake City for today. He and his girlfriend are going to look at houses. They're going to live there, because it's close to where she works, and he's going to commute up to Logan, where he works." He paused. "My man's man kind of liked him. Says he's a nice guy but very egghead, as you'd expect with someone like that. Anyway, after they get through looking at houses, she's going to work, and he's going to his mother's."

"Exactly what kind of work does he do? Who does he do it for? What's his specialty?"

"I'm coming to that. Damn it, Potter, you're paying a hell of a price for all this; I'm trying to give you your money's worth, same as I always do with everybody. He works for some cockamamie milk and cheese company in Logan called Logan Canyon Dairy. It's not much of an operation, my man's man says, but Jennings kind of runs it. Spends most of his time doing research."

"Research on what?"

"Cheese, I guess, or something to do with cheese. Whey is what he said, whatever the hell that is. I don't know, but maybe you do."

"Whey is what Little Miss Muffet was eating."

"Don't play games with me, Potter. I've been up for twenty hours straight, and I'm tired. Anyway—"

"I'm not playing games with you, Quick. 'Little Miss Muffet/ Sat on a tuffet/ Eating of curds and whey/ Along came a spider/ And sat down beside her/ And frightened Miss Muffet away.' What Little Miss Muffet was actually eating was cottage cheese. Curds are the solid part, and whey is the liquid."

"Well, anyway, that's what Jennings does. Now, you asked me to find out who his girl friend is, and I got that information for you too. She's a nurse, and she works at Latter-Day Saints Hospital. She lives at 184 North K Street, with her father—her mother's dead."

I wrote all that down, and then asked her name.

"Paulette Evans," Quick told me.

I thanked him and informed him that he'd done an excellent job, adding that I now had all the information I needed.

Then I placed a call to George Cole and gave him an assignment that was to take precedence over whatever else he was doing: to get in touch with William Holman at Refrigerco.

35

While I was at it, I talked to everyone else too. I got the impression that my staff was coping but was somewhat rattled by having no one to consult with; that Brian's assumption of leadership, which had been resented the week before, would have been welcome this week. Harriet even went so far as to ask how he was.

I answered their questions to the best of my ability, then had my call transferred to Mark. Business was fair, he said, which meant that it was very good. He wanted to know whether he should have his interoffice memos mailed to me. I said no. Well, then, he thought I should be informed that the photocopying machine had broken down yesterday and the serviceman had charged forty dollars to fix it. I thanked him for telling me, and asked to speak with Tom.

Tom said that business was sensational, which was his way of saying very good. He had a number of questions about specific stocks, and two of the salesmen also had questions. I gave all of them the best advice I could, but my best advice at the moment was only mediocre, and no one was more aware of that than I. I felt as out of touch with the stock market as I'd ever been; out of touch with our customers; out of touch with the companies I'd always kept my eye on. Although I wasn't exactly playing truant, I wasn't paying attention to those matters that needed attention, and I felt guilty.

Even Helen had problems. She no longer knew whose calls to give to whom, and people were coming to her for decisions that she didn't think she ought to be making. She did tell me, though, among other things, that the policeman—Detective Hastings—had been trying to locate me, and she'd given him my address; she hoped she'd done the right thing. I said that it didn't matter.

The call lasted an hour, and as I was getting ready to hang up, Clair Gould cut in to say that Mr. Cole wanted to talk to me again.

"Put him on," I said.

He'd just finished speaking with Bill Holman, he said. It had been a long and productive conversation. He gave me the facts, which took quite a while, because I was making careful notes. Then he suggested that I call the organization Holman had recommended: the Whey Products Institute, in Chicago, the trade association of whey processors. The director would be able to give me additional facts.

I said that I would—and I did. Immediately.

The director was extremely helpful. He gave me half an hour of his time and a vast amount of information.

After talking to him, I felt I knew all I had to know.

There was nothing further for me to do but wait for Brian to report.

It wasn't much of a wait. Less than thirty seconds, in fact.

"Who've you been talking to?" he asked. "I've been trying to get you for an hour, and the line's been busy."

"Everybody," I replied.

He was calling from the Green Well Motel in Moab, he said. He sounded tired and discouraged. He'd spent four hours the night before searching in the dark for the mine, without success. He'd started again at dawn, and found it.

I knew what he was going to say, but I let him say it.

"I hope you found something up there, Brock," he told me wearily, "because I sure didn't find anything down here. As near as I can see, there hasn't been anybody doing anything at the Lucky Devil since back when I was in college."

"I know, Brian. And I owe you an apology. You were right, and I was wrong. I was looking to the past instead of the future. Come on back to Salt Lake City. There's nothing in either of the mines."

"I don't understand."

"We've got a real firecracker on our hands, Brian. Something far more important to this planet than silver or uranium will ever be. Protein."

"Now you're beginning to make sense," my piranha said with sudden enthusiasm. "The dairy?"

"One answer to the world's food problem."

"I'll drive like crazy," he promised. "I'll be there in nothing flat."

I didn't have the heart to tell him that I no longer needed him, so I said, "O.K. I'll meet you in your room late this afternoon."

36

Cottonwood Mall on a Thursday noon was quite different from Cottonwood Mall on a Saturday afternoon. The Hammond organ was gone, along with the tropical fish and the streamers proclaiming Lucky Value Days. Most of the people were gone too. A few leisurely shoppers strolled here and there in the covered concourse, which seemed even longer now than it had before. Salesclerks and store owners stood in front of their display windows, smoking and gossiping. Everyone was relaxed.

Except me. I felt like a piano wire that was about to snap.

I cased Happy Hours. There was only one customer in the place, a woman who was so pregnant that she seemed liable to give birth on the spot. Del had a newspaper propped against the cash register and was reading it. I didn't see Kisman.

And in fact he wasn't there. For presently I observed him coming along the mall with several rolls of coins in each hand. I intercepted him before he could change course. "Good morning," I said.

He glowered. "I've told you all I'm going to tell you."

"And a very effective liar you are, Dave. Now it's time you told me the truth."

He stopped glowering. He blinked a couple of times.

"The truth," I repeated.

He brushed past me and went into the store. I followed him. He gave the rolls of coins to Del. She offered me an indifferent glance and put the coins in the cash register. Kisman turned around. "Go away," he said.

"The truth," I insisted.

The pregnant woman lurched toward the macramé supplies. Kisman started in that direction too.

I took his arm and stopped him. "You're in serious trouble. Wouldn't you like to find out what it is?"

"Go away. I'm not in any trouble."

"One murder and two attempted murders. That's trouble, my friend."

He removed my hand from his arm. "Get lost."

"Andy will be annoyed, Dave."

It was a random shot, but it hit the bull's-eye. His sad eyes showed acute distress. "What do you *want* from me?" he asked, with a certain desperation.

"It must be kind of tough to have a brother who's that much smarter than you are."

"Half-brother."

"Half-brother. But closer to you in some ways than your real brother or your real sister. Because you see more of him than you do of them, and because you and he are partners."

"That's not true!"

"Keith and Betsy sold their stock to Albion, but you held on to yours. So you and Albion and Andy Jennings are the three owners of Lucky Devil Minerals—along with me, of course."

"That's not true!"

"And Logan Canyon Dairy is Lucky Devil's principal asset, an asset which because of your half-brother's remarkable mind is on the verge of producing a handsome profit. And I'll bet that you're going to make even more money out of the company than he is, because you have a bigger interest than he does."

The pregnant woman found something she liked and brought it over to us. Kisman seemed oblivious of her presence.

"The young lady over there will help you," I told her, and she continued on her difficult way. I turned back to Kisman. "It's strange that Andy applied for the patents in the name of Lucky Devil Minerals rather than his own name. You're probably the one who persuaded him to do it that way. I don't imagine that he's as interested in money as you are. He can't remember ever having had any, and money isn't his thing—science is. But then, maybe I'm wrong about that. Since he's one of the owners of the company, he'll benefit no matter how the patents are issued."

Kisman heaved a tremendous sigh. "I wish you'd go away," he said. There was such hopelessness in his voice that I almost felt sorry for him.

"I'm not going to go away," I said, "and you know it. I'm

194

going to stay here and make your life miserable until you tell me the truth." I smiled. "It's funny about whey, isn't it? It's one of the most troublesome pollutants in the country. For every pound of cheese that's produced, between six and nine pounds of whey result—and nobody knows how to get rid of it. It kills rivers and gums up sewage treatment plants. A thousand gallons of raw whey discharged into a sewage treatment plant equals the load imposed by eighteen hundred people. And then, because the biological oxygen demand of whey is so high, the sewage plants don't process it completely, so it's passed into rivers and streams, and makes such a mess of them that the government has been giving grants to dairies that are willing to experiment with new methods of disposing of it. I guess it's one of those grants that got Andy Jennings started." I laughed. My laugh had a hollow ring, even to me. "No wonder you were so willing to talk about the mines and made so little of the dairy."

"I didn't kill anybody."

"People have known for years that whey is enormously rich in protein. And about half the world's population is starved for protein. The problem has been to process the whey at a cost that isn't prohibitive and to come up with a product that hungry people will be willing to eat, because strange as it seems, people will starve before they'll eat something they don't like and don't trust. And your half-brother, working quietly away at little old Logan Canyon Dairy, has managed to solve both sides of the problem at once. What's the name of the product, Dave?"

"I don't know, and I didn't kill anybody."

"Have you ever heard of kwashiorkor, Dave? You probably have, but it doesn't really matter. I hadn't, until just recently. It's a disease that tens of millions of people around the world are suffering from. It makes their bellies swell up and damages their brains and kills them. It's caused by the lack of protein. Dried whey can cure it. This product that you don't know anything about but you're going to make so much money from,

Dave, is going to eliminate kwashiorkor. And if it's doctored up with thiamine, which it probably is, it'll cure beriberi, and if it has vitamin D, which it probably does, it will cure rickets, and if it has vitamin C, which it also probably does, it will cure scurvy. But of course you wouldn't know anything about that either, would you?"

He had tears in his eyes, and there was a catch in his voice. "Please go away."

"No siree, Dave. You're stuck with me. Not with Albion— with me."

"Albion wants to help people."

"Albion wants to help Albion. A million dollars isn't enough for him. He wants to have everything he had before, and to be everything he was before, and in order to do that he *has* to help people. With his contacts in the under-developed countries, he can get your dried whey to where it'll do the most good. Without him, your little Logan Canyon Dairy would remain what it is now instead of what it's going to become. But Albion isn't a humanitarian any more than you're a humanitarian. He's a fanatically ambitious man with know-how."

"What do you want, Potter? What do you *want?*"

"I want the truth."

"You already know the truth, and I didn't kill anybody."

I looked at him. I took my time. "You're a fucking liar," I said at last, "and I hate liars."

With that, I turned and walked out of the Happy Hours hobby shop.

37

Irving had been moved to a private room on the second floor. Naomi was sitting in a chair facing his bed. She was working on the piece of needlepoint she'd started the night before. Irving grinned when he saw me.

His head was still swathed in bandages. The bottles filled with water were still on the floor at his bedside, and he was still connected to them with tubes. Another tube, for intravenous feeding, was taped to his wrist as before. But he was no longer attached to a monitoring device that recorded his every heartbeat, and his color was excellent.

"I just dropped by," I said, smiling back at him, "to ask when you're planning to show up for work."

"Now, Brock," Naomi said, "be nice."

"Maybe Monday," Irving said. He pointed to the glucose bottle that hung from a post beside his bed. "Do you mind if I bring my lunch?"

"I wouldn't want to start a precedent," I said. Then I became serious. "How much do you remember about the day before the accident?"

"As much as I ever will. Quite a bit. What do you want to know?"

"Where did you get that *Stock Annual?*"

"It was so simple I felt like a fool. I expected to have a hard time and I was prepared for all kinds of obstacles. I thought the place to start was at the Intermountain Exchange. I parked the car and was on my way over there when I passed a brokerage house, and I decided to try there first. I walked in and asked for a broker, like any customer would. They sent me over to one, and I told him I was interested in a stock called Lucky Devil. He whipped out that book you found in my room and looked it up, and there it was. The whole thing took all of a minute. He even offered to give me a copy—books like that are a dime a dozen out here. So I decided to take a chance and ask him if he knew a broker named Barton or Barclay or something who might deal in stocks like Lucky Devil, and he said sure he did—Gary Bartten, whose office was right around the corner. It's not like New York out here—everybody knows each other. I realized then what an idiot I'd been. If I'd used my head, I probably could have accomplished the same thing over the telephone and I wouldn't have made the trip. I wasn't thinking clearly."

"You'd still have had to make the trip. Where did you meet Albion?"

"On the street near Bartten's office."

"Was he coming from Bartten's office?"

"I don't know. I suppose he could've been." He eyed me owlishly. "Albion's mixed up in this thing?"

"Definitely." I watched a chain of bubbles rising in one of the water bottles. I smiled. "I have a new nickname for you, Irv: Bubbles."

"Now, Brock," Naomi said reproachfully.

"Don't you dare," Irving warned me. "Ever."

I became serious again. "Albion got involved by accident. He had a heart attack here in Salt Lake City. One of the nurses who took care of him at the hospital is engaged to Gladys Jennings' son. Gladys Jennings' son works at a little dairy that Ethridge Kisman owned."

"Who's Ethridge Kisman?"

I told him. I also told him how Kisman had gone public and

begun buying businesses, which he incorporated under the umbrella of Lucky Devil Minerals. And how Andrew Jennings had come to be one of the stockholders of Lucky Devil Minerals.

"No wonder she tried to run me out of the house," Irving said. "She was protecting her son."

"In her own peculiar way, yes. At any rate, his fiancée, this nurse, told Albion about the work Jennings was doing, and Albion immediately recognized its potential."

"It's potential?"

I explained about the whey.

"Son of a bitch!" he exclaimed.

Naomi had stopped sewing. "But that's magnificent," she said. "Think of how much better life will be for all those millions of people."

"That's true," I agreed. "Cheese consumption in this country has been going up every year for years. As a result, almost twenty-five billion pounds of fluid whey are produced yearly. Properly treated, that whey, most of which is going to waste now, can make life better for millions of people. Albion realized that. And he's dealt with the heads of government in those countries where it's needed. His problem was how to get a piece of the action. I imagine he bought up all the Lucky Devil stock he could get his hands on. The trouble was, he couldn't get his hands on much. Most of it was owned by Sarah Weinberg and by the Kisman heirs. Andrew Jennings wasn't about to sell his, and David Kisman, once he realized what he owned, wasn't about to sell his either. In fact, he may even have beat Albion to the draw and bought up his brother's and sister's stock before Albion got to them. Or he may have made a deal with Albion —Albion would market the stuff, in return for a percentage of the stock. He needed them, and they needed him, so that's the way it probably worked. Except that your Aunt Sarah owned more than any of them."

"So Albion is the one Bartten was acting for."

199

"Not necessarily. He may have been acting for David Kisman or Gladys Jennings or her son, or even for himself. He knows Gladys Jennings, he knows the Kismans—he certainly must have got wind that Lucky Devil was about to become valuable."

There was a silence. Naomi resumed her sewing. Irving closed his eyes. I watched the stream of bubbles in the glucose bottle and thought about the sad-faced man in Cottonwood Mall. "I didn't kill anybody," he'd said.

The hell he hadn't.

All of them, one way or another, had contributed to Sarah Weinberg's death. Just as all of them had contributed to Irving's present condition. Because none of them had been willing to share their future profits with the elderly Brooklyn widow.

Irving opened his eyes. "Sessions told me what happened in New York the other night. You took an awful chance, Brock."

"I'm not very bright at times, Irv. If you didn't know that before, you certainly know it now. I was afraid that if I called the police, whoever was going to be driving the car would see a couple of men in a car in front of my house or following me . . . And there wasn't enough time to explain it to the police. . . . And it wouldn't have made any difference. When nothing happened, the police would have left. But you're right. I did take a chance." I paused. "I'm going to see Sessions this afternoon."

"There's something I regret too," Naomi said quickly.

I looked at her.

"Last night, when you asked me, I said I didn't think anyone should be allowed to kill another human being on purpose and get away with it. I'm sorry I said that. If finding Aunt Sarah's killer means preventing all those people who need a decent diet from getting it, then I hope you don't find him. Or that if you do find him, you let him get away with what he did."

"Even if it means letting him kill me too?"

"Of course not. I didn't mean that, Brock."

"That might be the alternative. We're up against a determined and ruthless man, one who knows how easy it is to fly to New York, commit a murder and fly back to Salt Lake City. He's done it. And I don't think he intends to let me interfere with his plans."

"I'm sorry I got you into all this, Brock," Irving said.

"I'm not," I said. "I'm glad. It's taught me how much of a rut I was in. It never dawned on me that milk could be more important than silver or uranium, although it always has been. I should have known that. How much did you tell Sessions?"

"Everything I remembered. But it was dark, Brock, and the voice on the telephone had said I should hurry, the same as with you. I think I heard the car before I saw it. I saw hardly anything."

"I don't mean that. I mean about Lucky Devil."

"Not very much. I said that I'd come out here to sell some stock for the estate of an old friend who'd recently died."

"Did you mention the name of the stock?"

"Yes, but that's all. I didn't make a big point of it, and neither did he. I said I didn't know anything about the company, which was the truth."

"Well, I'm going to make a big point of it. It's time somebody did."

Irving agreed.

But Naomi merely sighed.

38

Detective Sessions was out, the receptionist said.

How about the chief? I asked.

The chief was in, she replied.

And again, without delay, I was escorted into the office of the chief of police. He seemed pleased to see me and even reached across the desk to light my cigarette. But before we could get into conversation his telephone rang. I gathered that someone from one of the television stations was on the other end of the line, inquiring about an imminent promotion within the police department. The chief answered his questions and then thanked him for a story the station had aired. The story had been very nice, very fair, very constructive, he said. And when he hung up, he said to me, gratuitously, "We have a good relationship with the press."

"That isn't true in most places," I replied.

He nodded, smiled and said, "Now what can I do for you?"

"I really came to see Detective Sessions," I explained, "but he isn't here. He called me, and I called him back. That was yesterday, and I haven't heard from him since."

"You haven't read the papers, I take it."

"I haven't had a chance."

"One of the elders of the church was hit by a car last night. Sessions has been out all day, working on that. But I talked to him a little while ago, and he'll be coming in soon, if you don't mind waiting." He relit the remains of a cigar that had gone out in the ashtray and observed that his wife was after him to give up smoking. "He wanted to ask you some questions and to have you talk to one of the homicide men." He waited for my reaction.

I gave it to him. "I'll be pleased to."

I half expected him to begin questioning me himself, but he didn't. He merely invited me to come with him and led me down the corridor to Sessions' office, where he left me.

There appeared to be more snow on the mountains today. I wondered how soon Brian would be back.

And presently Sessions arrived. He looked tired and discouraged. Also, surprised to see me.

"I tried to reach you last night," I explained.

He told me about the new case. Not only had the man been an elder in the Church of Jesus Christ of Latter-day Saints, but he'd also been the owner of a large hardware company. I concluded that the hit-and-run detail was, as a result, under considerable pressure, and that Irving's case now had a lower priority.

"Any clues?" I asked.

"Pieces of glass. We'll be able to identify them, but it'll take time." He tried to pull himself together. "What I wanted with you . . ." For the moment he seemed unable to remember. "What I wanted with you—oh, yes, I wanted you to talk to someone from one of the other departments." He picked up the telephone, dialed and asked for Fields, but evidently Fields wasn't available, for he said, "Then how about Nicolson?" I gathered that Nicolson wasn't available either, though, when he said, "Well, all right then, never mind." He hung up and turned to me. "Everybody's busy. But I think I can handle it." He settled back in his chair. "There seems to be the possibility that this accident Mr. Silvers had wasn't altogether an accident. And if I recall correctly, you sort of hinted at that yourself."

I nodded.

"Suppose you tell me why, Mr. Potter."

"Because as you undoubtedly know by now, Mr. Silvers didn't just happen to be crossing that street in the middle of the night. He was tricked into doing it. A friend of his in New York, a Mrs. Weinberg, had been killed, and he came to Salt Lake City to look into a stock she owned which he felt might have been the motive behind her death. The company is called Lucky Devil Minerals, and while the stock appears to be worthless, it really isn't. When Mr. Silvers became . . . incapacitated, I began looking into the company myself. And the other night in New York someone tried the same trick on me that he'd tried on Mr. Silvers. Either he didn't think I was onto it, or he simply couldn't figure out another way on short notice to kill me and make the death look accidental, or he was just brazen enough to think he could successfully pull the same stunt twice. And as a matter of fact, he almost got away with it."

"What is there about this company that makes it valuable?"

"I'll be delighted to tell you. I came here to cooperate. But suppose you tell me, first, whether you have any leads on the car."

There was a silence. It lasted for a while. "Yes," Sessions said finally, "we do. We vacuumed Mr. Silvers' clothes. We found very small fragments of paint. We sent them to Washington. They've been identified."

I was surprised. "You do? What kind of car was it?"

"I'd rather not say at this point."

"Was it a black Toyota Corolla, two years old?"

Now he was the one who was surprised. But he said, "It wasn't black."

"But it was a Toyota Corolla, wasn't it?" I could tell by his expression that I was right. "The car has almost certainly been repainted. Probably by one of those backyard shops you mentioned. You'll find that the car belongs to a Gladys Cornelia Jennings, who lives at 4391 South 11th Street East."

He seemed even more surprised.

"But before you question her, I think I ought to tell you, she wasn't driving the car. She simply loaned it to someone. And I can tell you right now, you have no more hope of getting her to tell you who she loaned it to than a snowball has in hell. She's protecting the one person in the world she truly loves: her son."

"Her son was driving the car?"

"No. But he's the one she's protecting."

Sessions got out a notebook. He began to write down what I said, starting with the make of the car and Gladys Jennings' address. Then he asked me about Lucky Devil.

I told him everything I knew. Except about the whey. That, I figured, wouldn't help him, and I wasn't sure that it wouldn't hurt the product's chances. I concluded by telling him that I thought he should call in James Justin Albion for questioning.

"We've already talked to him," he said.

I stared at him in amazement.

"What you claim was a trick, Mr. Potter, really wasn't a trick. Mr. Albion is the one who telephoned Mr. Silvers and asked him to come to the Hilton. He was waiting for him in a room there. He came in voluntarily and told us about it."

"I can't believe it," I said, still staring. "What did he say?"

"He said that he'd heard that Mr. Silvers was interested in this company you mentioned, and that he had some highly confidential information about it. Apparently he's been trying to buy stock in this company himself."

"When did he come in?"

"Yesterday. It's been bothering him, he said. He didn't think he could be of much help to us, he said, but he thought we should know. He didn't see the accident, of course, so he wasn't an eyewitness, but he was the one who made the telephone call, and he felt responsible in a way for the fact that Mr. Silvers was hurt."

"I can't believe it," I repeated.

"It's true. We checked the register at the Hilton. He signed in under his own name. We haven't checked the handwriting or anything, but I'm pretty sure he was telling the truth."

"What did he say about the company?"

"He was reluctant to say anything about it. But when I insisted, he said that it owns some patents that have to do with making cheese."

I just sat there.

"Do you have anything to add to that?" Sessions asked.

I continued to sit there. "What makes *you* think that the accident wasn't an accident?" I asked finally.

"The fact that you almost had a similar accident and you and Mr. Silvers work for the same company." He paused. "Are you sure that the two of you aren't involved in something else that might have made someone mad at you—something back in New York?"

I shook my head, and sat there a while longer. I felt utterly frustrated. At last I got up. "Is there anything else you'd like to know?"

"Not for the moment. I appreciate your help."

I hadn't helped; I'd hindered. And I knew it. I was on my own now, and I didn't have much time.

39

The exchanges were closed. Two of the salesmen were getting ready to go home. The others were sitting around, not doing much of anything. It was like my own office, or any other brokerage house, in the late afternoon when the buying and selling were over for the day.

Bartten was in his partitioned area at the back, talking on the telephone. He didn't see me. I watched him for a few moments, then crossed the room and went through the little swinging door.

He looked up. His eyes widened. He put down the telephone without saying good-bye.

"Greetings," I said sociably.

"Brockton Potter, sir," he said, struggling to get out of his chair, "this is a distinct honor." He made it to his feet and extended his hand.

I'd forgotten what his grip was like. I almost said, "Ouch."

"Sit down, sir. Sit down." He sat down himself. "To what do we owe this pleasure?"

I noticed that he had two packages of Life Savers on his desk this time, one open and one in reserve. Also, he was wearing his weekday clothes. A nondescript beige suit, an orange shirt and a striped necktie that was at most two inches wide. "I just stopped by," I said, "to find out what progress you're making toward selling my stock."

He chuckled. "You New Yorkers, sir—you have a very fine sense of humor."

"It's a regional characteristic. But in this case, Bartten, I'm not being funny. The stock, as you're perfectly well aware, is worth considerably more than what I'm asking."

The chuckling stopped. "Come now, Mr. Potter. The highest my client would be willing to go is five dollars a share."

"He's gradually getting up there, isn't he? Another ninety-six dollars, and we'll have a deal."

He popped a Life Saver into his mouth and leaned back in his chair. He could control his facial muscles but he didn't seem able to control his eyes. They said some interesting things—the most interesting of which was that he disliked me with a passion. But they also said that he was afraid of me.

"I was in New York over the weekend," I said. "I discussed Lucky Devil with my partners. They agree that it's worth far more than I'm asking. Tom Petacque, who's in charge of sales and whom you may have heard of, wanted to mention it to some of our customers. By spreading it around among them—a few thousand shares here, a few thousand shares there—he thinks he can get more than the five million fifty thousand I'm talking about, and I'm inclined to agree with him. Especially if I add my own recommendation, which I'm quite prepared to do. But then, I told Tom, it would be a lot of trouble, and you sort of have first option—or your client does. What do you say, Bartten? We New Yorkers are known for our impatience. We like to get things settled fast."

"How true, how true." He chewed the Life Saver and swallowed it. "But you're insane, sir, utterly insane. Lucky Devil—"

"Come off it, Bartten. I'm tired of your airs. You know damn well that Lucky Devil is on the brink of making a ton of money from its dairy subsidiary, and you know damn well that I know damn well all about it. Either you buy the stock at my price, or I'll sell it to somebody else at an even higher price."

For the first time he dropped the courtly-old-gentleman manner. His eyes became very hard. "You're playing a dangerous game, Potter."

"So are you, Bartten. And I'm curious to know how much you're getting paid to play it. Whatever it is, it's not enough. Because you're closer to going to jail than you think you are."

I left him glaring at me with distilled hatred in his eyes.

Brian had a towel wrapped around his waist and shaving foam smeared on his face. Beads of water clung to his back.

"Hurry up and finish," I told him. "I need a witness."

"For what?" he asked.

"Assault, probably. We're going to see the Jennings woman."

"Great!" He quickly finished shaving and got dressed.

In the car I briefed him on my day. He said he envied me. I told him he was crazy.

An Oldsmobile Cutlass, somewhat the worse for wear, was parked in the driveway. I inspected it but didn't learn anything. I crossed the lawn and pushed the buzzer beside the front door.

The man who opened the door was immediately recognizable as a relative of David Kisman's. He was about the same height and had the same long face. But he had red hair, which was already beginning to recede, and horn-rimmed glasses and fuller lips. He was wearing a sport shirt and slacks and no shoes.

"Andrew Jennings?" I said.

He gave me a tentative smile and nodded.

"My name is Brockton Potter, and this is Brian Barth, my assistant. We're with the brokerage firm of Price, Potter and Petacque. May we come in?"

The names obviously meant nothing to him. "Well, I'm not a stock buyer," he said, "but I suppose so. Sure." His manner was that of someone who's never certain whether he's doing the right thing but hopes he is.

He led us into the living room. The television set was on. A pretty girl was talking about giving your hair new life. Jennings turned the set off. Then he noticed his shoes in front of the couch. He seemed undecided about putting them on but finally did so. He gave me another tentative smile and managed to include Brian in it. "It's nice of you to come," he said, as if he'd invited us, "but really, stocks aren't one of my interests."

"We didn't come to sell you anything, Mr. Jennings," I said.

"I see. Well, if it's my mother you want, she isn't home yet, but she should be any minute, if you don't mind waiting."

"We didn't come to sell her anything either. We're interested in the work you've been doing on whey. We think it's of tremendous importance."

"You know about it?" He flushed. He appeared to be terribly pleased. "It's very gratifying, I must say."

The offspring of a woman who'd guarded and sheltered him and made him the center of her entire life. The fiancé of a woman who was as strong-minded and ambitious as his mother. He'd never really had to confront the world, never really would have to confront the world—and wouldn't know how, if the necessity arose. A true innocent. But, in his own way, a genius. "I'm sure it must be," I said, "and I admire you very much. And I regret that I've been going around making life difficult for everyone connected with Lucky Devil Minerals."

He was genuinely surprised. "You have? Why?"

"Because there's a big scramble going on for shares in the company. You see, as a result of your discoveries everyone expects the company to make a fortune."

"I know. It's very gratifying. There are so many times when I wasn't sure I was on the right track."

"This product you've come up with—what's it called?"

"Right now it just has a formula number, but I'm planning to call it Protameal. Do you like the name?"

"Very much. I suppose you've tested it overseas."

He nodded. "In six countries."

"Places like Bangladesh and Nigeria?"

"Honduras and Mali and . . . But why are you asking?"

"As my company's chief securities analyst, it's my job to ask."

He looked from me to Brian and back to me again. "Well, yes, I suppose it would be. Are you a friend of Mr. Albion's? Are you going to help us market Protameal?"

"Possibly."

"Well, you see, the good thing about it is that it's virtually a complete food. It has fat, which dry milk doesn't, and when you reconstitute it with water it can make a delicious drink. But it can also be used as a cereal, or it can be mixed with the local leavening agent to make bread—in those countries where the people eat bread. It's very versatile, and it's cheaper than dry milk. It can even be mixed with fish powder!" he concluded triumphantly.

"Terrific!" Brian exclaimed with sincere enthusiasm.

"Do you use reverse osmosis or ultrafiltration to dry the whey?" I asked.

Jennings began to regard me with suspicion. "Are you a dairy man?" he asked.

"No," I replied, "but I try to bone up on whatever product I'm studying at the moment."

"Ultrafiltration," he said.

"So your problem has been to find a satisfactory membrane to filter the whey through—one that can be used for a good long time, one that's sanitary and won't clog up or break. What did you come up with?"

But Jennings wasn't as innocent as all that. "You don't really expect me to tell you everything, Mr. Potter, do you?"

"I guess not," I said. I heard a car pull up outside. A car door slammed. I glanced out the window. His mother was returning. She had a shopping bag full of groceries in one hand, her pocketbook in the other. I tensed.

The front door opened. "Your car's blocking the garage, darling," she said as she entered the living room. Then she saw Brian and me. Her reaction was that of a cat to a couple of strange dogs. She all but arched her back and began to hiss.

"Good evening," I said, as pleasantly as I could.

Brian moved closer to me, protectively.

"These men are stockbrokers," Andrew told her proudly. "They're interested in Protameal. Mr. Potter knows quite a bit about the dairy business."

She put the shopping bag down. She didn't look quite as clownish as she had before, but her face was still more white and more red than it should have been. "What have you been asking my son?" she said in a low voice. There was no trace of curiosity in the statement; instead there was menace.

Andrew suddenly seemed to sense that we weren't altogether what he'd thought. He moved away from us.

She shifted her gaze from me to Brian. "Who's he?" she said in that same low voice.

"Brian Barth, one of my assistants. He's been helping me."

"You have a brilliant son," Brian put in.

She shifted her gaze back to me. "What do you want?"

"The first thing I want is for you to stop looking at me like that. I approve of your son's work. I'm not out to destroy it."

If there was any lessening of hostility on her part, I couldn't detect it. She continued to eye me in the same way, and her grip tightened around the handle of her pocketbook.

"On the other hand," I went on, "an innocent woman was murdered in New York, and a man whom I value very highly was almost murdered here in Salt Lake City. Furthermore, someone is anxious to do away with me too. Naturally, I don't approve of any of that." I glanced at Andrew. He was watching his mother. What I was saying was obviously news to him. Yet I sensed a certain fear on his part. Fear of her and for her. Fear that had always existed. Not of what she might do to him but of what she might do to someone else on his behalf. "Your mother is a brave woman," I told him. "She's willing to go to jail in order to further your interests."

"Get out," she said to me.

I didn't move. "I'm convinced that you weren't the driver who hit Irving Silvers as he was crossing Fifth Street last Thursday morning. But it was your car that hit him, and Gary Bartten is the man who arranged for the man who did hit him to borrow the car. Bartten's the kind who'd do anything for a

212

few bucks, and in your case it didn't take much persuading. The police are going to question you. You'd be smart to tell them the truth."

"Get out!"

I stood my ground. The hit-and-run detectives would never be able to prove it was her car that hit Irving. And the homicide squad in New York would never locate witnesses who could positively identify Sarah Weinberg's murderer. Through a car rental agency in New York they'd probably find the resident of Salt Lake City who'd rented a car on the day I was almost run over, but there would be no evidence that the car had been anywhere near West Eleventh Street. I could arouse suspicion, I could make accusations, but I couldn't give them what they needed to build a case on. So I delivered my parting thrust to Gladys Cornelia Jennings: "None of you may like it, but the fact remains that I represent the controlling interest in Lucky Devil Minerals, and unless you, Miss Jennings, tell the police everything you know, I'm not only prepared but absolutely determined to take all of you to court and insist on the sale of the company to the highest bidder, which you can be damn certain will be me or some friend of mine. And if you think I'm kidding, just put me to the test."

To which Gladys Cornelia Jennings responded in the only way she seemed to know how. In one remarkably swift movement she whipped a can out of the shopping bag and hurled it at me.

I managed to duck, and the can crashed into a vase, shattering it.

Her white face whiter, her rouged cheeks redder, she rushed at me, swinging her pocketbook and screaming, "Get out of my house!"

I retreated, but Brian didn't. He stepped forward and with a movement as swift as hers had been he rammed his knee into her crotch.

She uttered a strange little squeak and doubled up, sobbing.

Andrew leaped at Brian and seized him by the throat. "I'll kill you," he rasped.

I grabbed Andrew from behind and tried to pull him away, but he hung on.

My plump little assistant was perfectly able to defend himself, however. He simply brought his knee up again, and Andrew doubled over in the same way his mother had.

"Are we finished?" Brian asked me, rubbing his throat.

"I think so," I said. "A hit-and-run detective is going to be here soon."

We walked out of the house and got into the car.

"He may be a genius," Brian observed as we drove away, "but he's no good at all when it comes to self-defense."

40

"Mr. Tallman is sulking, I'm afraid," Barbara Deutsch said. "He won't tell me anything."

"But you did talk to him?" I said.

"This afternoon. You said someone might ask me about Aunt Sarah's stock, and nobody had, and I was curious—I wondered if anyone had gotten in touch with him. So I called him. He was very snippy. He said he was Aunt Sarah's lawyer, not mine. Which doesn't really make any sense, because she's dead now and I'm alive, and I think I have a right to know. But he wouldn't tell me anything. What do you think I ought to do?"

"I'll be back in New York tomorrow, and we'll discuss it," I said. "I just wanted to check with you. I don't think Tallman matters anymore. My lawyer will handle him if you can't. Get a good night's sleep. You're going to be rich." I put the telephone back on its cradle and turned to Brian, who was sitting on the bed, nursing the Scotch he'd poured himself. "And that's the way it's going to end," I said, picking up my own drink.

"How's that?" he asked.

"With Barbara Deutsch getting rich," I told him. I finished what was in the glass. "Very quietly, very simply. With Barbara Deutsch getting rich."

He pressed his glass against his throat. "I can still feel his fingers," he said, and lapsed into silence. But the silence didn't last. "And what about all the bad guys?" he asked.

"They're going to get away with what they did. Except for Albion, of course. We're going to take him for every dime he has left. We'll sell him Barbara Deutsch's stock, all right. He'll end up in control of Lucky Devil. But he's going to pay top dollar for it."

"That doesn't seem quite fair somehow. Not to Mrs. Weinberg, not to Irving, not even to yourself, Brock. I mean, Mrs. Weinberg was murdered, and Irving—"

"I know what you mean, Brian. You don't have to explain. But life isn't a morality play. The bad guys don't always lose, the good guys don't always win." I sighed. It had been a tiring day. "And you can't always divide the world into black hats and white hats. The Stetson people know that. That's why they make so many gray hats."

"It still doesn't seem fair. A woman was *murdered.*"

"And you want an eye for an eye."

Brian colored slightly. "I want people to get what they deserve."

I smiled. There wasn't a full generation's difference in age between us, but at that moment I felt like his grandfather. "In

215

a way they do." I got up. "Come on, let's get something to eat. I didn't have lunch today." Or breakfast either, now that I thought about it.

He finished his drink and, with a meticulousness that surprised me, washed the glasses. He looked unhappy. "So actually," he said as he opened the door and stood aside to let me go first, "it's all over."

I crossed the threshold. "No, Brian. It's not all over. We still have to impose our own sort of justice."

Brian closed the door behind himself, and we started across the parking lot. "But suppose," he said, "that Albion doesn't like our sort of justice."

"He has no choice," I said firmly, and the conversation ended.

Brian still wasn't satisfied, however. I could tell by the expression on his face and by the glum silence in which he ate his dinner. I understood his feelings and to a degree I shared them. I would have preferred a nice, neat apportionment of guilt, with everyone being punished for his particular role in the conspiracy. David Kisman, Gary Bartten, Gladys Jennings and James Justin Albion—all of them had contributed in one way or another to the murder of Sarah Weinberg, although only one of them had snatched her purse and pushed her off the subway platform. The same one who had tried to kill Irving. The same one who had tried to kill me. But it would be impossible to prove that the four of them had actually conspired to kill the old woman, because in a formal sense they probably hadn't. They'd simply agreed, first one and then another, that she was an obstacle and that she should be removed from their path.

Each had his own reason. But in a way all of them had the same reason, and David Kisman had identified it: Camelot. Gladys Jennings had never been there, but she wanted her son to go. The others had been there and wanted to return. Desperately.

The first crime had necessitated a second, hastily contrived. And the second had necessitated a third, even more hastily contrived. But hastily contrived crimes can be successful too. Irving had been effectively prevented from pursuing his inquiries, and it was only a matter of luck that I hadn't been prevented from pursuing mine.

I *had* been able to pursue them, though. And to step on everyone's toes. Now they were going, quite literally, to have to pay the price.

Did they really believe that I'd bought Sarah Weinberg's stock? Probably. It didn't really matter, however—and I'd been foolish to think that it did. All I would have had to do was claim that Barbara Deutsch wouldn't sell it without my approval. At any rate, I'd done what I'd done, and it was going to work. Soon.

I paid the check and suggested that we take a walk around the block.

Brian gave me a questioning glance.

"No particular reason," I said. "Just to get some fresh air." Which was the truth. I simply wanted to remain outdoors for a few minutes and get a little exercise. The tiredness I'd felt before dinner was gone, and I was more relaxed than I'd been in ten days. The curtain was about to go up on the last act, and I already knew that the play, while not exactly a morality play, had a reasonably happy ending.

All things considered, it seemed to me, I hadn't done too badly.

So we took our walk. And when we reached the opposite side of the motel—the driveway that led from the parking lot to Fifth South—I paused, and Brian paused with me.

We just stood there, looking across the wide thoroughfare toward the entrance to the Hilton, and I imagined the street in the early hours of the morning. Little traffic. A car parked near the corner of West Temple, its motor running. Irving hurrying down the driveway from the Rodeway Inn, stepping into the street. The car starting up, gathering speed . . .

And suddenly I felt a great wave of anger sweeping over me. Brian was right. What I had in mind wasn't enough.

It was the most I could do, though.

"Come on," I said in a tight voice. "Let's go back to the room."

Brian gave an affirmative grunt, and we walked into the parking lot.

"I hope Sessions wasn't too busy with his new case to go out and have a talk with Gladys Jennings," I said. The sooner he did, the sooner I'd hear from Albion. But perhaps it didn't make any difference. Perhaps I'd already stepped on enough toes.

We went into my room instead of Brian's, and for a moment, when I saw that the message light was on, I thought that the curtain had already gone up on the third act. But when the message was given to me, I discovered I was wrong. Detective James Hastings had called while Brian and I were having dinner.

I glanced at my watch. It was eleven-thirty in New York. Certainly Hastings would be off duty by now. Besides, I knew what he wanted. He wanted to know when I'd be back. And when it would be convenient for me to see him—he'd like to ask me a few questions.

O.K., I told him mentally. I'll be glad to answer your questions. However, you'll end up with a suspect but no case. As far as the New York Police Department is concerned, the subway murder of the Jane Doe in box nineteen will remain unsolved.

But her niece will wind up with at least a million dollars by way of compensation.

"I'll call him back tomorrow," I told Brian.

"And in the meantime?" Brian asked.

"We wait."

"How long?"

"As long as it takes. Albion will call. I'm sure of it. He can't afford not to. Probably quite soon."

Brian sighed and settled himself politely in the less comfortable of the two chairs.

I was wrong, however. At least about the time.

At ten-thirty Brian began to get restless. "Suppose he doesn't call until tomorrow or the day after," he said.

"Then I'll call him." I was beginning to get restless myself. I thought of Naomi's method of handling impatience. But I didn't know any recipes, except the recipe for scrambled eggs. And I didn't know the Greek alphabet. Or Freud's list of defense mechanisms. So I asked Brian whether he could name the top thirty corporations in the world, in order of their size.

He named the top eight.

I named the next five.

Then both of us got confused. We batted some names back and forth, but we had no authority to check them against, so we began to play a different game. I took out the *Stock Annual* I'd found in Irving's room, and we began to look for the most worthless company.

It was difficult to do, because the book was full of worthless companies.

And then, shortly after eleven-thirty, I heard from the future owner of a worthless company that really wasn't worthless at all.

James Justin Albion didn't telephone. He came in person.

The first words out of his mouth were: "I think we have some business to discuss."

The first words out of mine were: "Indeed we do."

41

He didn't appear to be angry. He appeared to be amused. Which annoyed me. I wanted him to be angry.

He glanced at Brian, then said to me, "Can we dispense with the third party?"

I gathered from the lack of curiosity in his eyes that he'd already heard from Gladys Jennings and knew who Brian was. "If you want," I said, and told Brian to get a good night's sleep.

Brian nodded. He was looking particularly inexperienced and eager to please, which meant that he was at his most dangerous. I could picture him in the next room, with a drinking glass against the wall, his ear pressed to the glass, listening to every word.

But so could Albion. For as soon as Brian was out of the room, Albion turned on the television set.

I promptly turned it off. Not because I was determined that Brian should overhear the conversation, but because I was determined that Albion shouldn't think himself in control.

Albion shrugged and said, with a little smile, "How much do you really want, Potter?"

I decided to open high. "Exactly what I said I want, Justin. A hundred and one dollars a share."

Still smiling, he said, "Don't be absurd. The company isn't worth that kind of money, and you know it." Then he made his opening bid. "How about five dollars a share? That's more than it's worth."

Apparently Bartten hadn't been kidding. "Don't make me laugh," I said. "That may be what it's worth now, but two years from now it'll be worth thirty times that."

"Perhaps. But only with my supervision."

"You overrate yourself, Justin. Have you ever heard of Bill Holman? He owns a company called Refrigerco. His contacts in the underdeveloped countries are every bit as good as yours. He could introduce Protameal as well as you can. And when I spoke to him about it this morning he seemed eager for the opportunity."

Albion didn't say whether he'd heard of Bill Holman or not, but I guessed that he had, for suddenly he stopped smiling. "You're the same prick you always were, Potter."

"People don't change. You're the same crazy, stop-at-nothing fanatic you always were, too. But we're not going to get anywhere by calling each other names. You want to buy, and I'm willing to sell. Only at a reasonable price, though."

Albion seemed taken aback. "Fanatic, am I?"

"You stop at nothing. Not even murder."

There was a silence. It lasted for a while. Finally he said, "Those are dangerous words, Potter. I hope you don't think you can back them up."

"No, Justin, I don't think I can back them up. Unfortunately. Because I'd sure as hell like to. I don't like men who push old ladies in front of trains, and try to run over innocent men. Which is what you did."

He continued to eye me for several seconds, then he went into action. Moving methodically around the room, he searched it thoroughly for a hidden microphone. The search took him a good five minutes. I simply sat down, crossed my legs and waited for him to finish.

"Satisfied?" I asked at last.

He seemed to be, for he too sat down. "What made you think it was me?" he asked.

221

"You told me so yourself. Last Sunday. When you asked me who I planned to leave my money to. I realized that the only reason you'd asked me to breakfast was to find out who you'd have to deal with in the event of my death, which evidently you were planning to bring about."

He gave me a smile of genuine warmth. "Potter the analyst. I can't say that I like you, but I do admire you."

The smile disconcerted me, but I continued anyway. "Then there was that funny flash of anger when I came early, and the Evans girl's surprise—obviously neither of you had wanted me to see you together."

"And you came early on purpose, of course."

"No. I came early because my plane was leaving early, just as I said. And finally there was that gold bracelet on your wife's arm. It seemed to me, when I thought about it, that considering how you used to live, she'd at least be wearing her engagement ring."

"She never had an engagement ring. We were too poor when we got engaged."

"Well, she must have had plenty of other jewelry. Oh, I don't know, Justin—it just seemed to me that by selling off most of what you'd managed to salvage, you'd raised enough money to begin the comeback you were determined to make. And having met the other members of your peculiar little team, I couldn't see any of them with the will and the guts to commit murder, except for Gladys Jennings, and she didn't fit the description of the eyewitnesses on the subway platform. No way."

"Eyewitnesses?"

I was tempted to lie. To tell him that the New York police had an accurate description of Sarah Weinberg's killer. But I saw no point in it. He'd eventually learn that they didn't. "A youngish man in a leather jacket and a cap. You do look remarkably young."

"Ten dollars a share would be a fair price."

I shook my head. "That wouldn't even compensate me for the inconvenience you've put me to by almost killing my right-hand man. Or the suffering you've caused him."

"Which are you trying to do, Potter—make a business deal or get me to confess to being a hit-and-run driver?"

"Make a business deal. But you *are* a hit-and-run driver." I paused. "I'd be willing to consider eighty dollars a share."

He ignored me. "The police know I'm not a hit-and-run driver."

"The police know what you told them. And I don't believe I can give them a case against you. But I'm convinced that you weren't in the hotel room you rented at the Hilton and you didn't make the telephone call. Gary Bartten made the telephone call, while you sat in the car waiting for Irving to start across the street. For all I know, you had Gladys Jennings and maybe even David Kisman handy as witnesses, in case you should need them."

He gave me another of those warm smiles. "Gladys's car was stolen that afternoon. She reported the theft to the police."

"And no doubt she managed to find it parked near her house the very next day, with a few nicks and scratches that made it necessary to have it repainted?"

Albion continued to smile as if I were his best friend. "Fifteen dollars?"

"Did Gary Bartten make the telephone call, Justin?"

"I admire your powers of deduction, Potter. . . . Fifteen dollars a share is as high as I'll go."

I refigured what I thought he had stashed away. I came up with the same figures I'd come up with in the first place: between a million and a million and a half. "Let's quit playing games," I said, "and get down to brass tacks. I'll sell you the stock for an even two million dollars."

My estimate had evidently been wrong, however, for to my considerable surprise Albion said, "Let's do quit playing games. O.K., two million even."

I looked at him. He was still wearing that smile. "I insist on a certified check," I said.

"Do you have the stock with you?"

"Naturally not."

"How soon can you have it here?"

I suddenly began to feel uneasy. The stock could be tied up until the will was probated. Even if I bought it from Barbara Deutsch for two million dollars borrowed from Mark and re-sold it to Albion, the transaction would take time. So I said, "About as soon as you can raise the money to buy it with."

"I'll have the check ready tomorrow," Albion said.

I swallowed. "It'll take me a bit longer than that."

He nodded. "Then here's what I propose. A simple contract between you and me, with the check going into escrow pending delivery of the stock."

"What do we need a contract for, Justin? We've already agreed on the price."

"You know damn well what we need a contract for, Potter. I don't trust you not to change your mind."

"My word is generally considered to be good enough. But all right, I have no objection to signing a contract."

"Fine. In fact, I've already been in touch with my lawyer. He's going to Los Angeles for a conference tomorrow but he'll be back tomorrow night. Suppose we get together tomorrow night at his house. He lives at 780 Northview Drive. That's at the northeast end of town, near the Morris Reservoir. Say about nine o'clock. He won't be back much before then."

"I was planning to go back to New York tomorrow."

"Take the two million while you can get it, Potter. Before *I* change *my* mind. It's a damn sight more than you expected to get, and you know it."

He was right, of course. "Very well," I said. "Nine o'clock tomorrow night."

"Northview Drive—780. It's a red brick house." He smiled one last time. "And don't forget your pen."

42

The next day I did something I never permit myself to do when I'm on the road: I loafed.

Not all day, of course. During the morning I spent the better part of two hours on the telephone. I talked, one by one, with Helen, Joe, Harriet, George, Tom and Mark. The research department and Helen were still feeling harried, but they were coping. Tom said business was great, Mark said business was fair; neither of them had anything unusual to report, although Mark did complain that the photocopying machine still wasn't working properly.

I also talked for some twenty minutes with Barbara Deutsch. I didn't tell her that I'd made a deal for her newly inherited stock, but I said that I was about to and that the amount of money was considerable. In order to act on her behalf, I told her, I needed a legal document authorizing me to do so. I asked her to arrange with Mark to come to the Price, Potter and Petacque office sometime during the day and meet with one of our lawyers, who would be there with the document ready for her signature. She agreed, with no reluctance whatsoever.

Then I called Mark back and explained what I'd done. He said he'd have the lawyer there.

Helen had given me a list of the people who'd been trying to get in touch with me. I called a few of the more important.

And since I had nothing planned for the weekend, I placed a call to Carol. She was so pleased to hear from me that she almost cooed. I was at last turning over a new leaf, she said happily; I was actually beginning to be *aware* of her.

"That's not fair," I objected. "I'm always aware of you."

"Only when you're with me. Never when you're away."

Which was closer to the truth than I cared to admit. "Anyway," I said, "what are you doing tomorrow night?"

She giggled. "My laundry. But if you have something else in mind, I'm open to suggestions."

"I don't know what time I'll be back, but it'll probably be in the late afternoon. How about having dinner with me?"

"Why don't you come over to my place for a change? I haven't cooked in ages."

She certainly hadn't, but I had enough sense not to say so. "Sounds great," I said. "How about eight o'clock?"

Eight o'clock would be fine, she said, and she'd do veal piccata.

With that one telephone call, I realized then, I'd done more to keep her from moving back to Minneapolis than I could have done by any other means. So I went a step further and arranged with my New York florist for some flowers to be delivered to her the following afternoon.

There was only one more loose end to tie, and I deliberately didn't tie it. I didn't call Detective Hastings, because I simply didn't know what to say to him. I needed time to think about it. The truth wouldn't do him any real good, and a lie would make me guilty of obstructing an investigation. I'd call him when I got back to New York, I decided; by then I'd have some sort of plausible story worked out.

Shortly before noon Brian and I drove over to the hospital.

Naomi was there, along with the children. Irving was pleased to see me but even more pleased to see Brian. They kidded each other a bit, then Irving became serious. He told Brian that no matter what he might have said in the past, he was really proud of the way Brian had taken hold. Brian blushed and grinned and said, cheerfully, "I can hardly wait for you to get back to the office, so we can start fighting again." And Irving smiled.

Naomi said she had a hunch I wanted to talk to Irving alone, and without waiting for me to say yes or no she shepherded the children out of the room. Brian went with them.

I told Irving about the deal I'd made with Albion.

After thinking about it, he said it was the best possible resolution to what might have been a stalemate. "But," he said after thinking about it some more, "do you think you can trust the man?"

"Why not?" I replied. "He's getting what he wants."

"Not really. He wants the stock for nothing. He's a dangerous man, Brock. Be careful."

"Don't worry," I assured him. "I know how to read a contract."

"That's not what I meant."

I laughed. "How about if I take Brian along for protection? He's pretty good with his right knee."

Irving didn't see anything funny about the suggestion. "You could do a lot worse," he said soberly.

"Well, anyway," I said, "if Sessions questions you again, will you be able to handle him?"

Irving said that he would, and I put my hand on his shoulder. "I guess I won't be seeing you for a while, pal. Get well quick."

"You'll be seeing me sooner than you think. I promise."

And on that note we parted.

I collected Brian, and we drove back to the motel for lunch. After which we went out to the pool. Every day that I'd been in Salt Lake City had been, from the standpoint of weather, perfect. Indian summer, I decided, was even nicer in Utah than it was in most places.

We stretched out on adjoining lounge chairs, the only people in the pool area, and soaked up the warm sunshine. I felt slightly guilty to be spending a Friday afternoon so lazily, and to be contributing to the delinquency of one of my staff. But presently the guilt feelings went away. I was actually about to accomplish something worthwhile. And as far as Brian was concerned, even if I'd insisted on his returning to New York, he wouldn't have got there in time to do any work.

Neither of us spoke for a long while. I watched some insects that seemed to be playing tag on the surface of the water in the pool. Then I watched the clouds. There were exactly three of them. They were small and fleecy and were drifting eastward at a leisurely pace. And finally I watched Brian. He had his eyes closed, but his body wasn't slack, the way it would have been if he were sleeping.

I wondered what he was thinking about. He was an enigma to me—more vulnerable than anyone thought he was, but with a savage streak that made him capable of absolutely devouring an enemy. He was sensitive, he was loyal, he was even gentle. But he was deadly.

He opened his eyes suddenly and caught me looking at him. I was embarrassed.

"Sun feels good," he commented. Then he asked me what I was thinking.

I had to come up with something. "I was thinking about what Irving said. He said I should take you with me tonight for protection."

"You weren't planning to?" he asked innocently.

"Frankly, no. The whole transaction is kind of . . . marginal, Brian." I explained about the arrangements I'd made with Barbara Deutsch. It was going to be legal, I said, but the fact remained that I was going to sell stock which I didn't yet own, and someday there could be repercussions. "The fewer people who are involved in the deal, even as witnesses, the better," I concluded.

He smiled. "You'd have an awfully hard time going without me, Brock. I'd follow you."

"Not if I asked you not to. And I *am* asking you not to. For your sake."

"Is that your final word?"

"I'm afraid so."

He shrugged. "O.K., then. You're the boss." He closed his eyes again and went back to his daydreaming or meditating or whatever it was he'd been doing before.

And once again I realized what an enigma he was. Utterly determined, yet strangely malleable—at least in my hands. And always behaving in some way that I wasn't expecting. Like the night before. After Albion left, I knocked on Brian's door, only to find that instead of eavesdropping, as I'd imagined, Brian had taken me at my word and gone to bed. I was a little disappointed. I told him about the inverted glass and listening through the wall.

"I haven't done that since I was a kid," was his answer.

"But weren't you curious about what was going on?"

"I figured you'd tell me."

So I did tell him. And waited for him to congratulate me.

Which he didn't do. He merely said, "Sounds like you made a deal with the devil," and that was that.

I sighed and went back to watching the insects skimming across the water in the pool.

Presently Brian yawned and stretched and said that if I didn't need him for anything he'd go to his room and take a nap. I said I didn't need him for anything. He hoisted himself out of the chair and left the pool area. I adjusted my chair to the changed position of the sun.

I grew drowsy.
I dozed off.

It was almost five o'clock when I awoke. I'd managed to get through an entire afternoon without talking on the telephone. I was shocked. I hurried up to my room.

There was another message from Hastings. I ignored it, and called the airline. I made reservations for Brian and me on the first eastbound flight in the morning. Then I began to work on the story I'd tell Hastings.

At six, Brian knocked on my door. There was still some Scotch in the flask, he said.

We finished the Scotch and went to dinner. I found that I didn't have much appetite, however. It was nerves, I told myself. Not fear—just nerves. The same feeling that I got before an important conference. An awareness that things might not go exactly as I anticipated, along with an exaggerated sense of urgency.

It was possible that Albion had changed his mind. It was possible that he'd try in some way I couldn't foresee to outwit me. Contracts were tricky things. One sentence, one word, could completely undo one of the parties.

It wasn't likely, though. Albion wasn't the sort of man who changed his mind easily. That was his whole trouble. He got going in a certain direction and couldn't stop.

Furthermore, while I was no expert in legal matters, I did know how to read a contract. And this wasn't apt to be a complicated one. It wouldn't be much more than a simple escrow agreement.

"If you don't want your roll," Brian said, "I'll eat it."

I gave him my roll. Also my salad. And he had blueberry pie à la mode for dessert.

I asked him how he planned to spend the evening. He said

he thought he'd put a few more miles on his car by driving over to the hospital to see Irving. I nodded and told him to leave a six o'clock wake-up call, as we were on an early flight.

I walked him to where his car was parked, then went up to my room to study my map of the city.

43

The Richard P. Morris Reservoir was clearly marked. It was evidently in the mountains, for a notation beside it said: "Elevation 5187." There was a nest of streets some distance below it. Northview Drive wasn't among them. But there was a Northmont Way, a North Hills Drive, a Northcrest Drive and a North Cliffe, all in the same area. Northview was undoubtedly a small street nearby. According to the map, the city ended there. The space above the reservoir was blank, with only a narrow river called City Creek winding across it to the upper right-hand corner. From the motel to where the lawyer lived was about four miles as the crow flies, I estimated; six or seven miles, following the main thoroughfares.

I plotted my route: Sixth South to Seventh East, then north in a straight line to North Hills Drive. Fifteen minutes, at the most. Allowing an extra ten minutes for a delay in finding the street, I could leave at eight-thirty and have more than enough time.

So exactly at eight-thirty, with the map in my pocket, I climbed into the car, fastened the seat belt across my shoulder, rolled the window beside me partway down, took a deep breath of the clear night air and backed out of my parking stall.

Emerging from the motel's driveway, I turned left onto Sixth South. The nervousness I'd felt earlier began to disappear. I rolled down the window a few more inches and took another deep breath. Confidence took hold. The last round was about to start, and I had the advantage.

Crossing Main Street, I saw the dark bulks of the high-rise office buildings a few blocks to the north. They were sharply outlined against the moonlit sky. And at the corner of State Street, the vast Capitol with its graceful dome loomed in the distance. I drove slowly, enjoying the cool night air and the realization that I was beginning to know my way around the city. I recognized, as I crossed Third East, that I was within a few hundred yards of police headquarters, and as I turned north on Seventh East that I'd be passing within three blocks of Holy Cross Hospital.

Beyond West Temple, the street began to climb at a steep angle. I continued my leisurely pace, pausing at each corner to check the street signs. They were numbered in consecutive sequence, though, and it was impossible to get confused. Second, Third, Fourth, Fifth—each was where you expected it to be, and was perhaps fifty feet higher than the one below. It was like climbing steps.

At Eleventh Avenue I stopped to consult the map. It showed that I was within two blocks of Northcrest Drive, which angled off Thirteenth Avenue in an easterly direction. North Hills Drive snaked away from Northcrest and led into Northmont Way. I looked around. The houses in this neighborhood were obviously more expensive than those farther down the hill. There was no doubt that this was one of the city's choicer areas. Which figured. Albion would never have picked a lawyer who wasn't in the top income bracket.

Albion had always surrounded himself with the best legal talent.

232

In the end, though, the best legal talent hadn't been able to save Cougar Consolidated.

And in the end the best legal talent wouldn't prevent Barbara Deutsch from getting two million dollars for her stock in Lucky Devil.

I glanced over my shoulder. Through the rear window I could see the city spread across the vast plain, its streets and boulevards defined by parallel rows of lights. I knew I'd been climbing, yet I was surprised to find myself so high above the point I'd started from. And viewing the scene ahead through the windshield, I realized that I had to climb considerably higher before reaching my destination.

I shifted into second gear and was about to step on the gas pedal when something that had only half registered a moment earlier suddenly penetrated my consciousness. I'd caught a glimpse of another car several blocks behind mine. It too, had stopped and was idling. I turned around for a second look through the rear window. The car was still there, but its head-lights, which had been on before, were now off. The driver had evidently got to where he was going and parked.

Pressing down on the accelerator, I guided my car across the intersection and up the steep grade on the other side. And presently I came to Northcrest Drive.

It was a narrow residential street that wound along the side of the low mountain. The houses that lined it were brightly lit. All of them were new, all of them were handsome.

I came to North Hills Drive and turned left. The grade here was even steeper. North Hills Drive soon merged into Northmont Way. But there was only one cross street, and it wasn't called Northview Drive. I kept going for a while, then began to wonder whether I'd got the address right. With so many streets that had "North" in them, I might have misunder-stood Albion. Or he himself might have had the wrong name. I decided to stop and ask.

233

Picking a house that had lights on in every window, I pulled into the driveway. A basketball net was attached to the front of the garage. I got out of the car and rang the bell.

A boy of about fifteen opened the door. He was wearing jeans and a T-shirt that said SKI ALTA.

"I'm looking for a street called Northview Drive," I explained. "I wonder if you can tell me where it is."

"On the other side of Terrace Hills Drive," he said. "It's one of the new streets."

"How far is it from here?"

He made a vague gesture with his thumb. "Just over there." Then he decided to be more specific. They were building a new subdivision off Terrace Hills Drive, he said. Northview was one of the streets in the subdivision. It was off Bonneville Drive, no more than half a mile from where we were.

I looked at my watch. Ten minutes to nine.

I thanked the boy, went back to my car, then hesitated. There had been no other cars on the street when I'd pulled into the driveway, but now I saw one. It was parked in front of a house perhaps a hundred and fifty feet in the direction from which I'd come. I could see its shape but not its color. The headlights were off. I stood there for a moment, doubting my own recollection that the street had been deserted, then decided that it made no difference whether it had been or not, opened the door of my car and slid into the front seat. A buzz reminded me that I hadn't fastened my seat belt. I pulled it over my shoulder, snapped the catch and backed out of the driveway.

Following the instructions the boy had given me, I found Little Valley Drive, then Edge Hill Drive and finally Terrace Hills Drive. It was immediately apparent why the street Albion had mentioned wasn't shown on the map. Everything in this area was entirely new, including the pavement.

A sign indicated Bonneville Drive. I turned. A few houses had been completed and occupied. A few more were in various stages of construction, the framework up but no siding covering it, mounds of recently dug earth piled here and there like giant anthills. A large tract was still undeveloped.

Within seconds I came to Northview Drive. I paused for a moment to orient myself. The street was a crescent that curved away from Bonneville and then came back to it. It skirted a shelf of land that seemed to hang above the city and offered a spectacular view. Several houses had been built along the edge of the shelf, and several others were being built, but there were wide gaps where the land fell away from the street so sharply that it appeared nothing could be built. Three cars were parked at intervals along the curb. It flashed through my mind that I might find myself in a larger group than I'd imagined; that if the parked cars belonged to friends of Albion's, he might have more than one lawyer present, plus a number of witnesses. I felt a prickle of anger; he was stacking the deck in his own favor. But the anger disappeared as quickly as it had come. He could have as many lawyers and as many witnesses as he wanted; unless the contract met with my approval, I wouldn't sign it and he wouldn't get the stock. Besides, I was jumping to conclusions. The parked cars might have nothing to do with Albion. I was losing my cool, and that was something I couldn't afford to do.

I studied the street for another moment, noted that the house at the midpoint of the crescent was the largest, decided that it was probably the one in which the lawyer lived, and turned into Northview Drive.

Suddenly I heard the roar of an engine and felt a rush of air as a car swept by me. I hadn't heard it, I hadn't seen it, I didn't know where it had come from, but there it was, headlights off, moving at twice my speed, missing me by inches. I gasped. My hands tightened convulsively on the steering wheel. The passing car kept going for a distance of maybe thirty feet, then cut directly in front of me and stopped, blocking the street. I swung

235

my wheel to the right and jammed on the brakes. My car swerved, went over the curb, hit a patch of soft earth and came to a stop. A cry of anger froze in my throat. The front wheels of my car were at the very brink of a steep drop. Directly ahead of me was an absolute void. I threw the gear lever into reverse and stepped on the gas pedal, but nothing happened—I'd killed the engine. I reached for the ignition key, and as I did so I saw the driver jump out of the other car and run toward me. He was carrying a bottle.

It was Albion.

He threw himself against the door on my side of the car and raised the bottle.

With my right hand I unsnapped the lock of the seat belt and threw my left arm up instinctively to protect myself. The shoulder harness caught in the crook of my upraised arm. I pushed against the door anyway and tried to force the handle down, but Albion was leaning against the outside of the door with his full weight. And within an instant he'd poured the contents of the bottle through the half-open window. The floor of the car, the steering wheel, the legs of my pants and my left sleeve were immediately soaked, and the car filled with the stench of gasoline.

The door gave slightly as I again threw myself against it, but it didn't give enough. The seat belt slid off my arm and recoiled. I looked at Albion. He was wearing a hideous grin. He struck a match.

I let out a yell and scrambled to the other side of the seat, reaching for the door handle. And at that moment I heard shouts. I got the door open on the right-hand side of the car and hurled myself out. I landed on my right shoulder and began to roll, covering my head with my hands and trying to get as far as possible from the whoosh of flame that was about to envelop the car.

"Stop!" someone yelled.

There were shots.

A blinding light seemed to wrap itself around me, and I felt a searing heat. I clutched my head tighter and continued to roll. Then the earth seemed to give way beneath me, and I lost all control of my movements. I'd gone over the edge of the embankment and was rolling faster and faster down the precipitous slope.

I saw nothing, heard nothing; I was aware only of accumulating pain in all parts of my body as I struck small rocks and sticks and wisps of dry shrubbery, of clawing at the earth in one long desperate attempt to stop the downward spin. But there was nothing solid to get a grip on.

Over and over I went, losing all sense of distance, all sense of time. I was conscious of nothing but my own unstoppable motion and of the outrageous fact that I was about to die.

Then a sudden, terrible pain washed over me, and everything went black.

The blackness didn't last, however. The next thing I knew, my eyes were open and were seeing fire. Something was burning at the top of the slope. Figures were silhouetted against the fire. They were moving. Two of them seemed to be coming toward me. I caught my breath, experienced a rending agony in my right side and moaned. Memory returned, and with it came the knowledge that everything was not as it had been before. I was no longer rolling. I'd come to rest against something solid, and whatever it was was cutting into my side. I reached out to touch it and felt a thick wooden post. I wrapped my arms around it and tried to pull myself up. The pain brought tears to my eyes. I managed to get to my knees, but could rise no higher. I could only kneel there, clutching the post, hoping that the people at the top of the slope could see me as clearly as I could see them. I sucked in breath and tried to call out, but the pain was so bad that I could make no more than a faint sound.

I'm here, I screamed internally. Look this way and you'll see me.

No one was looking in my direction, though. The figures at the top of the slope were engaged in some sort of violent activity.

My perception sharpened. I realized that I hadn't fallen all that far. I couldn't gauge the distance accurately, but the top of the slope and the fire that was blazing there and the figures that were moving about seemed less than a hundred feet away.

Two of the figures were struggling. Others were running toward them. Then one of the struggling figures raised his arm and struck the other. The one who'd been struck buckled and fell.

An avalanche of small stones and sticks cascaded past me, followed by something larger. The something larger was a man. He was rolling down the slope as I had. He passed within a foot of the post I was clinging to and kept going.

Someone at the top of the slope yelled, "Brock! Brock! Where are you? Are you all right?"

I couldn't recognize the face or even the shape of the body, but the voice was a familiar one. It was Brian's.

Ignoring the pain, I filled my lungs with all the air I could and called back, "I'm here."

I didn't make as much sound as I wanted to, but he evidently heard me, for he immediately began scrambling down the slope, and within seconds he skidded to a stop at my side, panting.

He didn't ask me whether I was hurt, or tell me whether he was. All he said was, "I hope I killed the son of a bitch."

Then he took hold of me gently and held me against the post and shouted for help.

238

44

It was two in the morning when they finally released us from the hospital. Brian was sporting a bandage that had been applied at a rakish angle beside his right eye, but he was otherwise unscathed. He helped me negotiate the relatively short distance from the emergency room to the driveway where the police car was parked. Our pace was far from brisk, for in addition to a variety of minor cuts and bruises, I had three broken ribs.

Sessions and one of the men from the homicide department accompanied us. They'd already taken our preliminary statements but had assured us that the real investigation hadn't yet begun.

Albion was beyond questioning. He'd been pronounced dead on arrival at the hospital. An autopsy would be performed as a matter of course, although the doctors were reasonably certain that he'd died of head injuries. It was unlikely, I felt, that the doctors would ever be able to determine whether the fatal injury had been caused by his striking the pavement of the new street that had recently been completed at the bottom of the slope or by the blow administered by Brian with a jack handle. And Sessions had cautiously hinted that the chances of Brian's being charged with a crime were very slim. For Sessions had been present at the scene. He'd witnessed Albion's frenzied attack on Brian with the empty bottle and could state, at least with some degree of truth, that Brian had merely been defending himself.

A television crew met us at the hospital exit. Sessions had already dealt with the press while Brian and I were being treated, but evidently this particular crew hadn't been satisfied.

A bright light went on, and a microphone was thrust in front of me.

"Is it true," the reporter asked, "that you're a member of the stockholders group that was suing Albion?"

I blinked and said, "No."

"But it is true that you and Albion had business dealings?"

Brian reached out and pulled the microphone toward himself. "Mr. Potter was about to conclude an agreement whereby Mr. Albion would acquire the controlling interest in a very valuable company called Lucky Devil Minerals. The firm of Price, Potter and Petacque represents the seller."

Sessions opened the door of the car, and the man from the homicide department helped me to ease myself into the front seat. The reporter followed us, asking further questions, but no one answered him, and presently the car sped away.

"A little plug never hurts," Brian remarked from the back seat.

I was in too much pain to reply.

No one spoke again until we reached the motel.

Brian assisted me from the car. Sessions told me to get a good night's sleep. The man from homicide said that he'd be around to see me later in the morning.

Brian took hold of my elbow, said, "Lean on me," and began to guide me toward the path that led to our rooms.

I resisted. "Let's have some coffee."

"At this hour?"

"The coffee shop is open all night. And I'm far too unraveled to sleep."

"You ought to at least change your clothes. You smell like a gas station."

It was true. The odor of gasoline clung. But I said, "I don't care," and moved in the direction of the coffee shop. For I really did want coffee. As well as the answers to some questions.

Brian heaved a sigh of resignation. "If you insist."

The hostess, who looked as if she'd been dozing at her post, opened her eyes wide as we approached. Then she got a whiff of me and hurried us to the back of the room.

The waitress turned her head away as she took our order.

"It's all right," Brian assured her. "He's unleaded."

But she held the coffeepot at arm's length as she filled our cups, and immediately fled to safety.

I studied Brian for a moment, then said, as sternly as I could, "Now suppose you tell me the truth."

His expression became one of utter innocence. "There's no truth to tell. You're just lucky you hit the sign, otherwise you'd have been hurt a lot worse. Maybe even killed."

There was no doubt about that. My fall had been stopped by one of the posts supporting a large sign that had been planted on the side of the slope, advertising homesites.

"You only rolled about fifty feet," he added.

"That's not what I meant."

"The hill was pretty steep. I'll bet it was eighty degrees."

"I'm not talking about the angle of the hill, and I'm not talking about the sign. I want to know why you followed me."

"*I* didn't follow you. *Albion* followed you. I'd been there for more than half an hour. Didn't Sessions explain?"

"Sessions explained, all right. But *you* haven't."

He put sugar in his coffee, which was something I'd never seen him do. And concentrated on stirring it. "You sound as if you didn't expect me to be there," he said in an injured tone.

"Of course I didn't expect you to be there."

"But, Brock, I never take afternoon naps."

"You mean that during the afternoon . . . ?"

"Well, *somebody* had to check the place out." He put the spoon down. "Isn't that what research is all about?"

"Really, Brian, I—"

"Brock, there *is* no 780 Northview Drive. It's a vacant lot."

"I know that now. But why in God's name did you let me go? I almost got incinerated. Pushed over the embankment in a flaming car."

For a moment Brian didn't reply. Then, still looking innocent, he said, "Well, you seemed determined to go. And you *are* the boss, after all." He paused. "If I had told you that there's no 780 Northview Drive, what would you have done?"

"I wouldn't have gone. I'd have called the police. I—"

"So Albion would have tried again, somewhere else. And you would have been just as unprepared. It seemed better this way. I went down to police headquarters. I told them what I thought would happen. I managed to convince them. They agreed to . . ." His voice trailed off, and his expression changed. The innocence disappeared. "I'm sorry, Brock. I didn't intend for you to get hurt. What I was trying to do was *prevent* you from getting hurt. We all were. You've got to believe that."

"I do believe that, Brian."

"It's just that we thought it would be another hit-and-run attempt. I didn't know—we didn't know—none of us imagined —that Albion would try anything as crazy as he actually did."

"It wasn't so crazy. It almost worked. If all of you hadn't been there . . ."

Brian went back to stirring the coffee, which he obviously had no intention of drinking. He avoided looking at me. He still hadn't told the whole truth, and I knew it. The whole truth was that he'd wanted Albion to get caught in the act of committing a crime. He hadn't been satisfied with the way I'd settled matters. And his next words confirmed my opinion.

"What bothers me," he said, "is that nothing will happen to Bartten or Kisman or the Jennings woman."

"They didn't break any laws."

"Even so." He put the spoon down again, met my gaze and said earnestly, "I couldn't let anything happen to you, Brock. I just couldn't. Please don't make me explain."

I shook my head in wonderment. He was not only an enigma; he was an enigma within an enigma. "I'm grateful to you," I said after a moment. "I really am. Of all the men who were there, you're the one who took on Albion."

He shrugged. "I was the one who was parked closest. Besides, there was no fire equipment. The others were afraid, I think—that the gas tank would explode."

"And you weren't."

He shrugged again.

I smiled in spite of myself. "Brian, you're the most unmanageable employee Price, Potter and Petacque has ever had on the payroll."

He appeared genuinely startled. "I don't mean to be."

"I'll never know what makes you tick." I paused. "But whatever it is, and whatever you are, I'm damn glad we have you."

He blushed.

I gulped some coffee.

"Do you think Refrigerco will take over Lucky Devil?" he asked.

"If you're the one who undertakes to persuade them, I don't see how they can refuse."

Brian gave me a look of pure joy. "You mean you'll let me try?"

"Certainly," I said. And already I felt sorry for William Holman. The poor man didn't know what was about to hit him.